# THIS
# *BEATS*
# *PERFECT*

## *REBECCA DENTON*

ATOM

ATOM

First published in Great Britain in 2017 by Atom

3 5 7 9 10 8 6 4 2

A CIP catalogue record for this book
is available from the British Library.

ISBN 978-0-349-00272-9

Typeset in Palatino by M Rules
Printed and bound in Great Britain by
Clays Ltd, St Ives plc

Papers used by Atom are from well-managed forests
and other responsible sources.

MIX
Paper from
responsible sources
FSC
www.fsc.org    FSC® C104740

Atom
An imprint of
Little, Brown Book Group
Carmelite House
50 Victoria Embankment
London EC4Y 0DZ

An Hachette UK Company
www.hachette.co.uk

www.atombooks.co.uk

This book is dedicated to my Mum.

# Track List

The Intro
1. I Am Rock 'n' Roll (Edward Gains)
2. Tightrope (Janelle Monáe featuring Big Boi)
3. Charmless Man (Blur)
4. Going to the Party (Alabama Shakes)
5. Futile Devices (Sufjan Stevens)
6. Before I Sleep (Marika Hackman)
7. The Masses Are Asses (L7)
8. Tally Ho (The Clean)
9. Empty Room (Arcade Fire)
10. Celebrity Skin (Hole)
11. Fallin' (De La Soul and Teenage Fanclub)
12. I Think I Smell a Rat (The White Stripes)
13. Consequence of Sounds (Regina Spektor)
14. Rudderless (The Lemonheads)
15. Please, Please, Please, Let Me Get What I Want (The Smiths)

16. Red-Eyed and Blue (Wilco)
17. Please Wake Me Up (Tom Waits)
18. No Diggity (Blackstreet featuring Dr Dre)
19. Good Vibrations (The Beach Boys)
20. Heavenly Pop Hit (The Chills)
21. The Weight (The Band)
22. The Tide Is High (Blondie)
23. Summer Friends (Chance the Rapper)
24. Big Time Sensuality (Björk)
25. To Hell With Good Intentions (Mclusky)
26. Sleepless (Flume)
27. Jealous Hearted Blues (Ma Rainey)
28. Goodbye England (Laura Marling)
29. And Your Bird Can Sing (The Beatles)
30. Please Mr Postman (The Marvelettes)
31. Sun It Rises (Fleet Foxes)
32. The Ballad of Beginnings (Amelie Ayres)

# The Intro

The list that accompanied the highly anticipated invitation from her dad was strict as hell.

Do not touch the rider unless Mel says it's okay.

Do not touch any instruments, cords, cables, speakers or equipment of any kind! Not even the kettle! Nothing! If you need to charge your phone, speak to Mel.

No photos.

Absolutely do not enter any dressing rooms.

Arrive before 6.45 p.m., go to the side entrance and ask for Mel.

Text me if there are any problems.

No alcohol – this means beer as well.

No photos includes selfies. No selfies.

Amelie Ayres had picked out her outfit the week before. The deliberation in Topshop had been short and to the point; after five minutes, and to her mother's disappointment, she'd opted for (in her mother's words) 'another pair of bloody jeans'. And now, here she was, on her seventeenth birthday, wearing true-blue denim and her favourite faded T-shirt, on her way to London's old Hammersmith Apollo. She flicked open the mirror in her bag to check her look. Her brown fringe was sufficiently straight, and her blue eyes were looking less tired and bloodshot than usual. It would do. She quickly re-applied some of her best friend Maisie's glossy candy-pink lippy.

She was buzzing with excitement. Not about seeing The Keep (they were dreadful beyond measure); no, tonight, for Amelie, was all about being backstage with her dad. She reached for her phone.

TO MAISIE: OMG, on my way. Legs shaved. Arm pits wiped. Not allowed to take pics, but will try a sly snapchat.

FROM MAISIE: You better! Have fun, beee-atch! X

FROM MUM: Have fun. Be Good! No photos! Say hello to your father! Mum xo 🖤, 🐑, 🎋

Although Amelie's parents had never been together, her father had been in her life as regularly as he could manage with his international career. He called or Skyped when he could – and he never let it go more than a few weeks between visits. But since he'd built his prestigious East End recording studio, he'd been way more settled in London and, for the first time, she was going to get a real glimpse into his world.

His band, Ash Fault, had had some small success. In the 1990s they had a few songs in the top forty, he'd appeared on *Top of the Pops* and even dated an actress from *Hollyoaks*, who Amelie had failed to find with Google more than once.

'I actually don't believe anything happened in the whole world ever before 1998,' Amelie had complained. 'What did you do before Google?'

'You remembered things all by yourself, Amelie,' her dad replied.

'You could lie effectively,' her mother moaned.

Amelie thought her dad used to be quite handsome, with his longish, shaggy hair and his classic nineties baggy T-shirts and flannel shirts, but she couldn't for the life of her imagine her parents together. She'd never known it.

These days, Mike Church was one of the most sought after sound engineers in Europe. He preferred not to work with just one act, so he was forever being flown here and there to do big, one-off shows. That's what he was doing tonight; and why, in forty-five minutes' time, Amelie would be joining him backstage at the pop event of the year – The Keep's only UK tour date.

The Keep were one of the biggest, most over-exposed boybands in the world. They had dominated entertainment news online, on TV, on radio and in every social media stream, everywhere, all day, all the time for the last few years. Comprised of five members – Charlie, Kyle, Lee, Art and Maxx – to Amelie they were nothing but a run-of-the-mill boyband. A BIG, massive, hugely successful one, but still with the slightly tragic matchy-matchy outfits, super-styled hair and swathes of tweenage fans. The band's image was starting to look vaguely pathetic now they were around twenty-one.

Amelie hated everything they represented. But even she knew their names. Everyone did.

Charlie, the blond with the hair that sat entirely horizontal, was the clean cut All-American one with the white teeth and the slightly preppy look.

In contrast, Kyle's brown, highlighted hair was completely vertical. He was tall and lean with an impossibly perfect body to go with his pretty, happy and open smile. Kyle looked like he might know what a curling wand or a collagen wave was.

Lee – the rebel – had longer, perfectly messy hair and wore rock star hats and long scarves around his neck. He was skinny and had the lion's share of the band's tattoos. Lee was the womaniser, the drinker and the one all the girls fancied.

Art was the most educated of the five, the oldest and also the strangest – prone to political outbursts and speaking his own, actual thoughts. His tight, curly hair and perfectly symmetrical face had a slightly creepy air about them – he was always relegated to the back row/outer edge of the talk show couch for PR safety reasons.

Maxx, the Memphis boy, was dark haired and, with his current rockabilly cut, had a touch of the young Elvis about him. Those with forensic knowledge knew that he was actually a very good musician, but in a horrific series of life choices he had turned his back on a solo career and ended up in The Keep.

Amelie had to admit, grudgingly, that Maxx was kind of hot; but how could you fancy anyone whose current hit song contained the lines:

> You don't have to say you love me, I can read it on
>      your face.
> Baby the way you look at me; you must think I'm
>      pretty ace. I'm your Ace Ace Baby [repeat × 4]

Lyrics really were the least important thing in pop.

# CHAPTER 1

# I Am Rock 'n' Roll

'Excuse me!' Amelie shouted. 'I'm with the band ...' Her voice trailed off as she cringed in embarrassment. She had to get closer if this was ever going to work.

Rows and rows of teenage girls funnelled by metal barriers were slowly pushing towards the entrance of the venue, moving to the soundtrack of The Keep's new, ingeniously titled compilation album – *Kept*. The scene managed to be orderly, boisterous and chaotic all at once.

'Tickets!' a scalper shouted. 'Seated circle!'

'T-Shirts! CDs! Get your EXCLUSIVE merchandise right here!' shouted a man holding a dodgy printed Keep T-shirt in one hand and glow sticks in the other, his eye scanning the crowd for police.

'*Big Issue*!' yelled a lady in a Keep baseball cap. 'Exclusive interview with Maxx from The Keep!'

'Mum!' screamed a hysterical girl drowning in her oversized Keep onesie.

'Keep moving forward. Stalls to the left, dress circle to the right,' a burly security guard ordered half-heartedly.

Amelie stood a little straighter and raised her chin. Confidence was the key here, just as Dad had told her. She tried to get closer but felt elbows rise to block her path.

On guard were two bald men wearing audio headset's and garish yellow high-visibility jackets, clutching clipboards. To one side, a group of mostly male photographers were chatting, smoking and laughing among themselves; and to the other a large posse of diehard fans and autograph hunters pressed up against the Mojo barriers.

'Excuse me!' shouted Amelie, waving at the nearest guard.

'I said no signings today,' he shouted without looking over. She felt her cheeks flush as she took a deep breath and tried again.

Amelie had practised this many times in her head, but it was hard to hide the nervous edge in her voice. She had to be cool.

'I'm here to see Mel! Mel Knight.'

The guard swung around, eyes suddenly bright. 'Ah. Name?'

'Amelie,' she stumbled. 'Amelie Ayres.'

'Amelie Ayres,' he said in a big, booming voice. 'Sorry, love. Yes, we're expecting you!'

She became aware of some murmurs of intrigue from the crowd behind her, and caught what she thought was a camera flash in the corner of her eye.

He pulled out his radio: 'Security to production.'

*Crackle*. 'Go ahead, security.'

'She's here. Miss Ayres.'

*Crackle*. 'Thanks, security. Mel's on her way.'

'Just wait here a sec, love.' The security guard pulled the rope up and ushered her through. She was on the other side of the barrier, but still just a few metres from the flock of ultra-fans and tabloid shutterbugs, and she could feel their eyes on her.

Suddenly a camera flashed, momentarily blinding her. As Amelie put her hands up to cover her face, another flash exploded, then another and instantly the air became a solid wall of sound and flare, snapping and shouting and sharp white light. Startled and shocked, it took Amelie a second to focus and she realised the paparazzi were aiming their huge lenses in her direction. She felt a familiar surge of terror, exactly as she had felt at the audition last summer when the room went quiet and all eyes were on her.

'Guys, for god's sake. She's no one. A roadie's kid. Forget it,' the security guard snapped angrily. He winked at Amelie and whispered, 'If they think you're *someone*, your photo will end up all over the bloody internet.'

Amelie felt relieved as the photographers immediately lost interest.

There was commotion at the stage door as a very tall and striking woman came striding forward – Amelie couldn't guess her age – with arms full of bangles, a huge, bright-red afro and a shock of magenta lipstick. She beamed at Amelie and waved her over while shouting colourfully in an American accent into her mobile phone.

'Fifteen? I'll let security know. Not much to worry about at the entrance ... No, don't bother stopping, I'll arrange the paps and press now ... Just one interview today ... The *Sun*, of course.'

Amelie opened her mouth to speak, but the woman held up an elegant finger with a bright blue painted nail. *One second!* she mouthed.

'Cars arriving in around ten, stage door entrance!' she said into her phone, before turning to address the waiting paps and fans. 'There won't be a fan greet today, but you'll see them arriving. No. No. They're running late! Sorry.'

She gave a quick wink to Amelie before finishing her call. 'I've just got to drop a little someone at the green room then I'll be right there.'

The woman snapped the cover on her phone shut, looked Amelie up and down, threw her arms around her and landed two air kisses a precise three centimetres from each cheek. 'Hi, I'm Mel. Cute outfit, honey. You look FABULOUS! *Aaaand* you're right on time! Let's get you inside. Did you get here all right?' She walked just ahead, her hips swaying from side to side as her bangles rattled in time.

'Yes, thank you.'

'Let's get you to the green room, doll, and you can have some dinner – have you eaten?'

'No, but I'm not really hungry. Thank you.'

'Not hungry? You're a pop star already! All you need now are butt implants the size of China – I know someone who can help with that – and a fling with John Mayer,' she pursed her lips, 'but ain't nobody need help with *that*. Are you excited for tonight?' she beamed at Amelie, her huge eyes sparkling.

'Yes! Will I see my dad?' Amelie hoped she could shadow him for the night and get in on the real action behind the scenes.

'I think he's gonna be pretty busy, honey. He's doing the support act tonight as well, Dee Marlow? But he might pop across to see you before things kick off.'

Mel led the way down a very tight hallway and up a small flight of stairs to the most unromantic and un-showbizzy green room Amelie could have imagined.

Against the two facing walls sat sad, old, red corduroy couches and shoved against the far wall, underneath a pokey window, there was a small portable table over-filled with food and drinks. There were a couple of sick-looking house plants in their pots-come-ashtrays cowering in the corner and the stained, greasy wallpaper looked as though it had absorbed several decades of debauchery.

'So, you can wait here. I'll come and get you when we have a show. Okay?'

Amelie hesitated. 'It's all glamour back here, right?' Mel laughed. 'Well don't be fooled – this room's hosted some real music royalty over the years. If these walls could talk ... ' she looked around nostalgically, then wrinkled her nose, 'not to mention the carpet – god only knows the dirt this flea-bitten thing could dish out to the tabloids. You know what, I'm just gonna choose to be glad they can't. Your dad told you no photos of the artists, right?'

'Oh yeah, I'm just going to text Mum that I'm here safe.'

'Sure thing, sweetie.' Mel smiled. 'See you in a bit. Everyone knows you're here and to look after you, so don't feel shy about saying hello. Promise?'

Amelie nodded, sinking back into the musty couch and took it all in. The carpet was covered in a smattering of cigarette burns and a patchwork of other stains – a glass of beer spilt here, a magnum of Cristal sprayed there. The food and drinks that formed part of the rider (something Amelie had imagined to be extraordinarily glamorous) looked like an assortment of Iceland party food that had been left out too long at a kid's birthday. She listened with longing to the action out in the hall. Voices shouting about this and that, the thud of equipment being unloaded, issues arising and being solved, it sounded so exciting.

TO MUM: I made it. In the green room waiting for Dad!

TO AMELIE: Just settling down to Bake Off with soupe a l'oignon! Bon Soir! Be Safe dot com! 🔔, ☺, 🍸

The door swung open and a thin, bespectacled, bearded young man marched in, made a bee-line for the food and clumsily piled three mini sausage rolls and a couple of pigs-in-blankets on a napkin.

'Amelie, right? Mike's daughter?'

'Yes, hello.'

'Pig-in-a-blanket?'

A sorry, grey sausage was thrust under her nose.

'Oh, no thank you.'

'Probably wise TBH. Well, hello, Amelie Ayres. I'm Clint. I'm a director, well, cameraman. I'm Julian's other half?'

Julian worked with Amelie's father at his east London recording studio, and he was a total scream.

'Oh. Yes. I've met Julian!' She stood up, feeling immediately at ease.

'Course you have.' He grinned. 'I'm filming the boys backstage and what not. Mike said you were keen to see how it all works. Want me to show you around?'

'Yes. That would be awesome. Only, I'm supposed to wait for Mel.'

'She's outside with the band doing press. The "band" has just arrived.' He smirked. 'Come on, we'll be quick.'

Clint led her out into the hallway. At one end there was a lot of commotion as the band's huge, colourful and lively entourage piled in. She craned her neck but couldn't make out any of the stars among the scrum.

'I should have been filming their arrival, but it's quiet out there. Londoners can be either hysterical or non-plussed. There's no in-between.'

Clint led her through another door onto the side of the backstage area. The enormous stage was right in front of her. She could make out the heaving crowd through a large, black mesh screen – in the darkness she could see heads bobbing about and the blue glow of thousands of mobile phones between camera flashes. Katy Perry was blaring over the sound system – and every minute or so the crowd began to chant.

Amelie was transfixed by the sheer size of the venue and the close proximity of the energised crowd made her feel almost giddy. She looked up to the ceiling – a labyrinth of lights and walkways and props hung overhead. To the side, the wings were covered by huge heavy black curtains and the mesh screen would presumably rise when the band came on.

'No one can see through that screen from out front,' Clint was explaining earnestly. 'The way it's lit; it just looks solid black. Magic, right?'

On the stage side of the screen there was a huge chrome fan (every boyband needs a wind machine, thought a smirking Amelie) and set up on a raised stage was a full drum kit. The plinth was on tracks, presumably so it could move forward. Behind that, hanging from the ceiling all the way to the floorboards, was an enormous, white silky screen – with a projector sat in standby mode shining a faint blue light across it.

'We use that thing during "When I Grow Up" – they have

these pluck-at-yer-heartstrings photos of the boys when they were babies. I mean, at least a few years younger than they are now! God, the mums *love* that number,' he smirked, turning to Amelie. 'It really gets them going. I mean, what the actual eff. Who gets into music thinking, "I just hope I can sell records to MILFs and their children." It's a sorry state.' He shook his head. 'Anyway, enough of that. Time for the main event – this, my lady, is where the magic *really* happens!'

Clint gestured elaborately to a laptop on a small desk.

Amelie looked at it, then back at him, her face completely blank.

'I know. It's pretty dull to look at. Everything is pro-grammed in, I mean, some of it is manual but most of it is programmed for each song. Look.'

He leaned over and hit a few keys and a big spotlight came on above them and lit up the front of the stage. Cheers rang round the hall.

'Ha! Man, these crowds are so easy to wind up.' He flicked the switch off. They both giggled.

'All the lights are rigged up through the console there.'

He flicked another switch and the projector lit up, and bright red flames flickered on the screen. 'Some people make a lot of money designing projections for these big shows.'

'CLINT!' A shiny, red-faced man in a boiler suit approached. 'What are you doing! Don't touch the lights.'

Clint waved Amelie towards the side door. 'You know the way. I need to set up my camera. No big multi-camera job tonight, just background stuff – we're filming the whole show for DVD release later in the tour though. I've got a team of six joining me!' he said proudly. 'Nice to finally meet you.'

'Ah, you too.' Amelie smiled. She was desperate to stay with Clint and watch him work.

'Your dad's a legend by the way.' He grinned, fixing a lens onto his small digital camera. 'Now get out of here before I lose my job.'

Amelie picked her way back through the darkness, pausing to listen as a technician gave a beautifully carved acoustic guitar one final tune-up. Amelie was staring so intently at the floor, petrified of putting a foot wrong and tripping over a cable or rogue amp and falling arse over tit, that she failed to see the figure standing by the side of the stage, psyching herself up – until it was too late.

'Hey! Careful!'

'Shit, sorry, oh my god, I'm so sorr—'

The girl flashed a broad smile and instantly Amelie recognised Dee Marlow.

'Don't worry about it.'

Dee smiled again – friendly but impersonal, well-worn and weary, lonely and jaded and deeply unsatisfied. Amelie knew that smile well.

She smiled back shyly and ducked out of Dee's eye line as quickly as she could. The music in the auditorium faded down with the lights.

'Pssst!' Mel whispered and gestured from the shadows. 'Over here!'

Amelie quickly joined Mel to watch the performance.

On stage, a lone spotlight came on, illuminating a lonely looking guitar and an old 1950s microphone. It was a nice touch. Ella Fitzgerald and Duke Ellington had performed on this very stage all those years ago, and tonight all the imagery and styling was perfectly pitched – paying tribute to Dee's musical influences and cleverly emphasising her credibility at the same time.

Waiting for her cue, Dee put her hand to her ear and bowed her head. Her blonde hair was braided around her face and pulled back from her head. She wore a simple dress made of many layers of white chiffon – her look. Otherworldly.

A drummer slid out from behind the curtain, settled onto his seat and began to tap the high hat. *Tst. Tst. Tst.* The crowd fell completely silent.

Dee took a breath and walked onto the stage. Amelie was spellbound. The surge of applause made her spine tingle, she felt overwhelmed with envy, anticipation and awe.

Dee's voice was warm and husky and pitch perfect. She plucked a few accompanying strings on her guitar – so gentle you could hear the scrape of her fingers across the steel.

'She's a little superstar, right?' Mel whispered into Amelie's ear.

Amelie nodded. She closed her eyes and let the music fill her.

'A lot of talent in that one,' Mel continued. 'Hard to believe she didn't win *American Stars* and The Keep did. Mind you, it's young girls that phone vote in those shows . . . '

Amelie nodded, unable to conceal her excitement.

Song after song filled her soul and reminded her more than ever of what she wanted. She was determined to get selected for the solo spot at Music in the Park, and play and sing her own song for the first time in front of an audience. She knew her dream. There would be no freaking out at the audition. This time she would overcome her nerves and get that place.

Leaning against the wall in the shadows, Amelie noticed a guy listening intensely, his head resting against a beam. His outline – the modern quiff and the curve of his shoulders through a dark T-shirt – was strangely familiar.

For a brief moment a beam of light spilled from the stage and fell on his face. Suddenly, he looked up and caught her staring. They locked eyes. She looked away quickly, cheeks burning: it was Maxx from The Keep.

# CHAPTER 2

# Tightrope

Maxx stood behind his bandmates, forcing a smile, as they were put through their paces by an overly zealous photographer who had them pretending to pile out of a Union Jack-covered Mini.

It was, as usual, utterly excruciating.

'Nice work, monkeys! Smile like you mean it, we're just getting started!' their manager Geoff Smart shouted with sadistic pleasure, waving the press schedule at them as they slipped through the stage door.

The label had been reminding Maxx every day for the past five years to 'just have fun!' and 'be more whacky!' and he still couldn't find a way to smile sincerely.

The boys filed into their one shared dressing room – as was typical with the older venues, it was a little bit of a squeeze.

The others moaned – it wasn't quite the luxury they were used to these days – but Maxx loved every cruddy, crumbling, cramped inch of this place where, in 1968, four boys just a few years older than he was now played their twenty-eight gig residency. He was almost ashamed they were contaminating the memory of The Beatles with their presence.

The room was plastered with posters of gigs past and present. Some framed, some hung with Blu-tack. Paint peeled in the corners of the ceiling, and a faint smell of stale nicotine lingered in every crevice, years after the last cigarette had been lit. There was a make-up chair and a makeshift wardrobe area with their 'outfits' for the night neatly hung and separated with Charlie, Kyle, Lee, Art and Maxx tags. One all-white number to open, a colour coordinated jeans/shirt combo for the middle of the set, when they played their more serious numbers, a black dinner suit for the closing number and a reversible, sequined stars and stripes jacket to wear during 'I'm Your Man (Not Him)' which was their break-out hit, and final encore track.

Naomi, their extremely sassy make-up artist – skinny as a rake, with a frozen face, boob implants and hair extensions (Geoff called her 'The Corpse') was already shaking her head at the sight of Maxx.

'You're first!' she said, tapping on the back of the chair. He slid in and looked at himself in the ring lights around the mirror. He really did look terrible. Dark circles around his eyes, crusty mouth, matted hair and his T-shirt was covered in plane food.

'This is no challenge for you, Naomi, you're a magician.' Maxx smiled at her, and she may or may not have smiled back, he could have sworn he saw some movement in her right cheek.

She had begun to tug at his hair, tutting and huffing, when Mel swung the door open.

'Boys! Great you're all here,' she beamed. They knew Mel well, as she had been their European tour manager since the start. Big and brash with a huge history in the music business – she'd worked with almost every big British artist from Coldplay to Radiohead. And us, thought Maxx glumly.

'So, hello and WELCOME back to London!' She clapped, the jangle of her bracelets waking up Art, who was having his pre-gig Nana nap.

'Look alive you blubbering piss bags,' Geoff murmured, shaking his head.

'Thanks for the press shot out there. You know what the tabloids are like here, better to give them something. Amirite?' Mel laughed. 'Geoff, shall we go over anything? Can I arrange anything extra? There is ample food and drink in the green room. There's no one in there right now – oh! Except the daughter of Mike Church actually, your stand-in sound engineer. We are LUCKY he agreed to do this tonight, so for god's sake, if you see him, thank him. Anyway, please go on in and help yourself to food, tea and coffee and cold drinks. And remember, this is England, so the catering is absolutely dreadful.'

'Yay!' Kyle clasped his beautifully tanned hands together.

'Wow. Mike Church is doing the sound tonight?' Maxx asked.

'That's right, Maxx. You must have heard of *real* music,' Geoff said, addressing the rest of the band. 'Yes. Mike Church is doing your sound. But just tonight.'

'How old's his daughter?' Charlie chimed in with a big sleazy grin.

Maxx's sigh was a little too loud – Charlie overheard and fired him an indignant look.

'Seventeen, I think,' Mel jumped in. 'It's her birthday actually. Anyway, be nice and hands off! We don't screw the crew,' she joked, waving a finger at them all.

This was serendipitous, thought Maxx, wondering if he would have time to meet Mike after the show. After all, if he wanted to build his solo career in some form, there was no one better to talk it over with. After Steve Albini, no one was cooler than Mike.

'Can someone please bring me a cheeseburger and a coke?' Charlie said, signalling he was tired of the conversation.

'Sure, honey.' Mel spoke into her radio, 'Alexia, can you get in here? We need some burgers brought up.'

'I'm vegan,' Art said solemnly.

'Since when?' Charlie sneered.

'I just want a beer. It's eighteen here, right?' Lee said with a big grin.

'Can I also get some gum?' Charlie again.

'Anything else, Charlie? All blue peanut M&M's? Scented candles? Gold toilet seat? Puberty? Culture?' Geoff muttered.

Alexia, one of the band's shared assistants, gently opened the door. She was eighteen and the daughter of one of the label's senior executives in New York. Sporting black jeans and a black T-shirt with '1984' emblazoned across the front in fluorescent yellow, she stood with her leather notebook and usual grin, especially directed at Lee who, after over a year, still hadn't noticed her infatuation.

'Hi, guys.'

'Sexy Lexi!' Lee said with a grin.

'A cheeseburger and a coke, and some chewing gum. Get a few packets of gum actually,' Mel said.

Alexia smiled at Mel and took the notes down. 'GBK okay?'

'Charlie?' Mel looked across.

Charlie had checked out of the conversation altogether and was busy updating his social feeds. It was part of their job to keep their social media streams active and check in with their fandom. Lately things had been getting a little weird for Maxx, with all the Kyle-and-Maxx-gay-fan-fiction and photo-shopped paintings of his head on a dead Jesus. Maxx didn't love it, but they all had to do it.

'Charlie?'

'CHARLIE!'

'What?' He looked up, annoyed. 'I don't mind where it's from. Sorry. Oh, but curly fries if possible. Oh, and no mayonnaise or alliolio or whatever they use here.'

'Aioli,' Alexia confirmed. 'Anything else?' she said, looking across at Lee, who was leaning back looking at the ceiling while trying to spin his chair in circles as fast as he could.

'I need some bottled water, and some fresh boxers,' Kyle said apologetically.

'Over there by the dolls,' Alexia said, pointing to a pile of merch in the corner with a couple of unopened bags from Selfridges.

'For god's sake, can we call them figurines? Or action figures?' Maxx said, half cringing, half laughing at Alexia.

'Or no-action figure in your case,' said Charlie, smirking at Maxx. 'Can you make sure my coke is extra cold, Lexi?'

Alexia nodded, softly closing the door before scuttling off to fulfil her list of requests.

'So, Mel,' Geoff started, 'we need to get the children out of here pronto to make their Berlin flight.'

'Yep, the cars will be here at ten on the nose.'

'No signings etc.'

'No problem, we've let security know.'

'There isn't anything else really, we're good to go.'

*Crackle.* 'Five minutes, everyone.'

'Okay, that's Dee's cue. I'll leave you to it. You're on in thirty, since it's just a short set tonight.' Mel closed the door to the tiny room behind her.

'Lee, you and Art are going to do the sit-down with the *Sun*, okay?'

Lee stopped spinning to give the thumbs up.

'Be interesting, Art. Don't talk about politics or any other weird shit again. Or better still, don't talk. We need the column inches. And can EVERYONE please do their YouTube diary with Clint today? We need to get them up. Seems that you're losing viewers, along with record and ticket sales,' Geoff said, rather too joyfully.

'Got it, Pops,' Lee replied, as he enjoyed the dizzy rush from ten minutes of spinning.

'You're done.' Naomi spun Maxx around in the chair. He was copiously quaffed and powdered; his hair combed into a modern quiff which was frozen stiff with litres of hairspray, and he had a large, white and silver glittered star on his cheek – as per their opening 'look'.

'I look like a cross between Elvis and a My Little Pony,' Maxx said.

'Yeah,' said Geoff. 'And it makes us all millions.'

Despite the fact he seemed to have actual contempt for the band, Maxx liked Geoff. It didn't matter who they were meeting or where they went, he would be there in a pair of Adidas tracksuit pants and a sweat-stained T-shirt, complaining about the heat, or his psoriasis, or the fact that he forgot to bring his earplugs to their gig and would have to waste 'another fucking hour of his life listening to their puerile crap'.

When they had played at Yankee Stadium, he had arrived late wearing a T-shirt that read 'Boybands Suck'.

'I nearly managed The Smiths,' he'd once muttered with grim disbelief. 'Fuck me.'

It often seemed to Maxx like Geoff hated the business and didn't know what he was doing. But their success was undeniable, so he must know something. And the label's head honchos (or *tasteless trend-hoppers*, as Geoff called them) seemed to think he was one of the best.

Maxx made his way to the door. 'I've got time to watch Dee's set, right?'

'You always seem to find the time,' Art said with a grin and a raised eyebrow.

'I haven't seen her play since Boston,' Maxx added, embarrassed, as he closed the door behind him.

Dee's set was overwhelmingly beautiful and so polished. She had grown into a really good performer and even though some of it felt a bit gimmicky, there was no denying the vast improvement. Unlike The Keep, her star was on the rise.

When Dee pushed her way off stage, flushed, sweating and positively radiant, Maxx leaned into the shadows so she couldn't see him. He watched her hug Geoff and then Mel and unscrew the top of a cold water bottle. She gulped it down, slowly catching her breath as Mel introduced her to *that girl* Maxx had caught staring at him during the set.

No doubt she was a competition winner or something. A

fangirl who had called in a hundred times to win some local radio station giveaway – *'Meet your idol backstage in London for one minute and forty-five seconds, and get a quick photo (approved by management) and a signed album (if you're lucky) and be completely patronised by everyone along the way – on us!'*

But this girl didn't look like the usual fan. For one, she looked cool. That typically British brand of vaguely subversive cool – effortless and unapologetic.

Next to Dee she was very slight, with elegant hands that, when released from her jeans pockets, she used in wild gesticulation.

Dee was so much better with fans than he was. She could easily play the part of the grateful artist, and really took her time to speak with them, so it came as no surprise they stopped chatting to take a quick selfie. Yes, definitely a competition winner, Maxx thought.

Dee touched the girl's shoulder warmly and gave her one final smile before turning to make her way to the green room, the smile disappearing the instant she was not on show. The stage was dark, and although Dee was barely off, the audience was starting to chant for The Keep between surging applause and cheers. He felt bad that she didn't get the same fanatical reception that his band did, when she was far and away the superior artist.

She was also the only one that would understand how stifled he felt in The Keep and how desperate he was to do his own thing again. He needed to talk to someone about it, and would try to catch her tonight if he could. He was sure she would not deny him that.

He sighed, and forced himself back into the dressing room to pull his horrible, embarrassing, stupid outfit on. And grab some food. He had about three minutes.

# CHAPTER 3

# Charmless Man

If Amelie saw nothing else that night, the trip had been worth it times a million. To see someone like Dee playing and singing, and watching the crew backstage working their simple magic with the show, was so incredible she felt she had memories to last her forever. But to meet Dee properly was something else. Dee was friendly, even warm with her – and Amelie was delighted at her suggestion they take a photo, even if that did mean she spent a few minutes cropping, retouching and filtering it before handing her the phone back. Amelie had immediately sent it via Snapchat to Maisie.

TO MAISIE: Look! It's my new BFF ;-)

She dreamed one day of writing songs that good, and playing them onstage or having people like Dee come to watch *her* play.

As Amelie dreamily made her way to the green room she immediately recognised Charlie from The Keep loitering in the hallway. He was fully and audaciously made up – leaning back, furiously typing on his phone. He was unmistakable as the All-American one – the blond-haired, blue-eyed dreamboat. He was the kind of guy you see in high school movies – a cherry coke-drinking, high school football-playing, cheerleader-dating guy – fused with half a pot of hair gel and some very questionable make-up. Amelie found it a total turn-off, and she was far too proud to be mistaken for some kind of fan.

The hallway was buzzing with backstage staff making the final touches for the headline act. Roadies pushed past with guitars, microphone stands, London-themed props, and three identically dressed backing singers squeezed by giggling and gossiping. The hallway was not wide, but Amelie hoped she could slip past unnoticed.

She looked straight at the ground, desperately trying to make out that she was busy with something else as she started her confident saunter past, which in truth just felt hugely fraudulent and awkward.

'Hey there!' Charlie raised his eyebrows and plastered on a toothy smile that was so fixed it made Amelie wonder if it was permanent.

There was no avoiding him. 'Oh, hi.'

He seemed to be waiting for something.

'It's Charlie, right?' she obliged, immediately irritated. Yes, Mr Superstar, I recognise you, she thought.

'Yeah. I'm Charlie. You working here?' His accent was thick and his teeth were completely distracting. They were so white they almost glowed. She tried not to stare.

'Um, no, my dad is working here.'

'Your daddy, huh?'

His eyes narrowed as if he had hit upon something. 'What's your name?' The glow of his teeth keenly matched the all-white opening number outfit he was wearing and he smelt like dry cleaning and fresh wall plaster. He nodded to a man in an oversized fur shrug who sashayed past, giving Amelie the once over.

'Um, Amelie . . . Ayres.'

'Oh! Our soundie's daughter, right? It's your birthday, isn't it?' Although he was ridiculously handsome, he was so clean and polished that Amelie was repelled. The antitheses of real. The opposite of rock and roll. She tried to take a step towards the green room but he had put his arm up, partially blocking the route. She would have to duck under it to get past.

'Um, yes. It is,' she said, blushing, suddenly aware Charlie was observing someone over her shoulder.

'So you saw Dee then, but you're not watching us?' He was definitely blocking her. It was subtle, but although Amelie felt too polite to push his arm out of the way, she was beginning to feel extremely annoyed at her space being invaded.

'But, sweetheart, we're the headliners,' he tried to joke; but Amelie's hackles were up. There was no stopping her.

'Boybands are not really my thing,' she said flatly. 'I'm just here to see my dad.'

'Oh, I see.' For a whisper of a moment he looked hurt, then disbelieving. 'You don't like us, even just a little?'

'Yeah. I'm more Talk Talk than Take That.' She stood firm, and she felt someone brush past, and from the corner of her eye caught a glimpse of Maxx's loose charcoal T-shirt and the unmistakable quiff.

'Hey. You met Amelie, Maxx? Mike's daughter?' Charlie's tone was almost antagonistic.

'Um, sorry ... I ...' was the clipped response, the thick southern tone to his voice marking him unmistakably as the guy from Memphis. He turned, his dark eyes locking on Amelie, who couldn't remove the 'fuck you' face she had just prepared for Charlie. 'I have to get ready ... and eat.' Maxx smiled wanly and sped off down the corridor.

Amelie could make out the hint of a smirk on Charlie's face.

'So, what were we saying? You wanna talk later?'

'ONE MINUTE! WHERE IS MY SODDING BAND?' Geoff screamed from the stage door. 'Unhook yourself from that poor child, Charlie!'

'Show time!' Charlie said with an arrogant grin. 'How do I look?' He stretched his arms out and straightened his shirt cuffs. She wanted to comment on his hint of a paunch, or the whisper of hair loss evident at his crown, but instead she opted for a clean escape.

'Good. Nice. Yeah, I have to go.' Amelie pushed him just as he stepped out of the way, which caused her to stumble forward into the wall, just catching herself before she landed face first on the carpet.

She marched into the safety of the green room without looking back and flung the door open. Who did that guy think he was? What a totally arrogant, rude bastard, she fumed, ranting away under her breath, when another one of *them* burst into the green room and marched straight past her to the food table.

'You're on in one minute!' she barked, far more angrily than she had intended.

'What?' Maxx spun around, hurriedly buttoning his shirt while trying to shove a stale egg sandwich into his mouth. 'Shit! I totally missed the call. As usual. Thanks!'

He was dressed differently now – almost unrecognisable all in white. Up this close Amelie could see the same thick make-up that Charlie was wearing, though Maxx's was covering a hint of dark stubble. None of them looked as baby-faced as they did in their press shots.

'Thanks,' he said again, fixing his stare on her. Amelie quickly turned away. 'I'm Maxx. I saw you. Backstage, right? So you're Mike's daughter? Amy-Lee? I thought you won a radio competition.'

He took a half step towards her, then stopped. 'I mean. Well. Sorry if I was rude, I'm just always late.'

Amelie kept her eyes averted, fumbling for her phone. He paused again for a moment before heading to the door.

'Sorry. Phone call,' she said quickly, turning away, desperate not to engage him further. He seemed to immediately get the hint.

'Well, thanks again,' he said as he slipped out.

For a moment she just sat there, shaken. Then, as if it had all the answers, she pulled out her phone.

> TO MAISIE: I just met Charlie from TK and he's a total nob.

> TO DAD: Where are you? Will I get to see you?

> FROM MAISIE: Ooooh my favourite one! Bummer. Mum and I are making homemade deodorant from vodka! So my night is worse.

Amelie sat staring at the screen, feeling like she'd rather miss the band perform altogether, when another message popped up.

FROM DAD: Are you backstage? Did Clint come and show you round? Mel? Everything okay?

TO DAD: In the green room, Dee amazing, can't wait to see you x

Her phone beeped almost instantly.

FROM DAD: Okay see you in the GR after show. Don't miss the boys – I know it's not your thing – but it's pretty fun. Gotta go! They're on!

TO DAD: Sure thing. X

She dragged herself out to watch the show, and ninety minutes later she was surprised to find that she'd been thoroughly entertained – if not by the music, then by the tour-de-force performance. She had never seen a crowd like it! The screams were deafening; girls were crying, one hapless tweenager fainted and had to be dragged from the front row.

She watched each of the band – their dance moves were

ever so slightly out of time with their enthusiastic finger pointing, but they were pitch perfect as they swept up the crowd; mothers, daughters and gay men alike. The consummate professionals.

Though the music did nothing to showcase any kind of vocal originality, Maxx was clearly the best singer. Art had a deep vocal, warm and bluesy, but he clearly couldn't dance, Charlie was the OTT-double-decker-cheese-on-toast who didn't sing solo, like, once; Kyle was the nice one – so smiley and sweet; and Lee was the crowd favourite – every time he sang a solo (which was not as often as the audience would have liked) the cheers turned to deafening screams. There were knickers thrown.

Amelie found herself giggling and foot-tapping along to the saccharine love songs and explosive pop hits (complete with fire and sparklers) – even the hardest cynic couldn't fail to be caught up in the spectacle.

# CHAPTER 4

# Going to the Party

'Sweetheart, I need you to head out and jump in any of the cars lined up out back, there's been a slight change of plan,' Mel said, looking a little stressed.

'But, my dad . . . ?' Amelie asked meekly as the house lights snapped on. She was unprepared for the stampede as the backstage area was dismantled and sweaty, sparkly, slightly liquored bodies were ushered out.

'He'll meet you there.' Mel winked. 'Hurry now.'

'But where?' Amelie called out as Mel disappeared down the side of the stage.

The only thing for it was to do as she'd been told, and soon Amelie found herself in a motorcade heading across London to the Sanderson Hotel's private Purple Bar, for an impromptu opening night soiree.

The Sanderson was a huge, once achingly trendy hotel and

bar in Fitzrovia, central London. In the lobby, two plucky blondes with matching boob jobs were sipping orange-coloured cocktails on a massive red couch shaped like a pair of luscious lips, and groups of men in dark suits drank brandy – no doubt discussing yachts, golf and/or watches, casually spending the average annual wage every time they bought a round.

Amelie found herself a little bit awestruck and intimidated by the ostentatiousness of it all. She kept running her fingers through her hair and straightening out her top. Nothing can be done about the trainers, she groaned inwardly, immediately searching out Clint for a little moral support.

The band, the managers, the make-up artists – they all milled around, radiating delight at the success of the show. Dee sat on a long leather couch, lazily holding court, now changed into soft blue trousers, a silver top and sandals, her hair freed from the plaits and falling softly around her shoulders. She looked every inch the superstar on down time; haughty demeanour in place, nose slightly raised, undeniable magnetic aura initiated.

Charlie, Art and Kyle were also milling about, still in their sweaty closing-number outfits, but Lee had changed and was washed clean of make-up, and so was Maxx, who looked infinitely more handsome in his Ramones T-Shirt, jeans and Converse. Amelie noticed with interest the edge of a small tattoo, peeking out from a sleeve rolled-up on a very defined arm.

She couldn't help taking a lingering look, and felt a pang of guilt for her earlier rudeness. Of the five, there was definitely something about him – he seemed a bit of a misfit next to the others, who all wore their atypical boyband personas with pride.

Moody electronica played over the speakers, while model-esque waitresses carried trays of champagne cocktails and ludicrously tiny macrobiotic canapés around to ravenous musicians.

'More like it, eh?' Clint smiled, using the smallest of pincer grips to pluck a miniscule gluten-free vegan slider out of its edible paper wrapper.

'Wow,' Amelie said, genuinely. 'No wonder rich people are so skinny.'

'That's negative eight calories,' beamed the hovering waitress, pointing at an unspecified stick of vegetation, impaled by a sterling silver toothpick. 'If you count the energy your body needs to digest it!'

'Sounds delicious,' said Amelie politely. 'I wish my friend Maisie could see this, she would be in heaven!'

'So how did you like the gig?' Clint asked. 'We always open at a smaller venue with a slightly pared-down show. Test the set list, see how the audience responds, if there's anything missing from the show – that kind of thing.'

'Slightly pared down! Are you kidding?' Amelie laughed. 'Who comes up with it all? The music, the outfits, the lighting? It's all so carefully choreographed – it's perfectly in sync.'

'N Sync,' Clint snorted. 'Look, it depends. The Keep have an artistic director, that guy there – Ashton.' Clint waved towards the man in the enormous (Louis Vuitton) fur shrug from earlier, who was now brandishing an elaborate gilded cane, and slowly sipping something from a silver thermos. 'Urine diet.' Clint screwed his nose up.

'Ewwww. So, *he's* in charge of how they dress?' Amelie said cheekily. 'No wonder.'

'Yeah, well, Ashton does all the concepts and stuff. He used to work with McQueen, you know. Brought in to make the boys more edgy,' Clint said blankly, before turning to Amelie and raising his eyebrows.

Amelie really liked Clint. He was slightly nerdy, what Maisie would call gawkward – but he was warm and friendly and he must be very good at what he did, how else would he be touring with this band as their on-the-road video director aged just twenty-three? He talked fast, jumping from thought to thought, constantly fidgeting – pushing his glasses back up on his nose or twisting a strand of his beard round and round until it stuck out like a spear.

Amelie burst out laughing. 'But does he decide – like make final decisions – or does the band?'

'The band?' Clint laughed. 'Erm, no. Not the band. They don't decide on much. But that's the gig, right? Handsome front men, but when you peel back the curtain, as they say ... there's nothing there but that guy.' He pointed across to Geoff, who was slyly picking his nose while barking orders at a young assistant. 'If you *had* to do one though, which one?'

Amelie giggled, ignoring the bait. 'But ... surely they have some input?'

'Well, no. Geoff and the label do it all really. Well, the team, you know. I mean Dee has more involvement because it's more *her* thing rather than a *production*. But The Keep? Nah. They're one hundred per cent music industry construct. Puppets really. Not that you'd ever say it to their faces.'

Amelie looked across at Dee, who was starting to tire of the attention around her and looked ready to leave. She stretched out a hand in front of her, surveying her perfect manicure, before chewing on the side of her pinkie and peering around the room as if searching for someone. She rubbed her eyes and yawned, waving away the offer of more champagne from a fawning waiter.

'Bloggers,' Clint continued – pointing at two completely straight-looking men observing from the fringes. 'You can tell a blogger from a vlogger by their looks. And age. But mostly their looks. Bloggers are the new Radio DJs,' he laughed.

'The Keep have had a good run though,' he said diplomatically. 'I mean, in boyband years, they're the same age as Madonna.'

'But they're only twenty or twenty-one though, right?'

'Yeah, but it's been five years! One of them has *got* to leave soon. I've got my money on Lee.'

'Where's my girl?' A voice boomed from across the room.

'There she is! Happy birthday, my darling.' Amelie's dad strode over, hitching up his jeans as he walked, popped down a glass of champagne he hadn't touched, and – much to Amelie's embarrassment – picked her up and spun her around.

'Dad! Finally!' Amelie tried to pull away from his vice grip but felt herself slipping into giggly baby girl mode.

'Ahh. How are you?' He planted kiss after kiss on her forehead. 'I'm so sorry I didn't get to see you before the show. Did you have fun?'

Her father's arrival had drawn attention, particularly from Charlie, who had been hovering near Dee but now appeared to be making his way over. Amelie glanced at her phone. 10.15. Why hadn't the band left for Berlin yet? They were supposed to be gone by now.

'It was good,' she said with mild enthusiasm, becoming uncomfortably aware that Charlie had manoeuvred himself to be just within earshot.

Her dad grinned. 'Come on, there's got to be some regular seventeen-year-old underneath all that cool?'

'Okay. Yeah, it was really fun,' she conceded, desperately trying to move so that Charlie was no longer in her peripheral vision.

'So I think everyone's hanging about for a bit. Hey, Mel.'

'Hey, Mikey,' Mel said, cruising over with her phone wedged between her ear and shoulder and a cocktail in her hand. They kissed each other's cheeks. 'I'm on hold,' she whispered.

'What's happening? I was going to take Amelie for supper, but if everyone's hanging back a little longer now ...'

'Not long, we're just here for a bit.' Mel checked her watch. 'Their plane won't be ready until morning now so we'll have to stay in London. The rooms here are taken – some luxury goods conference – Ashton is beside himself. But we'll sort it.' Winking, she raised a finger and spoke into her phone, 'Yes, we'll need nine rooms. How many can you do?' She looked at Amelie's dad and rolled her eyes.

'That's Alexia,' whispered Clint, continuing his guided tour of the room. 'We like her. She wants to be a director one day, so I try to get her to help out when she's not fetching things for the *talent*.'

Alexia was tucked away in the corner of the room, crouched on the floor with one of her three mobile phones plugged into the wall socket and a plastic wallet spilling paperwork, pens and a small bottle of Bach remedy on the floor.

'Hey, the sound was brilliant. Expect Geoff to come and hit you up,' Mel said to Mike.

He shook his head, modestly. 'Appreciate it, love. But, you know me.'

At just that moment Geoff was swaggering his way through the entourage, swearing at the inconvenience of the half-metre detour required to circumnavigate a group of people. He absent-mindedly positioned himself right in front of Clint and Amelie to talk to her father.

'Remember when a pub was enough? What is this fucking

place?' he said, scratching a scaly pink patch of skin on his arm.

'Geoff! Mate,' Amelie's dad said, warmly patting the manager on the shoulder. Amelie knew they had worked together for years, as he'd often remarked that Geoff would be a 'good contact' for her one day.

'Great stuff tonight, Mike. So ... what will it take to convince you, mate?' Geoff held his hand up. 'What's your price?'

'Arghh! I'm sorry, man, I just can't do it.' Mike shook his head.

'Everyone has a price. Even for this sack of moose shit,' Geoff said, waving in the general direction of the band. 'Honestly, I need you. It almost sounded like actual *music* tonight – I took my earplugs out for more than three minutes.'

Amelie knew her dad was good, but it was quite another thing to see someone like Geoff grovelling to him like this. She felt a surge of pride.

'Sorry.' Mike shook his head with a half grin. 'You're like an old dog with a stick, mate.' He turned to Amelie and Clint. 'Will you guys give us a minute? Amelie, you can have *one* beer if you want. If they serve it here.'

'The boys don't like old pubs ... ' Mel remarked as Amelie and Clint wandered to the other side of the room, skirting around the three backing singers who were now deliciously lubricated and starting to thirst for a boogie.

While Geoff, Mel and her father chatted, Amelie watched on, amazed by the throngs of people that came in a constant stream to ask something of them; nobody daring to interrupt too quickly. It was easy to see that though the *star* power was assembled like an Annie Leibowitz *Vanity Fair* cover around the band and Dee, the *real* power was in that circle. So when Maxx edged self-consciously up, stopping for longer than a quick thank you, she was intrigued that her father immediately engaged in conversation.

As Amelie craned her neck, trying to catch a word or two, someone turned the music up, making it impossible to make out anything. She gave up and took a quick swig of the single barrel boutique pale ale Clint had handed her.

'You stuck around, huh?' Charlie made his move, his sweaty, smeared face literally popping up right in front of her. 'Great show, right?'

'Yeah, I was waiting for my dad,' Amelie replied flatly, her eyes still on her father and Maxx. They couldn't know each other, could they? Dad hadn't worked with a boyband before, let alone The Keep.

'Ah, yes,' Charlie said, also eyeing her father and Maxx. 'So, what did you think?' He turned to Clint, 'Hey, we need to do a video diary, don't we?'

'Yep,' Clint smiled. 'Hi, Charlie.'

'Hiya ... ' Charlie paused for a moment to think. 'Clint!' He smiled, pleased with himself for remembering. 'Well? Tell me! What did you think, Amelie Ayres?'

'It was good, actually.' Amelie was feeling charitable. 'I enjoyed it.'

'Oh yeah?' At that, Charlie's manner changed, and his slightly smug grin reappeared. 'So, won you over, did we?'

Amelie gritted her teeth, while Clint coughed, trying to obscure a giggle.

'I like playing in those smaller places sometimes,' Charlie continued, oblivious. 'It makes a change. We never had to do the rounds in those kind of places. You know, because we were so *instantly* huge.'

Amelie tried to imagine The Keep doing the rounds of the local venues and pubs in east London, singing their tacky love songs in a single-line formation to a room full of acutely critical hipsters. They would be crushed.

'Champagne?' A waitress approached with a tray, beaming at Charlie.

'No, I'm good,' Charlie said, and she sashayed off. 'There are a couple of "serious" music bloggers here – invited of course – but I gotta be careful,' he continued, nodding to the jeaned and sneakered thirty-somethings still skirting the edges of the party. 'That's why it's good to talk to you guys. Deflection. You're nobody to them. I mean ... no offence.' He smiled.

On he droned. Amelie couldn't resist an eye roll, which she indulged just at the moment Dee looked over at her. Ashamed of herself, Amelie quickly looked away.

Amelie willed her father to come and save her from

Charlie's incessant rambling. She wondered if the band didn't get to meet people their own age often – or at least ones that weren't dressed head to toe in Keep merchandise.

'Are you two together?' Charlie asked. Prompting Clint to burst into laughter and Amelie to blush wildly.

Amelie had never had a boyfriend and had only once been kissed – Leslie Kilpatrick on the back stairs at the third-form disco. Leslie was the dumpy lead in choir, and Amelie did it purely out of boredom, and then deeply regretted it after it took all of the next year to shake him.

She had had a small crush on her guitar tutor, Jasper Poshwood (not his real name), who was really handsome and a great guitarist. He was something of a local celebrity – he often busked at Columbia Road flower market alongside a friend on double bass – but last summer Jasper had grown a twirly moustache, so that ruled him out immediately. And he was also called Jasper, which was far too west London for her tastes.

'Eh, no,' Amelie stammered.

'So, you on Twitter?' Charlie asked. 'I'll follow you. What's your name on there?' he said, pulling out a brand new iPhone.

'Umm . . . ' Warning bells sounded and Amelie racked her brain for a stalling tactic.

Just then Kyle walked over. 'Hey, Charlie. Cars are here.'

'Well?' Charlie's finger was lingering on the keypad. 'Come on, I like to follow someone after every gig.'

She couldn't get out of it. 'Um, it's @callmeamelie98.'

'Sorry,' Kyle apologised to Amelie. 'He really has to get CHANGED! Oh my god, happy birthday, right? It's Amelie?'

She nodded and smiled at Kyle, his warmth irresistible.

'Two L's?' Charlie asked as he was leaving, Amelie pretended to be distracted by the dessert canapés that were now doing the rounds.

'Looks like you've got a fan there,' Clint grinned. 'Look at you! You lucky, lucky thing. I forgot it's your birthday, how rude of me. How old are you. Let me guess. Seventeen?'

'Exactly.' Amelie smiled. 'This was my present. It's my first gig backstage.' It was almost 100 per cent likely that Charlie would forget her Twitter name and not follow her, but she had to admit the idea was a little amusing.

'Your first gig!' Clint laughed. 'Well, happy birthday, Amelie.' He handed her the world's smallest cupcake canapé; it was no bigger than a 20p coin and had a tiny flag in it, which read 'sugar free'.

'How perfectly depressing,' Amelie said, as she popped it into her mouth, and watched Maxx file out the main door.

# CHAPTER 5

# Futile Devices

Maxx stood hunched over by the entrance of the Sanderson, watching the London nightlife stumble past. He stared longingly across at the White Horse, a proper British pub, where weary staff wiped down tables and collected empty pint glasses while trying to usher out the last of the singing drunks. One made a beeline for a parked Porsche and gleefully took a piss on it while singing The Keep's second ever single, the dubiously titled 'Golden Rain', at full volume.

A black cab pulled up and two impeccably suited young men and their beautiful, high-fashion partners stepped out onto the street. The women's thousand-pound Louboutin's were welcomed warmly by the fawning, stuttering doorman.

'Soccer players,' Art's deep, gravelly voice sounded out from the shadow where he was waiting. 'They're like gods in England.'

'Oh,' Maxx mumbled, watching two paparazzi arrive on motorbikes. He bowed his head slightly as they set up their lenses, willing the rest of the band to hurry.

He tucked the piece of paper with Mike's phone number into his back pocket. Mike seemed intent on pushing him to come and 'just record some songs and see how it goes', and his fatherly and encouraging way had made Maxx feel like it was something he could almost do.

Maxx wanted to make sure he got in a car with Dee who, after unhooking herself from numerous lecherous admirers, was waiting with her small bag for the chauffeur to open the door.

'Can I ride with you alone?' Maxx blurted out.

Dee glanced briefly at Charlie, who was also waiting by the car. 'Go ahead,' Charlie remarked.

She then nodded towards the paparazzi, who were starting to shout.

'Dee! Dee! Give us a snap.'

'Come on, love! One of you and the fella!'

'Maxx! Come on, mate.'

'One photo!'

'Sure, Maxx,' Dee said warmly. 'Quick.'

She spun around and, grabbing Maxx by the arm, flashed a huge smile at the waiting paparazzi – their cameras went crazy and she gave a small wave as they slipped into the waiting car.

'May as well give them one,' she smiled. 'Might be the last.'

'Yeah,' Maxx said, caught off-guard, his eyes stinging from the flash of bulbs.

'Great gig as usual. I loved your solo number!' she teased.

'Thanks, Dee.' Maxx felt ashamed. He hated his solo number, a moody, faux-country hit he had to sing while straddling a pink fibreglass horse.

'I hate that we have to stay tonight! Arghh ... we have to get up at five a.m. now – did Mel tell you?'

Maxx looked at his watch. That was in five hours' time! Damn it. Another night of little sleep.

He watched Mike get into the car in front with Amelie. They were heading back to the East End for 'a proper supper of pie and mash' before he dropped his daughter off. For a moment he imagined going with them, to see the real London with a couple of locals. To slip into a booth somewhere cosy, eat that pie and 'chew the fat' into the small hours, talking music with Mike and maybe with that feisty daughter of his.

'So, I just wanted to talk.' He looked out of the window, feeling too pathetic to look Dee in the face. The driver turned the radio on, sensing a moment of intimacy, but unfortunately for Maxx he chose the *Love Songs Until Dawn* programme on Heart FM, kicking off with that awful 70s classic, 'I'm Not in Love', which was the worst possible score to this scene.

'Yes? What's up?' Taking a big deep breath, Dee turned her phone face down and looked at him over-earnestly.

'I just needed to talk to you.' He was sounding out his thoughts. He hadn't actually thought this through properly.

'What is it?'

'I dunno.' He gazed out the window as they drove down rainy Oxford Street past the massive flagship stores – Topshop, H & M, Selfridges – London still brimming with life even as the heavens truly opened. 'I guess, I feel ... '

What did he feel exactly? He wasn't sure. He looked over at her now; she looked smaller, more real, more like a girl you might meet at school or at the mall. Her hands clasped together on her lap.

'Maxx.' Dee shifted in her seat.

'No, no, it's not what you think.'

*I'm not in lo-ove ...*

The song on the radio seemed to be working overtime to humiliate him further. He rubbed his head in his hands and felt sweat forming on the back of his neck.

*So don't forget it ...*

'Jesus. This isn't going well,' he said regretfully.

*It's just a silly phase I'm going through ...*

'I still don't understand, I guess. I mean, what happened,' he tried.

'I told you, I'm busy with ... you know, the new album ... ' She paused.

'Yeah, I just don't understand. I guess I wasn't expecting it. I didn't think you were so unhappy.'

'If I'm honest, Maxx,' she spoke gently, 'you seemed pretty unhappy yourself.'

He hadn't considered this; he had been unhappy in the band

of course – but he'd never felt unhappy with her. He sighed, thankful the song was starting to fade.

'It wasn't you,' he started.

'It was me?' she smirked.

'Sorry.'

'Well, neither of us were having a good time, you know, so it was better to call it off. And, of course, management were pissed that the press found out we were dating,' she said practically, before quickly adding, 'Not that that had ANYTHING to do with it!'

He sat in silence, trying to make sense of his feelings.

'Can you at least admit you weren't happy?' she tried.

'Yeah, I guess. Arghh . . . this band. I can't escape it.' He put his head in his hands.

She tried to steer the conversation. 'You should really get on with it. You know, writing again. Everyone knows you hate it in the band – it's pretty obvious.'

He looked up with shock. 'It is?'

'You seem bored. Even, embarrassed sometimes? You shouldn't, by the way. There are plenty of much worse bands out there – and you've had, like, how many top ten singles? How many platinum albums? How many Teen Choice awards? But you want to do your own thing, right?'

Maxx nodded. 'Yeah. I don't know if I can do it any more. I just don't know how to pick up a guitar any more and play. Do you get that?'

'Yeah, I do.' She touched his hand. 'You need to just enjoy

your time with The Keep. Like, you know, Charlie does. He knows it's a short-term thing.'

Maxx curled his lip up at the mention of Charlie.

'No one likes a Man Band,' Dee tried to joke. 'It's not forever. And lord knows, you're all getting on a bit. Art is talking about doing a degree in Roman Economics, for god's sake.'

'I'm boring. Jesus, Maxx. Get a grip.' He sighed, looking across at her, starting to wonder what the fuck he was doing. She fidgeted with her phone impatiently.

'Can you hold that thought?' She held a finger up. 'I'm so sorry, but I really need to finish this Instagram post. Which one?'

She held up her phone to show him three photos – one of her Union Jack-painted nails, a moody shot of her from behind, standing in the rain with a yellow umbrella, and finally one of her waving from inside a red phone box.

'The phone box one?' Maxx said half-heartedly, wondering where she found the energy for it all.

'I don't like my hair in that,' she said doubtfully. 'I'll do the nails.'

The car holding Lee and Charlie pulled up next to them at the traffic lights. Lee did a blowfish on the window.

'Sorry. That was insensitive of me. So, what were you saying?' Dee asked distractedly, her fingers still fondling her phone. 'By the way, do you hashtag England or Great Britain or the UK? It's a mystery.'

'London?' Maxx offered limply.

She finished up, and turned back to him. 'Sorry,' she said once again, smiling at him to continue.

'I guess I miss someone to connect with in the down time, like we used to . . . ' His voice trailed off.

'But I'm completely deranged, remember?' She tried to make light of it, but on a rare and slightly risky evening out together she had knocked a huge glass of red wine over Maxx when he tried to kiss her – and unfortunately for everyone the incident was caught on video and ended up on notorious gossip website The Buzz. *Dee-Ranged to The Maxx!* was the headline.

They had managed, through various diversionary tactics, to keep their short relationship so secret that the press was caught completely off-guard, and there was a surge of attention at the discovery, despite the fact they were actually at the end of the road.

Management had made the call not to let them go public about their break up, since Dee had a new album coming out in the autumn. Dee didn't seem to care about playing the part; she was good at the game.

'Ha!' He stared back out the window as they drove along the edge of Hyde Park, neon lights shining across puddles on the pavements as young Londoners hid under awnings or made their way arm in arm under umbrellas.

'But seriously, it's strange. Talking to you now, I'm not sure what's been going on with me. I was a good musician once.'

'I know. You still are, you're just rusty.' Her voice was becoming a little clipped.

'I sometimes feel like I don't know myself,' he said, accidently and far too dramatically, just as Coldplay came on the radio. 'Oh god. Kill me now,' he laughed.

But he knew Dee got it. At his level of fame you become your image, you lose yourself in the promotions, appearances, photo shoots, red carpets. You 'turn it on' because it's what everyone expects, and the more you do that, the harder it is to turn it off again.

'What do you want from me?' Dee sighed. 'Because as your *friend* I'll do whatever I can to help you.'

'Okay,' he conceded.

'So what can I do?'

There was a long silence before Maxx sighed. 'I feel like a dick.'

She brightened up and her eyes widened in excitement. 'I've got a BRILLIANT idea. Why don't we collaborate? Just you and me? A song together?'

Maxx looked at her, surprised but strangely intrigued by the idea.

'Oh my god,' she continued, 'that's totally what we should do. A duet. It will be amazing!'

'Would you be into that?' Maxx was slightly wary, since Dee was known to get wrapped up in things and then quickly drop them, like a bored child.

'Of course! My god, you'd be helping me. Anything that helps raise my profile. What do you think?'

'What do you think *Geoff* would say?'

'Let's talk to him together. He won't hate the idea. I don't see why they can't accommodate at least ONE of my ideas into something I do!'

'What? You write all your songs!'

'Well, yeah, *just* – but that's where the freedom ends, my friend. I can't tell you how much I want my red hair back. Not to mention to get out of those ridiculous white dresses!'

'Hey, I'd love to do that.' Maxx allowed himself to feel a little excited. 'I'd just love to. I hope Geoff goes for it.'

'We don't actually have to tell him yet. Let's come up with some ideas, and have a few jams first. See if it fits. Before we, you know, tell anyone.'

Maxx knew exactly what she was getting at. The rest of the guys would be a little miffed by a collaboration with Dee. It would be the first major project that one of them had taken on outside the sacred five-piece. But it was something he felt sure he could handle.

'Oh, I'm really excited about this. Let's find some down time this tour and just get on with it.' Maxx fingered the phone number in his jean pocket. 'Hey, you know Mike Church. Tonight's sound engineer?'

'Oh yeah, wow! Wasn't the sound great tonight!?'

'Yeah, unbelievable. He's definitely as good as they say. I had a quick talk with him after the show and he was trying to persuade me to do some recording of my own.'

'Really? Looks like the stars are aligning.' She winked.

'You think we should work with him?'

'Yes. That's EXACTLY what we should do,' Dee said wistfully. 'Text him now and tell him!'

Maxx looked at the number again. Was this right? Doing it with Dee? Or was he still just too scared to go it alone. It felt like a good step, it gave him confidence. He decided to throw caution to the wind and began to write Mike a message.

'That girl was nice. The guy – his daughter, did you meet her?' she said, as the car pulled up to the hotel.

'Mike's daughter? No, well yes, briefly.'

'She was sweet. Yeah, sounds like she's taking after her dad.'

'Oh, I'm not surprised. Did I see Charlie hitting on her?' Maxx asked.

Dee scoffed and curled her lip. 'Um, maybe. I don't think so. You know what he's like. Ridiculous flirt. I guess she's a diversion.'

'From what?' Maxx said as he hit send, just as an old Dee single came on the radio.

TO MIKE: Hi, this is Maxx. Nice to talk earlier. I'd like to go for it, but will have to keep things quiet until I speak to management, if that's okay? It's tricky. Also, will start with a duet. Will explain later. Can we email? maxxedout95@gmail.com

FROM MIKE: Sure. I'm in.

'Oooh I love this song!' Dee tapped the driver. 'Can you turn it up?'

# Chapter 6

# Before I Sleep

Amelie snuggled up to her dad in the back seat of their car home, the night's performances like a whirlwind in her head.

'Thank you, thank you, thank you. Do you think I can come again? Or to your studio maybe? To watch a session this time?' she pleaded.

'Well,' he laughed, 'maybe we can look at the bookings and see if there's some assisting you can do. Oh my god, I almost forgot.'

Her dad pulled out a small box with a ribbon.

'I hope you like it.'

Amelie looked down at the beautiful little jewellery box, and tugged on the soft black ribbon. Inside sat a pair of tiny, gold bass clef stud earrings, with a little diamond inside.

'Dad, I love them! Wow. Thank you so much. Are these diamonds?'

'They are. So look after them, okay?' He stroked her head. 'So, how's the practice going?'

'Oh good, good.' She tried to brush him off, staring down at the beautiful gift and avoiding his eyes. She knew what was coming.

'When am I going see you play then? Or record you? Or at least hear some of your new songs?'

'Soon, soon.' Amelie closed the box and looked up at him. 'I just want to do this audition first, and if I get chosen I get a place on stage at Music in the Park. If you play there, it's really a big deal.'

'Amelie, I admire you for not wanting help, but remember, there's no harm at all in leaning on the people you know.'

'I know, I know. I just want to do this first. Okay? Without help,' Amelie said.

'You don't even want *me* to help?'

'Mum says you can't count your success unless you've earned it all yourself. I want you both to see me do this on my own.'

Her dad looked at her wearily. 'Well, your mum is ridiculously stubborn. Lord knows, I'd have liked *her* to accept some help from me over the years.' He sighed. 'At least come and spend some time at the studio this summer.'

'Okay, Dad. Let's see,' she said cheerfully.

They pulled up to the house as Amelie tucked her birthday present into her bag.

'Dad, I love my earrings. Looks like Mum's gone to bed already, I'd better get in.'

'Amelie, think about it, okay? Ella called me after the, um, setback last year. Everyone gets overwhelmed when they're performing. You needn't worry, it'll come.'

'I wasn't ready,' she whispered. 'It will be different this time. It's so silly, I love to play but I totally freak out at the attention.'

'Well, it's scary performing, but there are other options. Getting a publishing deal is one. Producing is another. You don't need to stand on stage to be an artist.'

'But I want to perform. Isn't it cruel how all I want to do is stand on stage and perform my own songs and I can't actually do it?'

'You can. And you will.'

'Yes.' She kissed him on the cheek and felt a hot rush of inspiration and a desperate need to pick up her guitar. 'I will. Thanks again, Dad.'

As she crept into her bedroom, she flicked on her tacky, microphone-shaped reading lamp. Another one of her mother's 'incredible flea market finds'.

The corner of her little sanctuary was in dire need of sorting. She had, over the years, acquired myriad pieces of recording gear – some of it was her father's castaways, while others bits she had scrimped and saved for. It was patched together and connected to her laptop and created a surprisingly excellent sound for such cobbled-together kit. It was a health and safety nightmare – constantly buzzing and hot to touch – but it was her special little place. Her own teeny, tiny home recording studio, and she loved it.

She switched it on, and the computer whirred louder than their precious three-footed washing machine as it struggled to come to life.

'Come on, little buddy,' Amelie whispered, stroking the side of the machine as it powered up. 'Two minutes today? That's fast!'

She opened Pro Tools and dug around to find where she'd got to on her last song. Slipping her huge headphones onto her head, she hit play and sat back.

'Two Tuesday Blues' was a track she'd been working on for weeks now. It was almost finished and it was going to be her audition song – it needed to be perfect.

She logged onto SoundCloud and checked her profile.

Her last track, 'Bare', had been liked 737 times, and reposted eighty-nine times. She felt a surge of pride and the giddy thrill of the safe place she called insta-fame.

She checked her comments – *So beautiful! Exquisite melody! When could I buy an album? Why is she not signed to a record label? Heartbreaking lyrics! When will you play live? Are you playing By the Sea in Margate this year? Do you have a Facebook? Where's your website?*

Then she looked through her favourite artists to check for updates – the guitar singer/songwriters she admired most: Marika Hackman, Laura Marling, SZA, Aldous Harding. And then she went over to YouTube and watched some of the huge artists the girls in her music class loved: Alessia Cara, Melanie Martinez, Tove Lo. They looked so confident with their brightly lit videos, outrageous make-up and polished performances.

She opened her own account. In the last month she had taken her best friend Maisie's advice and branched out to YouTube, although the videos were not exactly what she'd had in mind.

There were just four so far, but she had already accumulated 700 subscribers, most of them followed her there from SoundCloud.

On YouTube, the commenters were, unsurprisingly, rather less supportive. *She must be ugly*, said one commenter. *Does she think she's SIA?* asked another. *Good song, boring video*, said a third. But between the protestations at her lack of visuals, there was plenty to be proud of.

She pulled out her dad's old Canon 5D and rested it on top of the shelf above her laptop. She tipped the lens downward and took a test shot holding her guitar. In shot was her guitar only, the frame cropped at the chin. Behind her the yellowy light of her lamp created an even more darkened image in the foreground. She was happy with the result.

She aligned her microphone to right in front of her mouth, so close she could taste the cold metal on her lips. The second mic was propped up to the sound-hole of her guitar, positioned exactly as it had been so many hundreds of times before. She sang a few lines, and quickly listened back. There was very little echo thanks to the foam boards she'd glued to the back of an Ikea bedroom divider the week before.

She hit record. Three minutes and four seconds later she was done. The song was hastily uploaded after an even quicker mix and a thrill coursed through her veins as it appeared online. She played it back and was mostly satisfied with the result. For now, this would have to do. Especially at 3.29 a.m. She yawned and flicked off her machine, suddenly desperately tired.

Amelie thought back to the stage, filled with glitter and pyrotechnics and the boyband bouncing about like a bunch of half-wits – and was appalled by how jealous she felt.

All she wanted was to feel that buzz. That thrill of performing live. It was easy to be one of the most popular London artists online when you were completely anonymous.

# CHAPTER 7

# The Masses Are Asses

The next morning, Amelie mooched through into the lounge where her mum had made her slowly warmed stovetop hot chocolate for breakfast, using a whole block of real chocolate and a hint of spice. It really was a treat having a proper cook for a mother.

Her double chocolate birthday cake was on the counter. It had said 'Happy Birthday Amelie' in bright pink icing when she had left for the Apollo, but now only said 'Amelie' – more than half had been eaten.

'Oh my god, Mum!' laughed Amelie. 'Where did it go?'

'I ended up having it for dinner!' Her mum groaned and rubbed her non-existent tummy. 'And also dessert. And an evening snack! Do you fancy it for breakfast?'

'Oh, go on then!' Amelie realised she had hardly eaten in the end, and cut herself a huge slice of double chocolate to go with her hot chocolate.

Her mum's kitchen was as eclectic as she was. Nothing went together, but somehow everything did. Each mismatched plate had a story – a cake stand from a flea market in Provence, a teapot from a car boot sale in Birmingham, silver cutlery 'borrowed' from a French restaurant she was working at for less than four pounds an hour. The kitchen itself was a perfectly preserved 1970s avocado green and teeny tiny, with a pint-sized fridge to match.

Growing up meant moving a LOT, including to rural France, coastal France, Paris, the outskirts of the outskirts of Monte Carlo and . . . Bolton. But they'd finally settled here in Hackney for what was, for Amelie Ayres, an eternity – three whole years!

Ella had taken them to France when Amelie was six so that she could study cheese making, which she quit six months and two dress sizes later because of the calories involved. She then tried her hand at wine making, which included an extravagant number of 'tasting sessions', and quit because of the hangovers involved. Then – after three years – she'd settled on French cookery. 'Anything as long as it's French,' her mother, born and raised in rural Devon, had insisted.

Ella finally flunked out of the cookery course just a few weeks before it finished, after a surprise fail grade on an apricot-almond clafouti. A strange turn of events, especially after all the extra after-hours tutelage head chef Monsieur Calliat had kindly offered.

When they left, Amelie remembered a lot of hurried

packing late in the evening before an overnight train to Calais – they'd managed to fill four suitcases with French farmhouse 'trinkets' and stuffed a couple of large black plastic rubbish bags with their clothes.

'Rapide!' Her mother had shouted at their taxi driver. 'RAAAAAPIIIIIIIIID-AY-MMEEENNT!'

'But why do we have to leave now?' Amelie had whined, still half asleep.

As the taxi had sped away they'd passed a very large, very angry woman in a dressing gown marching up their driveway, brandishing a rolling pin in one hand and a shotgun in the other.

The fact that her Mum could never settle on one thing meant they were always on the move, and always just scraping by financially, but Amelie didn't care. Wherever they were together was home, and right now that was Hackney.

'Oh my god! What a cool night.' Amelie beamed.

The lounge was more shabby than chic, but it was cosy and clean and in every corner collectables were carefully displayed – from the stack of *Vogue* magazines in an old wire stand to the pile of blankets, carefully folded on a Georgian foot stool that her mum had refurbished.

Her mum was dressed so beautifully, with a huge, multi-coloured vintage silk kimono and satin slippers. Her face was glowing and moist from a facemask and her long, elegant hands were examining the earrings from Amelie's dad.

'Oh, they are sweet,' she said. 'He's a good, good man, your father, in so many ways.'

Amelie smiled and then, as she always did, steered towards a new subject so that her mum never felt inadequate. She was nowhere near as well-off as her dad, but Amelie knew she always did what she could. After all, this year her mum had taken her shopping – to a place that sold actual new clothes – which was a vast improvement on last year's wonderful but slightly strange birthday gift of three beautiful matching porcelain cats, doing ballet.

'They're a delightful little keepsake, don't you think? Look after them, okay,' her mum had enthused as Amelie had tried to hide her disappointment at not getting a new microphone.

Her mum wanted every single detail from the last night's gig, but as usual, all the wrong details. 'How was the tube, did you change at Holborn?' and 'What was the decor like?' and 'Did you get one of those plastic things for round your neck? Were the staff nice to you?'

Amelie talked about Dee and how lovely but very aloof and professional she was.

'Oh, really? And did you meet any nice boys?'

Amelie quickly skimmed over her interactions with Charlie – 'What *is* a Twitter name, Amelie? It sounds like a children's toy.' – and then spoke excitedly about her dad and how everyone wanted to talk to him, and how they asked him to do the European tour but he said no. 'Sounds like your father!' her mum smirked.

Amelie's mum and dad had met in Paris while he was on tour. He had been in a Parisian bistro trying to order a steak and fries (which, as Amelie learned, is pretty much the easiest thing to order on the menu at a French bistro). They both told the story a little differently – in Mum's version she had to swoop in and 'save him' and in Dad's version she had 'stuck her nose in' where it wasn't required.

In both versions, however, they had got talking and then ended up spending two glorious weeks together, visiting museums and art galleries, brunching on small outdoor tables along the boulevards and drinking cheap wine in pokey French jazz clubs. When the two weeks were over, they went their separate ways, both agreeing that they wanted different things from life and that they should remember their special time for what it was. Amelie didn't understand exactly why they didn't try to make a go of it. Her dad told her that one day she would understand that love sometimes isn't quite enough to make a life together, and her mum would just say, 'I'll always love your father for giving you to me.'

Nine months after they had met, Amelie arrived, and they had both very easily and amicably worked out how to be sep-arated parents together.

Amelie yawned.

'Well, Mum. I'd better get on with my practice. Only a couple of weeks to go!' She grinned.

'Happy birthday, my darling.' Her mum kissed her fore-head. 'My darling, darling girl. I love you so.'

Amelie pulled off the second-hand or, rather, 'vintage' Spider-Man PJs her mum had given her for her birthday and tucked her beautiful new earrings into her top drawer. Then she took a long, deserved shower and washed her hair.

It was too late to call Maisie, who would already be at yoga, but she realised she'd not messaged her since before The Keep went on and she would be dying for an update. She fished her phone out of her jacket and switched it on, and almost immediately it started beeping with notifications.

She smiled, awaiting the usual influx of comments and messages she received after uploading a new track. But they were from Twitter. She hardly used Twitter. And they kept coming.

Her phone beeped so much that she flicked the side switch to silent in a panic, but the barrage of messages from total strangers just kept coming. Had she been hacked?

@Charleelove03: Lucky B*TCH! #hesmyboyfriend

@keepfandom1xx: OMG WHO ARE YOU? #cantcope

@SweetCharlie45: IM SO EMOTIONAL! WHO IS THIS GIRL THATS DATING CHARLIE OMG OMG KILL ME NOW.

@lovelovekeepgl: The fandom be like 'WTF!'

And, to her absolute horror, #Ameliewho was the number two trending topic, underneath #NoCharliesAngel

On they went. Pages and pages of messages from mostly

girls from all over the world. She was confused at first, trying to figure out who these people were that were tweeting her. She scrolled down further, frantically searching for something that would explain – then she suddenly froze.

@Keeponcharlie: Great gig & nice hangin' backstage with my girl @callmeamelie98 tonight in #London

Oh god. It had been retweeted 3,450 times.
At that moment, a text message:

FROM MAISIE: OMG OMG OMG

And then another.

FROM MAISIE: Um Amelie. You'd better call me in the A.M.! OMG!

In a blind panic, Amelie turned her phone off. Sitting there on her bed, breathing heavily, her mind was spinning out of control. Oh god, this wasn't happening. He'd not only mentioned her in a tweet, he'd written it in such a way that EVERY ONE of his MILLIONS of followers would see it, he'd called her 'my girl' and also mentioned that Amelie had been backstage. What the hell was he playing at?

Her mum popped her head in. 'I'm just heading out to the market, do you want anything?'

'Cheese,' said Amelie, without really thinking, and then, 'Oh god,' as she heard the front door shut.

She decided the best thing was to go back to bed, so she crawled in and pulled the covers up over her head and felt the thump, thump, thump of a headache between her temples. She felt exposed and vulnerable. School on Monday was going to be an utter nightmare.

She thought for a moment about tweeting Charlie back, something flippant, cool, nonchalant, but she couldn't compose anything in her head that might calm the situation.

Arghh. She squeezed her eyes shut and rolled over. Her mind was a wandering mess as it worked through all the different scenarios that might play out over the coming days. She tried to calm herself by repeating 'Tomorrow they will move onto something else. Tomorrow it will be another girl. Tomorrow it will all be over.'

## Chapter 8

# Tally Ho

On Monday morning, Amelie walked along the canal and picked up Maisie on the way to school. She had left her guitar at home that day and was wearing her school hoodie up along with her mother's huge dark sunglasses to complete the full incognito look.

Maisie Stone lived just three minutes' walk away in a huge house that her father had worked on tirelessly, renovating it into something a little bit *Grand Designs*, a little bit bonkers. The house was a perfect amalgamation of both parents; part warm family home and part inner-city wellness retreat, complete with a sun salutation roof terrace and meditation room.

Maisie was from a huge family who had immigrated to London from Australia. Her dad had opened a fancy butcher's on Broadway Market and her mum took private yoga classes. She had opened Sydney's first wellness clinic back when yoga was strictly practised by middle-aged women in open marriages and tomato juice was the only superfood.

A very un-meditated Maisie came careering out of the front door.

'BYE, MUM!' she screamed as the door slammed behind her. 'Holy shit! This is totally awesome. You're famous! And I'm your best friend! Don't forget it! What the hell are you wearing!?'

'Hiya, Bonkers, you should ease up on the acai berries or whatever.' Amelie flinched, her eyes still not adjusted to sunlight after twenty-four hours locked in her bedroom.

'The Keep fandom are total freaks! I can't believe the things they've been posting about you! OMG. But some love you, did you see?' Maisie laughed.

'No, I made my accounts private and logged off. I'm not really into cyber bullying,' Amelie said wearily, feeling slightly irritated that Maisie didn't find this woefully, life-changingly tragic.

'Oh, don't worry about that. They're just jealous. I don't think you look like a ferret, by the way,' Maisie said in all sincerity. 'You *can* look a little drawn. But that's lack of sleep and – I know I keep saying it – too much gluten.'

'I'm not gluten inadequate like you,' Amelie sniffed.

'It's intolerant.'

'Well, thank you very much. So are you right now, to be honest.'

Maisie grabbed Amelie by the arm and squeezed her close. Amelie felt sick. She had hardly eaten and had locked herself in her room with her phone off and watched every film in her collection, telling her mother she had a migraine (which was 99 per cent true) until she had no excuse but to go to school and face the music.

'You *do* look terrible, Amelie,' Maisie said, unable to hide the excitement in her voice. 'I didn't think you were coming today. I called round yesterday afternoon, did your mum say? You do look sick actually. What's up? We need to talk about the tweet! OMG! Don't you think it's awesome? What happened? Did you kiss him or something?'

Maisie was all this. One hundred miles an hour and full of beans. She was so bubbly and full of unyielding optimism that Amelie couldn't maintain her achingly cool persona around her. Maisie ignored melodrama and thrived on positivity and excitement, and Amelie was reluctantly but wholly drawn to her.

Maisie had lately, with the help of her mum, started a kind of wellness blog and Instagram feed – her photos were green food, green drinks, green spaces, dainty feminine crafts and Maisie fixed firm in unfathomable yoga poses against gritty east London backdrops.

Over the last couple of years she had grown increasingly beautiful – her broad, round features and huge caramel hair no longer looked oversized and awkward on her long and lean body. But Maisie wasn't used to her new skin; she still had the mannerisms of a child, and was blissfully unaware of the attraction she held for the boys in her form.

In moments like this, though, she was so chronically

upbeat that it was a frustrating, and a terrible dampener when Amelie's desire was to sink into the drama.

'No!' Amelie snapped. 'I hate the attention. I'm totally dreading school.'

'It's bloody awesome! Cheer up. Everyone will be dead jealous! They are! He called you "my girl" – I thought you said Charlie was an idiot?'

'He is.'

'Really? No! His message was sweet; he certainly made it sound like you got on. Was he being sarcastic then? This is hilarious. Everyone's going to want the dirt. You're going to be bombarded. I'll be your security!' she joked, pretending to clear the way for Amelie as they passed a stream of cyclists and early morning dog walkers.

'Arghh. It's a nightmare.' Amelie reached behind the sunglasses and rubbed her eyes for the hundredth time.

'Don't be ridiculous. What exactly is bothering you? Apart from the attention, I know you're not great on that. But you must secretly want it, if you're going to be a rock star.'

'Firstly, people are going to think I actually like The Keep. And secondly, they're going to know my dad worked for them.'

'Yeah, so?' Maisie was confused.

'Well, Maisie, apart from obliterating my credibility . . . ' Amelie shook her head.

'Oh pleeeeeeease!' Maisie said, her Australian accent coming through.

' . . . And I didn't tell those senior girls in music class – you know Brooke, Ashleigh and Tara? And they were going on and on about it during band practice, how they were going and they had seventh row tickets and I didn't say anything. I let them brag away.'

'Well, that's kinda funny,' Maisie giggled.

'I know,' Amelie conceded, 'but ...'

There was nothing worse than notoriety at high school. If you stood out from your usual place in the pecking order two things happened: 1. The popular kids resented you for encroaching on their turf without invitation, or worse – making them look off the ball for not discovering you themselves; and 2. The unpopular kids resented you for taking a step up in the world. The result? A social outcast without a place, in desperation you ended up bequeathed to the lunch duty teacher whose job it was to bust smokers.

' ... but the audition! I'm against Tara, you know. I don't want them to think I'm getting any kind of preferential treatment because of my dad.'

'That's your mother talking,' Maisie said. 'Just because she won't accept help from him, doesn't mean you don't have to. It's perfectly normal to get a foot up from your parents. Look at Brooklyn Beckham. Or any Kardashian. Nicole Richie? Bad examples. But you get me.'

Amelie felt momentarily angry at Maisie, who had stopped to tie her shoe laces. She watched her hoist her leg up on the railing with the strength and elegance of a ballerina, pulling her knickers out of her bum when she was done.

'There's no need for drama here, really. You met a pop star!'

'You don't understand. I just want to focus on the audition.'

'Unless you end up dating Charlie and becoming a hashtag *Keeper*, none of this is going to stop you. Amelie,' Maisie stopped walking. They were late – the bell had already rung and everyone would be making their way to their classes by now. 'You're really bloody stubborn. I know this is about the attention. It will totally pass. And if you want to be a musician you're going to have to get some kahunas and put yourself out there a bit more!

'This is actually a *gift*. All those people wondering who you are!? I keep telling you to put your name on that secret YouTube account of yours and just get on with it – imagine if you had done and all those Keep fans were on there listening to *your* music. Life,' Maisie began, as Amelie winced and braced herself for yet another corny self-help quote, 'is there for the taking – what's taking *you* so long?' She raised her perfect eyebrows and allowed the silence to settle for complete dramatic effect.

'Maisie. What if I'm terrible again? I can't bear it.'

Maisie threw her arm around her and pulled her in tight. Amelie knew her friend could see the shy vulnerability behind her self-assured and surly demeanour, though Amelie rarely actually broke down and showed it to her.

'You won't be. If you want to be on stage, you need to put yourself out there,' Maisie reasoned. 'You're going to need thick skin, babe. Or do you want a way out?'

Amelie shook her head, trying to hide her eyes.

'About today, do as Tay Tay says. Shake it off. Say as little as possible. It will all pass.'

'Okay,' said Amelie, sniffing.

'Just say you happened to meet Charlie for five minutes and he asked for your Twitter handle. Say he asked for everyone's. That's all.'

Amelie grimaced. 'But Brooke, Tara and Ashleigh. They're totally terrifying.'

'I know. But, you never know, they might just be happy for you,' Maisie tried. 'Or, maybe they'll be onto the next thing by now. I mean weren't they all about The Wanted a couple of years ago?'

'Just devoid of cool,' Amelie said in wonder.

'Honestly, just brush it off. It's cool. One of the most famous people in the world – sort of – tweeted a personal message to you. It's a great story! Be cool. Let them all wonder . . . !' She grinned. 'Now. Can we talk about the gig properly? Did you meet the whole band or was it just Charlie and Dee?'

'Oh, I met Maxx, briefly. The brunette one.'

'Ooh. What's he like?'

'Big southern accent. He was kinda nice I guess,' she said, remembering the outline of his shoulders in the darkness. 'I don't know really. I think he's dating Dee, isn't he? Well, he was totally glued to her performance on stage. Was unrecognisable at the after party.'

'Oohh, after party ...!' Maisie nudged her in the ribs. 'And how fancy was the show?'

'I think it's not quite as flash as some of the bigger gigs they play, but to me it looked pretty damn fancy. They even had fire synchronised to their dance moves – it was pretty hilarious.'

'Oh my god, the boyband dance moves,' Maisie laughed.

'I know! And I met the director guy who is filming them – Clint – Julian's boyfriend? He's like twenty-three or something, but he tours all over the world with them.'

Amelie tried to forget her worries as she and her best friend wandered down the canal to school. By the time they arrived, the playground was empty and first period classes were well under way. Luckily, Amelie had PE and she sped off towards the gym to join the others getting changed.

'Remember: the less you say the better.' Maisie wagged her finger as she turned to go. 'It's going to be fine.'

Amelie felt better, but the relief was short-lived. The moment she opened the gym door it was clear this was not going to go away quickly.

# CHAPTER 9

# Empty Room

Huddled up, sharing headphones and chatting away next to each other on the tour bus, Kyle and Dee were the only ones who seemed to be full of beans on their arrival in Germany. Art was reading *The Economist*, while Lee and Charlie were bickering like an old married couple about something to do with a video game and Maxx, just awake again, stumbled out of the toilet with his baggy, dark eyes and pale face.

'Oi, ignorant horseshits,' Geoff bellowed as he looked back over his shoulder from the front of the bus. 'You're at the start of your SOLD OUT EUROPEAN TOUR you know. Can we at least start out pretending to be pleased and/or get along?'

Of course, they all pasted on their happy faces as soon as they disembarked the bus outside their hotel. There were about a dozen girls waiting for them with flowers and placards welcoming them to Berlin.

'I LOVE YOU MORE THAN FREE WIFI' read one.

'KISS ME I'M LEGAL' read another.

'YOU'LL NEVER BE ONE DIRECTION' read a third. There was always at least one Directioner to put The Keep in their place.

They signed some CDs and a few bored photographers took official press images of them, selfies were snapped, Instagram pictures carefully edited and uploaded, and even Maxx managed half a smile and a wave. It wouldn't matter what he did anyway, the papers would all run the photos of Lee, who had jumped into the fountain in just his underwear.

Their Berlin hotel was totally luxurious, and unlike the last-minute accommodation that was arranged in London, here their every whim was anticipated and catered for. They had the entire tenth floor, including both suites, for the five boys, Dee, Geoff, Mel and Ashton.

Dee was given a suite, as was usual, and the boys and Ashton got 'Executive King' rooms with Geoff and Mel in the enormous two-bedroom suite, so they could work. The rest of the gang were in regular rooms on the floors below – but despite this upstairs/downstairs separation, they all did hang together.

Maxx threw himself down on the crisp white bedsheets, and let them envelop him in their feathery softness, while a porter and maid began to unpack his belongings and sort everything into the cupboards – they needn't have bothered, but Maxx had given up trying to stop all this extra-special treatment, even though he found it intrusive. He had learned quickly that the more he complained about the attention, the more he looked like an ungrateful jerk. Best to accept it and tip well.

He needed to call home right away, since it had been nearly a week since he'd been picked up by the chauffeur from his parents' place and left his mum crying on the porch. She rarely cried, so it was all the more unsettling to see, and Maxx often worried about the impact all this fame was having on them.

Outside, Berlin basked in the baking hot sun, perfect weather for their two nights at the Olympic Stadium. They had four hours until they needed to head there for a sound-check, so first a call home, and then a sleep. Maxx waited until he was alone, slipped the hotel staff a fifty-dollar bill each, awkwardly explaining that he didn't have any euros yet.

The phone rang off and went to the same answerphone message his parents had had for over five years – it was his mother's sing-song voice with the dog barking in the background.

'Hello. You've called Clare, John, Jimmy, John Junior, Christian, Bonny and Maxwell. We're very sorry we cannot take your call right now, but please do leave us a message and we'll ...'

Maxx hung up, shaking his head. After a couple of moments he tried again, and this time his mum picked up, panting as if she'd run in from tending the hedgerow in the yard.

'Maxwell? Is that you?' shouted down the line.

'Hiya, Momma!'

'MAXWELL!?'

'It's me! You don't have to yell, Momma,' Maxx said. 'It doesn't make a difference if I'm overseas – the phone still sounds the same!'

'JOHN! IT'S YOUR SON ON THE PHONE!' she yelled at his dad, who was probably still in the garage, working late on his car. Maxx imagined him in his denim overalls, the ones with 'John' in red writing on the breast pocket. He could see his greasy hands working on the engine, a cold beer by his side and The Rolling Stones or Johnny Cash playing on his old radio.

'Is it hot there?' his mum asked. There was always a conversation about the weather. 'It sure is here. I could've cooked a chicken on the porch. It's too hot to prove dough or bake or anything in the kitchen, mind. Your father had to make do with cornbread tonight. JOHN! I don't know where that man is.'

'Momma, how are you doing?'

'I'm fine. Least I was until those nosy Galloways came here wanting more money for repairs to the driveway. Why should we have to pay the same as everyone else when your daddy and I have one car and those families have at least two each. I think the Andertons have four! That's what happens when the kids don't leave home though, I suppose. A garage full of cars.'

'I can help with the cost of the driveway, Momma.'

'Did you hear that pretty little Leah-Anne is getting married? And only twenty-one! I always thought you and her . . .'

There was a click on the line as his mom's voice trailed off.

'Max? 'sat you?' His dad had picked up the second line in the garage.

'Dad.' He loved to hear his voice. 'How's the Chevy?'

'Pile o' crap.' He always said this about the classic cars he refurbished – until he'd finished with them.

'Don't you swear in front of Maxwell!' his mum pipped in. 'What city are you in?'

'I'm in Berlin.'

'That's in Germany, John.'

'Yes, Momma. It's great here. Lots of sausage and beer – Dad, you'd like it.'

'Oh, I don't think so,' he replied firmly.

'We're going to the Brandenburg Gate tomorrow and then to see where the wall used to be. And we have two shows here and then we move on to Copenhagen.'

'Uh huh.'

'That's in Denmark. I hope you're eating well. You looked too darn skinny last time you came home, didn't he, John?'

'If you say so, Clare.'

'I miss you guys,' Maxx said, wishing he were at home being fussed over by his mum. When he was tired he longed for her chicken and a cool lemonade while he sat in the games room and caught up on baseball. Not that he actually liked baseball, but his dad did, and he loved hanging out with his dad.

'Well, you can always come home.' His dad was ridiculously impractical. 'Your brother's here at the moment with his nice girlfriend. You met her, oh of course you did, at Christmas.'

His brother, Jim, was the firstborn and had finished his MBA. His parents were really proud of him. They were proud of them all, although Maxx knew they found his career choice a little difficult to understand and it had impacted on their lives too, since he was just so incredibly famous now.

Occasionally, Maxx would ask if they saw a new music video or a clip of him at an award ceremony, but he always got the same response.

'Oh, honey, I wouldn't even know where to look for that. Can you post it to me?'

Although his Dad would never say it, Maxx knew he was uncomfortable with the whole 'boyband' thing. He would have been far happier if Maxx had been in a blues or rock and roll band – something he understood.

'It would be nice to see you dating a good girl, you're old enough now.'

'I was dating, remember, I told you? Dee?'

'A real girl, Maxwell. A Southern Girl.'

'It's kind of hard to meet real girls, Momma.'

'There's plenty back home looking for a nice boy like you,' his mum sighed. 'Did we tell you it's really hot here?'

'You did, Momma.' Maxx smiled at the consistency and predictability of his parents. They were like old slippers. He longed to be home.

'Well, you need your sleep. Good night, honey.'

'It's morning, Momma.'

'Good morning then, honey. Get some sleep. I worry you don't sleep enough.'

'I will, Momma.'

'Be good, son.'

'I will, Dad. I'll call you from Copenhagen, okay?'

He hung up and lay on the bed feeling very alone. This year he would make sure he got home as often as possible in the breaks, instead of taking holidays abroad like last year. It was time to ground himself. Between doing some recording with Dee and pulling back a little on the obligations of The Keep he hoped he could find a bit of balance. Things were going to get better, he told himself. As he began to relax his mind wandered back to the events of last night in London, to the conversation with Mike and then to his awkward and embarrassing confession to Dee, the niggling feeling the duet they had vowed to work on was somehow not quite right.

Then his mind wandered to Mike's daughter.

He pictured her looking over at him backstage – those inquisitive eyes staring at him – and something stirred. He tried to remember all of her – her face, her hair colour, what she was wearing when she had stormed into the green room, but he couldn't remember details, just an overall impression of beauty and restlessness. She had been flustered and flushed and didn't want to talk to him – she was even rude – but those blue eyes were so alluring, despite their sulky insolence. He was definitely intrigued.

When he awoke he rolled over, confused and disorientated, and checked his watch. He'd been asleep for nearly six hours! He stumbled to the bathroom and threw some water on his face. Why hadn't anyone called? He picked up the room phone and dialled Mel's number but there was no answer, so he checked his mobile. There was a text.

FROM GEOFF: When you get up, have the hotel arrange a car to soundcheck. We thought you needed a good sleep, you grumpy jerk.

He probably deserved that. He had been extremely grumpy for more than a few weeks – maybe even the past month. The relentless rehearsals in New York before they took off, the last minute pick-ups at the studio for their new single, filming three music videos in one week! It was too much.

He decided to chill for a little longer and took the opportunity to check in on his social feeds. Lee, who had the most followers, but said the least, had posted a photo from the hotel room of the empty mini bar in his room (a record label rule since some were still under twenty-one, despite being in Europe, where they could all legally drink).

@LEEkeepofficial: Whaa not even OJ? ;-)

@kyleeyeofficial: A wonderful day in beautiful Berlin!
☺

@arthousesinger1: So much history here. #berlin

@keeponcharlie: Oops. Busy makin' headlines again.
#columninches #wasntme

He cringed, closed his phone and hauled himself out of
bed. He hoisted back the heavy black-out curtains to see the
late afternoon sun across another city in another country. He
pulled his jeans on and ran his fingers through his dark hair.
He picked up the room phone and dialled reception.

'Hello, Mr Cooke.'

'Hi, I'm ready for my car.'

'No problem, sir.'

'It's just … Can you tell them I want to go to a music shop
on the way?'

'A record store, sir?'

'No, for musical instruments, a guitar shop.'

'Of course. I'll arrange that for you now.'

'Thanks.'

If he was going to start writing music again he needed a
guitar, and now was as good a time as any to buy one. He
texted Geoff.

TO GEOFF: Making a quick stop, but I'm on my way.

TO MAXX: Good. Someone needs to calm Lee down. Code F*ing Red.

# CHAPTER 10

# Celebrity Skin

Amelie had been batting off some pretty full on, unwanted, but rather amusing attention at school. She was practically rugby tackled when she arrived at PE that first morning. She walked in late, and for a beautiful and brief moment *had* thought she'd slipped into the changing room unnoticed, until Bridget Greenaway shrieked from the furthest corner of the room so loudly Amelie had to cover her ears.

'OMG! Did you meet CHARLIE from The Keep!?' She marched over and pointed right at Amelie's chest. 'Were *you* backstage? Is it true?'

'Are you a fan?' another queried suspiciously, a circle of agitated, excited girls forming around her.

Amelie's lip curled automatically, and she hurriedly and hopelessly tried to disguise the reflex action as an itchy lip.

'She's not a *real* fan!' one declared, pointing at Amelie's Hole T-shirt.

'Why did you go?'

'How did YOU get a ticket?'

'How did you meet Charlie? Is he hot in real life?'

'My dad,' she began, her voice wavering as she felt the room go deathly silent and the penetrating gaze of a dozen teenage eyes. 'It was a birthday present. I only spoke to him for like five minutes.'

'Happy birthday, Amelie!' said one of the girls from her jazz band. Amelie smiled back meekly.

'How did your dad get you backstage? AND WHAT HAPPENED?' Bronwyn cried.

'Um, it was a birthday present,' she repeated. 'He was working there.' *The less information the better*, she kept reminding herself, just as Maisie had coached her.

But she was ambushed. The scrum was two deep, six across, all the girls wanting to know what Charlie was like, what he was wearing, what happened between them, how did he get her Twitter name, were there any other girls there, did she get any photos or an autograph, will she see them again?

'Ugh. I hate boybands,' moaned Kate Dawkins, the school's only goth and possibly the only person who knew as much about music as Amelie did. 'You only like them because they're good-looking,' she said cattily to Bronwyn.

'Yeah, I bought the record to listen to their faces,' Bronwyn sneered in retaliation.

'I thought you had good taste?' Kate scoffed at Amelie. 'I didn't take you for a Keep-worshipping fangirl.'

She looked at Kate and shrugged hopelessly.

But as Amelie clammed up and tried to brush off the increasingly hostile questions, she could sense that among some of the girls the excited jealousy had turned to resentment.

A small group of eavesdroppers were whispering among themselves and Amelie could feel the penetrating stench of high school bitchiness in the air. Today was going to suck.

But, no matter how little Amelie said, Bridget, head of the amateur dramatics society, would not be deterred. The interrogation continued.

'Why did he call you "my girl"? Did you kiss? Did you meet Lee? He's my favourite.'

'No. No Lee. And certainly no kiss,' Amelie scoffed. 'Honestly, it was nothing. I don't even like them. My dad won't ask me again.'

Despite this she got the inevitable barrage of requests for tickets, backstage access, introductions to Charlie. Some girls were impressed, some feigned disinterest, some were jealous and some were downright nasty.

'Really. Honestly.' Amelie held a hand up in frustration. 'It's never going to happen. I can't get tickets, not even for myself. I'm nobody! It was a one off!'

But on it went, throughout the day. Her English teacher, Mrs Wilkinson, had to ask the class to settle down twice.

'For every five minutes you talk, I'm holding you back at

lunch!' she threatened, firing her signature single eyebrow raise and pursed lip combination in Amelie's general direction.

During lunch, Maisie had been good to her word and had brushed off the story with a kind of theatrical nonchalance that shut even the most diehard gossip down. There was a small group of fourth form girls who had begun to hang around, trying to befriend Amelie, who was now something of a celebrity among the younger students.

'Wow, Amelie. I thought you had taste?' sighed Jasper, her guitar tutor, as he closed the storage cupboard in between third and fourth period. 'A Keeper, huh?' he said, shaking his head.

Despite all the attention, in general the situation was more manageable than she imagined it would be. There was a pecking order at school, and despite her short-term notoriety, the status quo *must* be maintained, so things quickly began to die down.

But she still had to get through the moment she'd been dreading. When she finally saw Brooke, Ashleigh and Tara, clicking their way down the corridor in their *barely* acceptable school shoes – kitten heels, hitched-up skirts, this week's matching dip-dye hairstyle – she froze.

'Hi there, Amelie Ayres.'

'Hi,' she said, turning to her locker and pretending to look for something, though there was just mouldy lunch and a box of guitar picks in there.

'You were backstage at The Keep?'

'I didn't know,' she said with a sigh.

'Why didn't you say you were going?'

'Didn't you want us there?'

'Were you embarrassed of *us*?'

'No, no. I just didn't know until last minute. My dad got me in.'

'I thought you hated boybands and pop music. I thought you thought it was all beneath your exquisite music tastes?' Ashleigh said. 'That's what you're always saying anyway, isn't she?'

Brooke nodded, while Tara looked off down the hall, a little bored.

'Well?' Brooke said, in her thinly veiled threatening tone.

Amelie kept steady and turned to face them, shutting her locker with more of a thud than she intended. 'Sorry, I'm late for final period.'

'Well, another time then,' Brooke said menacingly. 'Let's go,' she added to the others as they sauntered off down the hall.

'You're fucked,' said the ever-present Bridget Greenaway, who had overheard from across the hall.

'Completely,' agreed Kate Dawson, pulling her black hair back with a black band.

The online story was even more outside Amelie's control, and things were gathering momentum. After Charlie's initial tweet there had been a bit of a buzz online about how he had been hanging backstage with a local girl from east London.

Fans had poured through her Twitter and Instagram feeds, they had hacked her Facebook, which luckily Amelie hardly used, and they had even tracked down her address and her school.

And as for Charlie, infuriatingly and somewhat puzzlingly, he was clearly enjoying the storm he'd created and later that afternoon posted a couple of cryptic tweets, including one about 'missing London'. So, without public confirmation or denial from either party, the speculation grew even more wild and ridiculous.

By the evening a couple of websites, including notorious gossip columnist Theo Marlon's The Buzz, had posted stories about the tweet. The general tone at this point was intrigue, and people seemed genuinely keen to latch onto a potential love story between a big American pop star and an east London schoolgirl.

Maisie kept Amelie updated, as things kept changing by the hour.

'No fine details,' Amelie had begged.

'Okay, well, for now, you're a mystery poor girl from east London. General internet affection level? I'd say 6/10. It's up on yesterday,' she smiled. 'If you do a search for "Amelie", "Charlie" and "ship" – you do get quite a few positive responses. Oh, and there's a Tumblr.'

'Oh, Jesus.'

'Yeah. Someone has written some fanfic about your night together. You're quite the minx, Amelie! But you die. Yeah. Let's leave it at that.'

She still hadn't replied to Charlie's tweet, and had resolved not to. All the advice was that she should let things blow over. As old news, Amelie would fade back into the background at school and life would move on. But if she contacted him, or denied it, she could certainly end up fanning the flames.

But, sadly, they had all underestimated the fame of The Keep and the interest of the British tabloids.

# CHAPTER 11

# Fallin'

The headline and accompanying photograph were massive. Huge. Enormous. It may as well have been a huge red arrow pointing to Amelie's head and following her around wherever she went. She'd spotted it on her way to school and immediately rushed home with a copy. Her mum sat with her at the kitchen table staring at it too, more bemused than panicked, much to Amelie's irritation.

There on the front page of the *Sun* was her photo, clear as day. It was taken by the paparazzi that had snapped her when she arrived at the backstage gates.

'She's no one,' the security guard had told that photographer. How she wished that were still the case.

She was looking over her shoulder, long brown hair waving in the wind, with a startled look on her face that somehow made her look all the guiltier. The caption read: 'The Keep's Charlie Bags a Brit.'

'Well,' said her mum with a wry smile. 'This is a bit of a nuisance.'

'This is a total catastrophe, Mum,' Amelie wailed. 'Why won't he say something! He must have known he would do this to me! What the hell was that tweet about column inches? Why does he keep winding things up? Read it to me again!'

'Oh, Amelie,' she stifled a giggle. Her mother was not taking this quite as seriously as Amelie was, creeping to the window, she peaked through the blinds at the photographer that had set up camp outside the front door.

'Read it to me again!'

Her mother turned around and in a dramatic newsreader voice she began.

'*The* Sun *can exclusively reveal the girl behind the infamous tweet from The Keep heart-throb Charlie Childs. Schoolgirl and east Londoner Amelie Ayres, 17, whose father is said to be working for the band, was secretly ushered in backstage just moments before the boys arrived. Sources say Charlie, 22, met Amelie when they were last in London at an undisclosed location. They spent the evening cosying up backstage before the boys headed on to Berlin for the second leg of their European tour, leaving Amelie Ayres behind to pine for her pop prince. The Keep's management could not be reached for comment.*'

'Arghh. Pining for her prince. VOMIT!'

'At least they got your name right. I mean, some of the article is factually correct,' her mum offered.

'I can't leave the house for the rest of my life.'

'Well, you don't have to go to school today at any rate.'

'Dad is coming over. I called him.'

'I wonder if that nice man wants a hot drink, he might be out there for hours and it's actually cold today – I wish summer would hurry up.'

'Mum!'

'Well, he's actually very nice. Helped me with the groceries earlier.'

'MUM!'

'I'll just take him a blanket. Won't be a sec.'

'Oh god, this is an actual nightmare.' Amelie put her head in her hands again. Just as she thought things might begin to calm down!

As her mother popped out the door, her father arrived, unkempt and extremely wound up. He marched in holding the offending newspaper and threw it down on the kitchen table.

'There's a bloody paparazzi out there harassing Ella.' He gave Amelie a kiss on the cheek and flicked the kettle on.

'I think Mum might be harassing him.'

'I mean, I have no idea what's going on here, but I could strangle that idiot. I didn't even see you two speaking? I mean it, I'm furious. What happened, Amelie?'

'Well, he was quite pushy, but I don't know why I . . . Oh, Dad, I'm so stupid, he asked for my Twitter name. I didn't think he'd find me online or even mention me – let alone allude to some kind of thing between us.'

Her dad sighed. 'This is what they do, I'm afraid. They're not responsible with the fans online – they're notorious for it. I could wring his bloody neck.'

Amelie sunk her head into her hands. 'Why couldn't it have been someone cool?' she moaned.

'I'll fix this,' her dad said gently, seeing that his daughter looked exhausted and vulnerable. 'Honestly, I could throttle the little prick.'

'Michael! Language!' Ella said in her poshest English accent.

She was looking rather smug, stuffing the nice young paparazzi's phone number into her pocket as she fussed over the warming and comforting Boeuf Bourguignon she was heating up for lunch.

'Sorry, Ella,' Amelie's dad said, giving her mum a quick kiss on the cheek. 'How are you doing?'

'Oh, I'm fine,' she smiled. 'These kids though! Always a drama.'

'Let me call Geoff now. Bloody idiot.'

'Guys, come on,' Ella said, forever the care-free optimist. 'It's really going to pass. Mike, you know what it's like, this stuff happened to you ALL the time way back when. And to be fair,' she nodded towards the window, 'it was more than just one – *rather handsome* – photographer camped outside your door.'

Amelie's dad raised his eyebrows.

'It's different now, Ella. With the internet, the attention

is so much more personal and intense. All I ever had to put up with was a photo as I was leaving The Ivy or some bar or whatever.'

'Which was every other week,' Ella reminded him.

'Trust me, it's different.'

He pulled out his phone and began searching.

'Damn it, I don't have the bloody number. I was sure. Ah, maybe on the call sheet.'

Amelie tried to breathe deeply and quash the anxiety that radiated through her, and the nausea in her belly. She looked across the lounge at her guitar, sitting on the floor, and felt her resentment begin to rise. Was all this really what she wanted? If she was going to be a musician, a performer, an artist, was this what would become normal to her?

'It's not always like this, Amelie,' her dad said.

'I'll just make that nice chap a hot chocolate. Anyone else?' Her mum was still going on about the handsome but apparently perilously cold photographer outside.

'Hey, Mel, if you get this message, I need to talk to Geoff urgently. Can you have him call me?'

They waited for a few moments in silence. Amelie's mum put her hand on her daughter's shoulder and said gently, 'I know it feels like you're the centre of the universe right now, but this attention is not real. It will pass. You should just try to disengage with it, darling. People love a rumour and a gossip, but those people are fickle and easily distracted. It will be something else soon.' Ella looked at Mike and for a moment Amelie thought she could see *something* unspoken between them.

'She's right,' said her father, looking a little uncomfortable. His phone vibrated and, quick as a flash, he picked up.

'Hi, Geoff! Thanks for calling me back, mate. No. I didn't hear? No not about that, I was calling about something else. No, I'm sorry to hear that – but the answer is still a no. Yeah, it's about my daughter actually. Well, she's getting a lot of attention because one of your boys has said some things online that have led the press to believe they are dating or something. Yeah. Charlie? That's the little sleazebag. It's in the papers today. The fucking *Sun* actually. Well, my daughter is struggling, to be honest. There's paps outside her front door. It's too much. She's only just seventeen, mate.'

At this, he walked out of the living room and into the bathroom, where he shut the door and kept on with his conversation.

'What will happen, Mum?'

'I guess they will decide how to deal with it. It's pretty naughty of this boy, I mean, he must know what he's doing.'

'I think he thinks he's doing me some kind of favour.' She winced. 'I mean most girls would love it, to be honest.'

When Mike came back into the room he looked pleased, albeit a little grim. 'I think it's sorted. I mean, Geoff has promised to get their publicist to deal with it – I'm not sure how, but Amelie, they know what they're doing. He's a tough negotiator though. I've agreed to do the last few tour dates with them.'

'Oh, Dad.' Amelie felt terrible. 'Really?'

'Don't worry about it, love. They're paying me for it.'

'But you HATE it!'

'Well, it's okay. I like Geoff a lot, and their sound guy Bill is very sick – he's in hospital actually – and they're really struggling to plug some of the dates. I don't mind, I need to finish a couple of things at the studio but after that I'm not too busy. And it hopefully gives me a chance to kick-start my next project.'

'Are you sure, Dad?' Amelie was unconvinced.

'Yeah. I'm sure.'

'How will it help, though?'

'With what?'

'Your next project. I mean, being away from the studio?'

Her dad looked at her for a moment, like he was weighing something up.

'Oh, well. I guess I can tell you after everything that's happened. But Amelie – you have to keep this to yourself. I know you will.' He raised his hand. 'But I need you to promise.' He watched with amusement as her eyes showed a faint sparkle.

'What? Are you doing their album? You're not, are you?'

'No,' he curled his nose up. 'But I am – might be – work- ing with one of the boys, but as you can imagine this is quite sensitive information.'

'Wow! Really? Not Charlie though – so who? Which one?' She gasped suddenly. 'Oh! Maxx?'

'Yes, but it's complicated.' He smiled. 'Even super-famous people doubt themselves, Amelie.'

'But he's not a musician?'

'He is, actually. A very skilled one as it happens. You should take a look at him on *American Stars*? Check out his audition – he went on with just his guitar and sang a song he wrote himself – but they made him join The Keep. I don't know much more than that really, but I've seen the audition. It was pretty neat.'

Amelie remembered the story, and was utterly fascinated to hear that her dad would be working with him. That was clearly what they had been discussing at the after party, and considering her dad's taste in music and impeccable standards in who he agreed to work with, she was intrigued.

'Which one is he?' Amelie's mum interrupted, holding up the newspaper with a photo of the band arriving at the Apollo.

'That one,' Amelie pointed at Maxx. 'The moody, bored-looking one.'

'He's a good kid, actually,' Mike said. 'Got his feet on the ground. I think, well, I think he probably made a big mistake joining the band, that kind of music, it's not in his blood. No, really. I like him.'

Amelie stood up and hugged her dad.

'I should be more kind. Thank you so much for sorting this out.'

'It's not sorted yet, but Geoff assures me it will be right away. I'm just sorry this happened. Well, I guess we will know for next time!'

'Mike, thank you.' Her mum touched his arm. 'Really.'

'It's okay. I'm sorry again. Have a nice lunch – smells incredible as usual!'

Amelie decided to run herself a hot bath after her father left. Hopefully this entire misunderstanding would be sorted soon and she could forget Charlie and Maxx and The Keep and the whole sordid affair. She had an audition to prepare for, and laying low would give her the perfect excuse to get stuck in and get herself ready.

Her mum knocked gently on the door as she sunk deeply into the mass of rose bubbles.

'Amelie, darling. That was the school. They want to know if you are coming back in tomorrow, and I told them yes – is that okay?'

'Yeah, Mum. There's only three days left before we break for the summer. I can face it.'

# CHAPTER 12

# I Think I Smell a Rat

Geoff called Charlie off stage during the full dress rehearsal and soundcheck for the Copenhagen show. He was furious after ending the call with Mike, and came stomping across the hall with his face red and his temples throbbing.

'Can't it wait? We're nearly done!' Charlie replied as they worked out the final moves to 'You're My Little Baby', a number that necessitated dancing with huge oversized toddler toys.

'Get down here, you miserable little worm.'

The Berlin shows had not been great. The sound was dreadful – after Bill had pulled out at the eleventh hour they'd had to improvise. That had worked fine in London with Mike, but in Berlin they'd had to rope in someone they didn't know. Someone who came on the recommendation of the venue manager, but who turned out to be the ex-husband of a friend of his aunt and had never tackled a gig of that magnitude before. The microphones constantly dropped out; for an entire song you couldn't hear the bass drum; and the vocal harmonies were mixed all wrong so on some songs you could actually hear Charlie.

From the perspective of the tour, the call from Mike had been extremely fortuitous. He couldn't join them for a few days but then he'd be with them until the final night in Paris, and all Geoff had to do was shout at Charlie for his inappropriate behaviour with a girl. Or shout at all of them because it was fun. But that didn't mean he wasn't angry.

'Actually can I have all of you down here?'

The boys looked at each other. It wasn't often that Geoff was really, properly annoyed – and he seemed furious.

'I know you all sit around at home masturbating over your own reflections, but just a reminder – you're on the slide. You can't afford mistakes any more or you're out of the game. You'll be catapulted back into your pointless previous existences, grasping for something to fill the void. Maybe you'll find an addiction, swim the Atlantic for charity, or end up on Dancing With the Has-Been Stars. I don't give a shit.'

Charlie rolled his eyes. 'Yes. We have to be careful. What have I done now?'

'Can you guys all please remember what we taught you about tweeting people – especially your younger female fans – individually? It seems the *Sun* newspaper, TMZ, The Buzz and a host of other equally highbrow publications all think you are dating Mike Church's daughter, Charlie. Because of some tweets you've posted.'

Lee burst out laughing. 'Jeez, you're a fucking dick.'

Maxx felt a pang of irritation and wished he'd spoken up when Charlie had been bragging about her in London, or when he'd alluded to her again in Berlin. He put his hands in his pockets and looked at the ground, trying to disengage himself from the conversation.

'It isn't funny. Charlie, we're going to make a statement of some kind, Mel is talking to publicity now. I don't care if you two are dating, or want to date or whatever is going on, you need to put an end to it. Publicly at least.'

Then, at last, Charlie seemed to realise it was serious. 'Is she pissed?'

'She's upset about the attention, of course. She hasn't been to school or something. Regardless, her father – your new sound engineer – is VERY pissed.'

'I don't want to make a statement,' Charlie sulked. 'What are you going to say?'

'We don't know yet, but we have to protect her. I promised so that Mike would do the last few dates on the tour.'

'Mike's joining the tour?' Maxx asked, trying to move the conversation away from Charlie.

'Yep. So, Charlie, you'd better organise your apology,' Geoff warned. 'Guys, we have to take this stuff seriously.'

Maxx was looking forward to speaking with Mike again,

and filling him in on the duet idea with Dee. He'd already started writing, getting himself off to his room and plucking away on his new guitar.

It was easily the best one he'd ever owned, a beautiful vintage – the only one he could find that he loved in the little store in Berlin. There was something about the body and old school elevation of the neck that he liked – made him feel like he had to work for each note, each chord. The inspiration was beginning to come back already, and he would seek out every moment between photo shoots, record store appearances and TV interviews to sneak off and write.

'The statement will be out by the end of the week. In the meantime, can you all try to stay off Twanker and Prickbook or wherever you go to troll underage girls?'

'No problem for me. I try to limit my screen time,' Art said smugly.

'Jesus, you're not a fucking toddler,' Geoff snapped at him, his anger causing his neck to turn deep red as he started to mutter wildly to himself. 'I try to limit my fucking screen time? Jesus Christ. Kill me now. I hate my life.'

'Everyone got it?' Mel jumped in quickly.

'Sure,' Maxx said, while Art, Kyle and Lee all nodded in agreement. He glanced over at Charlie, who was still sulking like an insolent child.

Maxx was starting to really dislike him.

'Great.' Geoff turned and marched off with Mel by his side. Cursing and waving his arms as he went.

'So, is something going on with you two?' Maxx asked Charlie when Geoff and Mel were out of earshot.

'Why?'

'I just wondered. Well, why, really? What do you gain from it? If something is going on, why would you want the fans to know? We're supposed to keep these things quiet.'

'Like you and Dee did?' Charlie scoffed.

'Um, well I think that's a bit different, don't you? Besides, we kept it secret for a long time.'

'What's it to you, anyway?' Charlie glared at Maxx.

'Woah!' Kyle intervened. 'Guys. Let's just chill.'

'Why don't we take a break and go see an exhibition?' Art suggested.

'Do you just do it for the thrill of it?' Maxx persisted. 'I'm just wondering?'

Maybe it was because of his intention to work with Mike, maybe it was just that he hated to see people upset, maybe he just disliked Charlie's attitude – but Maxx had not a care in the world for the consequences of his actions. He wasn't sure why he was so irritated, or why he was sticking up for a girl he didn't know, but he couldn't stop himself.

'It's really none of your business, dude,' Charlie said, eyeing his band mate with suspicion. Then suddenly his face changed and a sly smile creeped across it.

'Oh, interesting.'

'What?'

'Well, well,' Charlie continued. 'Like her, do you?'

'Guys, can we move on now?' Lee faked a yawn. 'This is getting boring.'

'I don't know her.' Maxx was suddenly on the defensive.

Charlie took a swig of his water bottle and wiped his mouth with the back of his hand. He turned to the band and singers on stage. 'Well, it's not my fault she wants me.'

Maxx smirked in disbelief. 'Sure, Charlie.'

'Well, don't blame me.' He shrugged. 'That's all I'm saying, bro.'

Maxx had had enough. He pulled himself back up onto the stage, picked up his stupid oversized toddler props and marched off stage, tossing them into the prop bin on his way out.

'What's going on?' Dee sounded concerned, staring over at Charlie as Maxx picked up his sunglasses and wallet from the side of the stage.

'Charlie. He really pisses me off, is what.' Maxx was fuming, but he also felt foolish. It hadn't occurred to him that Amelie would have been interested in Charlie, but of course that made the most sense. They had been having a flirtation and the fandom had gotten wind of it and made Amelie's life hell. It happened all the time.

Lee's girlfriend Jessica nearly broke up with him over a couple of misinterpreted tweets from over-enthusiastic fans. He felt like an idiot for making such a scene over nothing.

Dee put her hand on his shoulder and whispered, 'What's happened? Did he say something?'

'No.' There was nothing Maxx could say without sounding like even more of a dick. He shook his head. 'I don't want to talk about it. I have no right to be annoyed. It's stupid. He's free to date whomever he wants. It's cool, Dee, honestly.'

Dee looked relieved. 'Oh really?' She looked back at Charlie again. 'Is he dating someone ...?' her voice trailed off nervously.

'What? Look, it's cool,' Maxx said putting his sunglasses on. 'I'm over it. I need to move on from all of this.' He was referring to the band, to Dee, to this whole bullshit life he was living. Dee smiled timidly at him.

I need to get back to London as soon as possible, with Mike, he thought as he headed out into the cool air.

# CHAPTER 13

# Consequence of Sounds

'Dad, can I drop by?' Amelie shouted down the phone, pulling off her PJs and tossing them across the room so they landed in the vicinity of the clothes basket, which was currently housing her neglected saxophone.

'PLEEEEEASE!' she begged, pulling on her jeans, which conveniently and finally tore authentically at the knee. She stopped for a moment to admire the perfect fraying.

'What?' her dad said. 'No, no, no! Not today, darling. I have a production meeting about a new session this morning and then I'm flying out for the last few tour dates with—'

'The *boyband*. I know.' Amelie smirked to herself. 'I'll be quick, I've got to get home anyway and practise.'

She hung up quickly, before he had a chance to argue further, and grabbed her guitar. 'Mum, I'm going to see Dad!' Amelie called, slamming the door behind her.

It was just over a week until her audition and she was feeling close to ready. It was finally time to share her track with her dad, because despite its incredible online reception, the only musical opinion that REALLY mattered in her life was her dad's.

'Hey, Superman!' Amelie grinned as she arrived at her dad's studio half an hour later.

Mike stood in the reception area, hunched over the coffee machine in light denim jeans and a faded Stone Roses lemon graphic T-shirt. The stereo was blasting 'There's No Other Way' by Blur so loudly that she had to tap him on the shoulder to get his attention.

'Amelie!' He jumped, aimed the remote at the stereo and turned it off. 'Shoes off,' he said, looking at her muddy Chucks.

'Did I just walk into the nineties?'

'I'm just doing some research for the meeting.'

'Maxx from The Keep likes nineties Britpop?'

He kissed her on the cheek. 'Have things died down?'

'Oh my god, like, totally,' Amelie said with awe. 'You were amazing!'

An 'exclusive interview' with Charlie by Dan Wootton had appeared in the *Sun* newspaper a couple of days after Mike's phone call with Geoff. Charlie talked about missing home and being on tour and how he was 'not looking for love right now, and happy'. The headline read 'Keeping Single'. The fandom swiftly moved on to the next drama – naked balcony photos of Lee – and the end of term had meant Amelie could escape any lingering limelight at school.

Charlie even reached out and apologised to Amelie with a series of direct messages. They appeared, on face value, to be a sincere attempt to make amends and be friendly.

> TO AMELIE: Hey You. How's London? Sorry bout the shit with the press & fandom. <3 C x

> TO CHARLIE: No worries, have fun on tour!

Then, a few days later:

> TO AMELIE: How's stuff? What's happening? Europe is sooo hot <3 CXXXXX

> TO CHARLIE: Not much. Weather here hot too.

And again, a couple of days ago:

> TO AMELIE: What is your favourite record of all time? Not including any of mine ;-) BTW Stage collapsed in Prague :-/ XXX

> TO CHARLIE: Oh dear. Couldn't choose a record.

It was best not to mention the messages to her father, so Amelie played it safe. 'The photographer's long gone and Iggy Azalea had a Twitter spat with Kylie Jenner just after the interview came out and so Amelie Ayres was forgotten in a click,' she said, snapping her finger.

'Yesterday's news,' her dad sighed. 'I'm glad it's over.'

He had that look he got when he was busy. Distracted, clipped smile, inattentive. 'I really need to crack on here.'

'I know, but the whole thing ... Dad, it gave me some confidence, I think.'

'I'm glad something good came of it.' He smiled warmly.

'I mean how much worse can it get than everyone at school thinking you like a boyband?' They both laughed as Amelie sat her guitar down and put her hands in her back pockets.

'Well, I wanted to thank you,' she said, smiling shyly. 'And I wondered ... '

'Yes?' he said.

'Could I play you my audition song?'

Her dad put his coffee down and ran his hands from his hair across his face shaking his head and smiling with surprise.

'Oh god, of course you can. As long as it's single length and not some twelve-minute epic B-side?' he added quickly, looking at his watch.

'It won't take long, I promise,' Amelie said, clicking open the latches on her case.

'You need a new guitar. And new strings,' he remarked as she dug around for a moment and pulled out a USB stick.

'I thought you were going to play it for me?'

'Yeah, I recorded it.' She grinned, finding the track and hitting play.

Amelie couldn't sit and she couldn't stand and so she paced back and forth the nine or so steps of the reception area, staring at the deep blue carpet and trying not to look at her dad. The guitar introduction came in, a melancholy minor chord, picked gently over a deep, almost drowning beat.

'Can you have the backing track at the audition?'

'No. Shhhhh,' she said.

'How did you get that sound?' he asked.

'A woodblock, a brick and a tea towel,' she said hurriedly. 'Shhh.'

'It's good.'

'SHHHHHHHH!'

Her vocal came in and Amelie drew in a deep breath. This was it. She looked nervously to her dad and then back to the floor, and then to her dad. She chewed on her nail and she waited. The first note was bright, optimistic, wavering high above the deep beat before it fell into a minor key, mirroring the aching sadness of the guitar. As the track moved into the chorus, a rolling, roaring bluesy beat picked up . . .

'Hey, I'm sorry,' came a thick southern accent.

Amelie scrambled to the stereo and switched it off quickly, her heart thumping.

'I hope I haven't interrupted something?' Maxx said, staring right at Amelie for a moment, a whisper of a smile appearing before he looked over to her dad.

'No, no. Not at all,' her dad pulled himself up.

Maxx looked relaxed in an old charcoal grey T-shirt half tucked into his worn jeans and his hair, liberated from the weight of a tonne of gel and spray, hung forward. He had a brand new hard guitar case in one hand and a leather bag across his body. Behind him, pulled right up to the door, sat an expensive black car with tinted windows – the driver leaning nonchalantly against it.

Amelie hid her stunned face and tore the USB out of the stereo.

'Maxx. My daughter, Amelie, you guys met?'

'Hey, Amy-Lee.' Maxx came forward and stared confidently at her, raising his hand to shake hers. 'Not properly. I *really* hope I'm not interrupting?'

'It's Am-elie,' she said, ignoring his hand as she silently cursed his interruption. 'It's French.'

'My mistake,' Maxx said.

'You're *not* interrupting. At all,' Mike said, shaking Maxx's outstretched hand. 'Amelie was just playing me her new track. Come in, come in. Welcome to Church Street Studios.'

'Thanks, but really, you wanna finish? I can go ahead and call my driver back? I'm just off the plane anyway. I can hit the hotel and freshen up and leave y'all to it?'

'Not at all,' Amelie said quickly, she looked apologetically to her father, who shook his head in reassurance. 'I better head.'

'Sorry, darling. We've only got this small break in the schedule, then we gotta fly to ... Rome, right, Maxx?'

'Maybe?' Maxx laughed. 'I forget, it's terrible.'

'Amelie, can you email it to me?' her dad asked.

'Sure,' she said, though she knew she'd lost her nerve.

'I mean it!'

'Did you enjoy the gig?' Maxx asked, popping his guitar down next to hers. She'd had it since she was nine, her first adult-sized guitar, and seeing her old soft case sitting next to his shiny new Gibson case – she definitely wanted an upgrade.

'Um, yeah.' She smiled politely. 'Dee was amazing.'

'She's certainly got it,' Maxx said.

'You want tea? coffee?' Mike asked Maxx, kissing Amelie on the cheek as she flung her case on her back and tied one of her shoelaces up.

'You know what? That sounds great,' Maxx said, flopping on the couch and looking over to Amelie. 'I guess I might see you around then?'

'Sure. Bye,' Amelie said quickly, pulling the door open, avoiding direct eye contact. 'Bye, Dad.'

She hurried outside and fixed her canary yellow bike helmet on her head, nodding to Maxx's driver. The afternoon was disappearing into evening and she suddenly wanted to get home to the comfort of her bedroom studio. She swung her leg over the back of her bike and kicked the pedal forward and took off towards Broadway Market.

Boutique beers were being poured as the cafés were pulling down their shutters, and Hackney on a summer's Friday evening was beginning to loosen up for a long night ahead. Couples strolled arm in denim-covered arm, and beards and buns sat astride the bench seats at the Cat and Mutton, discussing digital media and coffee beans with earnest. But as she rode, it was flashes of Maxx's face that distracted her.

She stopped at the barrier by the canal – her shortcut home – and dismounted, feeling an overwhelming need to walk instead. As she took a few steps, she realised her legs were a bit wobbly. She'd pulled her bike up to a bench seat and sat for a moment to gather herself when her phone rang.

'Amelie.'

'Hey, Maisie. What's up?'

'Nothing much. Um, where are you? You sound like you've been for a run.'

'No. I just went to see Dad. I'm on my bike.'

'Oh yeah. Did you play him the track?'

'Almost, we got interrupted.'

'Oh! Bummer,' Maisie paused. 'And is there something else, my eternally earnest friend?'

'No. No. It's fine,' Amelie said, basking in the surprising warm feeling coursing through her. 'I *am* fine, actually. In fact, I feel really rather good. What are you doing?'

'Ummm ... waiting for you at my house! You're staying over, remember?'

'Oh SHIT! I'm on my way.'

# CHAPTER 14

# Rudderless

'Okay, I'm coming out!' Ella burst out of the changing room wearing a black Dior slip dress with hot pink sky-high Louis Vuitton stiletto heels.

'Oh my god, Ella,' Maisie said with her jaw on the floor. 'Wow!'

Amelie's cheeks flushed instantly. 'Oh my god, Mum.' She covered her eyes in embarrassment.

'Oh don't be a prude, Amelie! It's beautiful.' She spun around in a circle. 'Don't you just wish!?' she said, staring at her reflection in the mirror.

'Madam, can I 'elp with sizes?' said the sales assistant, who was hovering.

'Oh no, it fits perfectly,' Ella sang out. 'Amelie, why don't you try it on? For me.'

'Oooh, yes, Amelie, you must!' Maisie collapsed into the

plush changing room sofa, the sales assistant wincing as a teal and silver silk organza full-length gown was crushed under her.

'It's okay, you can sit. I can steam it,' she stammered.

'I don't want to try it on,' Amelie sighed. 'Please.'

'Oh, I despair, Amelie, I really do.' Ella crossed her arms. 'You realise you're a young woman now, and there's nothing wrong with embracing your burgeoning sexuality.'

'Oh. My. GOD!' Amelie sunk as deeply as she could into the sofa. 'No more, Ella. Please. No more.'

'Can I get you anything else, ladies?' The assistant stood patiently by while Ella began to undress with the door wide open.

'No, I'm going to think about the dress,' she said, unzipping the back and sliding it off her shoulders. She winked at Maisie and added. 'Yes, I'm going to have a glass of champagne with my beautiful daughters and think about it.'

'No problem, madam. I'll put in on hold for you. Can I 'ave your name?'

'Honey Wilson,' Ella said, stifling a giggle, as the assistant began to pick up the scattered clothes with the smallest suggestion of an eye roll.

Maisie sniggered. Amelie wanted to die. Her mother found everything hilarious. This was the dynamic of their threesome.

As they sauntered out of Liberty and onto Carnaby Street, Amelie longed to be back home in the safety of her bedroom studio – practising her track, recording, tweaking, playing it back. All she could think about was the audition tomorrow, but on her mother and Maisie's insistence that she got out of the house before she turned into a character from *Twilight*, she was dragged to central London for a girls' day out. This basically consisted of Maisie and Ella being as girly as humanly possible, while she moped about and complained.

'Is that enough shopping?' Amelie asked meekly, nodding across at The Diner and dreaming of a hotdog smothered in onions and cheese. 'I mean … shall we get some lunch?'

'We only went to Liberty! There's still Topshop, COS, Selfridges, Harvey Nicks, Zara, Coast, COS, M&S for knickers, Boots because I love toiletries – ooh and I love a peek into Bang Bang,' as her mum rattled off the list it felt like a prison sentence, and worse was to come, 'but first, I have a surprise for you both!'

'Oooh, Ella, what!?' Maisie's eyes widened with excitement.

'Let's just pop down this way …' Ella said ominously, as they ducked down a side street heading further into central Soho. The streets were brimming with tourists shopping, wailing buskers, charity muggers and pretty PR girls handing out free trials of this and that.

'Free class at Psycle!' a fit one shouted.

'Two for one cocktails!' a fun one shouted.

'Second-hand mother!' Amelie muttered. The feeling of dread growing within her was fully realised as Ella waved them towards Nails, Nails, Nails OK!!!

'Manicures!' Ella giggled, turning to both girls. 'For your upcoming birthday, Maisie, and for you for the audition, Amelie, and for me, because, well, I have a, well, a date of sorts.'

She pushed open the door, and a small blonde woman who was round as a barrel with teeny tiny legs came wobbling across the floor, her boobs heaving as she stretched out her arms in greeting.

'Ella! Amelie! You must be Maisie!' She air kissed her mother. 'What can I get you to drink? I have liquorice tea, grapefruit juice, a lovely cava? Or we have *instant* coffee. Not my fault. His.' She waved to the other beauty therapist, who looked like a blonde Jack Sparrow.

'Thanks, Frankie. Thank you so much.'

'It's no problem, darling. Anything for you.'

The girls were ushered over to the back of the salon, where they were sat at the black perspex nail bar on candy floss vintage stools and ordered to dunk their fingers into a bath of warm water.

Amelie loitered back a little.

'Take a seat, love! Your first manicure!' Ella beamed.

Amelie looked down at her calloused fingers and broken nails. She instinctively started to chew on her thumbnail. 'Mum, I'm sorry. I can't really have a manicure.'

'Oh yeah,' Maisie turned, smiling. 'She needs to keep her fingers rough for playing her guitar.'

'What? Oh, come on love, you'll love it! We can keep the colour nice and subtle.'

'No, Mum, really. I can't. It's not me being difficult . . . '
She squirmed as Frankie slipped three glasses of cava onto
the nail bar next to them. 'I'm so grateful, but I really can't.
I need to keep them hard.' She held up her calloused fingers
to show her mum, who curled her nose up at the sight of
them.

'Oh, this is such a shame. Gosh. Can't you just get a little
file and a colour then?' her mother pleaded. 'A pedi? What
about those feet? They haven't seen the light of day since you
were eleven!'

'We have musicians come in here all the time,' Frankie said
matter-of-factly. 'George can give you a guitarist manicure . . .
GEORGE! We do it all the time. ALL THE TIME,' she said,
as though Amelie was hearing impaired.

Amelie shrugged at her mother's pleading eyes and caved.
'Um, okay. I guess so. Thank you.'

Maisie shot her a look. 'You *could* get your feet done
instead,' she whispered as Amelie dunked her fingers into the
warm water.

'It's okay. Really.' She tried not to furrow her brow as
George appeared with a small plastic tumbler filled with
horrifying-looking silver torture equipment.

As the three sat having their nails done, Amelie tried her
best not to bring the mood down. Her mum chatted away to
Frankie, who turned out to be an old friend from school and
who had been around when her parents had met.

'Oh, but your father was so charming!' Frankie said. 'So

charming and so cool. We were all terribly jealous of Ella when she snagged him.'

Amelie recoiled at the image of her mother literally snagging her father. Like some barbaric metal hook snags a dead pig.

'What were they like together?' Maisie asked innocently, whilst holding two identical looking hot pinks up. 'Left or right?'

'RIGHT!' Frankie and her mother replied in unison.

'They were cute. Ella was very smitten,' Frankie grinned. 'But it wasn't to be. Short and very sweet, it was.'

'But he gave me you!' Ella said with a smile. 'My baby girl.'

'If only he'd given a bit more than that,' Frankie muttered.

'What?' Amelie's ears pricked.

'Oh, nothing, love,' Frankie said, focusing her attention on applying a thin clear base coat to Ella. 'You know what men are like.'

'Amelie has a big audition tomorrow! Don't you, love?' her mum said quickly. 'She's been practising like mad. Totally dedicated to her music! Incredible determination, I'm very proud of her. As you know, I can't stick to one thing, me. Always looking for the next thing.'

She and Frankie shared a laugh as the cava began to loosen them up a little.

'Which reminds me,' Frankie said conspiratorially. 'Back to Paris, eh?'

Amelie looked down at her hands as George furiously

filed the edges of her non-existent nails. She closed her eyes and shook her head, trying to clear what she thought she had heard.

There was a silence from the end of the bar. She didn't need to look across to know that Frankie had spoken out of turn, and her mother was probably giving her the *look*.

'Eh?' Maisie raised her eyebrows and squeaked. 'Paris? What? Who's going to Paris?'

Amelie wanted to pull her hands out from under the fluorescent drying contraption, she felt trapped, but the conversation was running away from her like a steam train.

'Well, I wasn't going to say anything just yet.' Ella beamed across at both the girls. 'But yes, I have been offered a job opportunity for the summer in Paris. I don't have the job yet, but I have a final meeting tomorrow to finalise everything. Hence the nails. I'm going to nip over on the train. Maybe look for accommodation while I'm there.' She said it as if everything should be perfectly clear now.

Amelie managed a weak smile, but Maisie was confused. 'Hang on, who's going to Paris?' She shot a hurt and confused look at Amelie, who dropped her head and focused everything she had on not screaming.

'I know! Back to Paris, for the summer at least! It's quite a shock, but to be honest it's always been on my mind.'

'That's great, Mum,' Amelie squeaked. 'Well done. But . . . tomorrow?'

'Oh, darling, you said you didn't want anyone at the

audition! And anyway, I didn't have any choice – it was the only day.'

'But you can't go to Paris, Amelie. You've got exams. Final Year. Your audition is tomorrow! What about working at your dad's studio?' Maisie sounded panicked.

'Oh, Amelie can stay in London. You're old enough to stay, Amelie.' Ella smiled as if this made it okay.

Amelie looked down at her nails and felt a sharp elbow in the ribcage from Maisie. 'Tell her,' she whispered through gritted teeth. 'Tell her you don't want her to go.'

'It's okay,' Amelie huffed. 'Leave it.'

'What are you afraid of? Tell her!'

Amelie's cheeks were burning. She willed Maisie to stop probing as she felt her eyes begin to sting.

Amelie blew out, hard. 'LEAVE IT!'

Suddenly and mercifully the clattering of two loud, squawky girls weighed down with Primark bags came crashing through the door of the salon – the tension dissipated immediately and Amelie felt the tightness in her chest ease.

'FRANKIE! Emergency. Broken Nail,' wailed the taller one. 'OH LORD MY NAAAAAAAAAAAAAIL!' she screeched, holding up a snapped blue-and-yellow-striped acrylic monstrosity.

Ella slid down off her stool. 'Here you go, love, I'm done,' she said calmly, blowing on the end of her perfectly finished scarlet-red nails. She walked down to towards Amelie and laid a hand on her shoulder. 'I'm so sorry, I was going to talk to you over lunch. Nothing is set in stone yet. I have to GET the job first. Ooh, look at your nails! They almost look like the hands of a young lady.'

Amelie blinked, took a deep breath, looked up and smiled at her mum.

'It's great for you, Mum. I'm happy. Really.'

'I knew you'd be pleased for me.' She grinned. 'Maisie, I don't want to jinx things, but if I DO get the job, you two must come and spend a long weekend with me in Paris.'

Momentarily sidetracked, Maisie grinned. 'Oh my god, Ella, that would be amazing!'

# CHAPTER 15

# Please, Please, Please, Let Me Get What I Want

There were three ways you could get a slot on stage at Music in the Park.

1. You were asked by the promoters – for the mega famous.
2. You entered online via the hugely competitive unsigned bands competition – there was one place and it always went to established, gigging bands.
3. You won a place through the high school audition. This was Amelie's plan.

The auditorium was filled with a hugely diverse group of young musicians from six different schools in the east London area. The competition was fierce, with everyone turning on their very best to nab that one wildcard spot on stage. She only recognised a handful of other people in the auditorium: the fourth form three-piece pop/rock band (who were pretty good actually); Tara would be her main rival as the other singer/songwriter; and a few from the jazz band had gotten together to create a cool, small unplugged band which they'd asked Amelie to join, but she'd turned them down since she was auditioning by herself.

Amelie sat on a seat alongside the fifty-four other hopefuls, her guitar at her side, listening to a sixth form rock band – Blind Envy – playing a punk rock version of the *Play School* theme song.

'*There's ... A ... BEAAAAAR! There's a bear in there,*' the lead singer growled, swinging his head in circles, his long black hair whipping across his face.

Next up, an all-girl a cappella choir, dressed in matching silver, singing a cover of Rihanna's *Diamonds* – Amelie thought it was all a little bit out of tune, as she eyed the judges for some kind of hint of what they might be thinking.

There were three judges. One was a youngish blogger and general music industry whiz kid called Tom. He owned an indie record label in Shoreditch and had recently signed some awesome singer/songwriters. Amelie *had* to impress him.

Next to him was Hackney's Councillor for Children, a squat lady in a purple suit with sensible shoes and a bob cut. Strictly there as the council representative, and not for her impeccable taste as an A & R woman, Amelie wondered if she'd ever even been to a gig.

And finally there was singer/songwriter/DJ extraordinaire Trinx. She was a formidable player in the London music scene and cool as cool as cool can be. She was also the headliner on the dance stage at Music in the Park, so certainly boosted the credibility of the process.

A bespectacled third year with a harpsichord walked onto the stage, and Amelie took the opportunity to head out for a quick bathroom break and to call her dad.

'Amelie?' He turned off the playback in his studio. 'What's wrong?'

'Are you recording?'

'Yeah, Maxx is right here – he says hi. Just trying to get going. So what's up?'

'Audition is in about fifteen minutes, I reckon.'

'Okay! Oh, wow. Well, remember, just relax and take a deep breath. You can do it.'

'I feel pretty good, Dad.'

'Great. Is your Mum with you . . . ah, sorry, of course, she's in Paris.'

'Yep.'

'What's the competition like? Anyone we need to worry about?'

'Not right now, but there is this girl Tara, she's got pipes.'

'Pipes, huh?' Her dad laughed. 'Well, good luck, darling.'

'Thanks! I'll call you right back afterwards.'

She snuck back into the auditorium just as she was due backstage to get herself ready. She slipped up the side entrance and sat in the wings, tuning her guitar and picturing herself playing to a hall full of naked people, as Maisie had suggested. She laughed. That was NOT going to work.

Suddenly there was a clatter from the back of the hall and all heads shot round to see Brooke and Ashleigh clambering over chairs to get to the front of the audience.

'SCUSE ME!' boomed Brooke, as she pushed her way past a row of trombonists.

'SORRY!' Ashleigh shouted, tripping and crushing the cake box she was trying desperately to hold aloft.

Amelie peered around the curtain to catch Brooke handing a slightly squashed cupcake to each of the judges.

'Don't let us interrupt. Hello there, I like your music,' she said, shaking the hand of a very bemused Trinx.

Amelie cringed. Thankfully Tara was next up, which meant they would hopefully be gone before Amelie auditioned.

She turned her attention to Tara, and was intrigued to see her younger brother accompany her onstage and sit at the piano.

'Hi, I'm Tara. I'm eighteen years old.' She spoke way more softly than Amelie imagined, and there was definitely a hint of nerves in her voice.

'What are you going to play for us today, Tara?' asked Hackney's Councillor for Children, with a warm smile.

'I'm going to sing a song called "Breeze", which I wrote myself,' Tara explained. 'My brother will be accompanying me on the piano.'

'And why do you want to perform at Music in the Park?'

Amelie watched with surprise as Tara took a step back from the mic and looked back at her brother. She saw a hint of a lip wobble and perhaps even a glassy eye. Her brother nodded in encouragement and Tara turned back, taking a deep breath.

'Um, I want to get a chance to prove myself, I guess. That I can do this . . . ' Her voice trailed off, but there was no mistaking the crack in her voice as she spoke.

Amelie allowed herself a little sneer – it's not bloody *X Factor*, she thought, imagining 'You Raise Me Up' by Westlife playing in the background of her audition montage.

The piano began. The track had a modern R & B sound despite its somewhat staid accompaniment. Tara held the microphone, took another deep breath, and then out came this incredible sound. Smokey, bluesy and without a hint of nerves to betray her. This was nothing like the uniform vocals she'd heard from Tara in the school choir. This was different. Amelie closed her eyes and could hear a thoroughly perfect, current sound.

Amelie was suddenly thrown. She hadn't imagined this kind of competition, and Tara was REAL competition. Her music was, Amelie thought despairingly, good, polished and original. And above all, her performance was confident.

As Tara finished to rapturous applause from the other auditionees, and plenty of *whoop whooping* and whistling from Brooke and Ashleigh, Amelie felt the sense of dread start to seep into her veins.

'Thank you, Tara,' smiled Tom. 'That was excellent.'

Tara smiled, caught her breath and whispered 'Thank you,' before hugging her brother and exiting the stage right in front of Amelie. As she passed by, Tara missed Amelie completely, she was so wrapped up with her brother and buzzing from the reception of her performance.

'Who's next? Amelie Ayres, is it?' Trinx was speaking now. Amelie had to get onstage. She craned her neck to see Brooke and Ashleigh still there in the crowd. They had their feet up on the seats in front and were both waiting for her. She hesitated, but her name was called again.

'Amelie Ayres? Hackney College?' Trinx said once more.

She had no choice. She walked slowly from the wings onto the corner of the stage, and felt the blood begin to drain from her face. With one foot in front of the other, looking down at the cracks in the floorboards, hearing the creaking sound amplified around the auditorium, she began to feel the nausea.

'You need to turn the mic on!' One of the judges was speaking, but all Amelie could hear was the pounding of her heart in her ears. Her shaking fingers struggled with the tiny button on the microphone, and when she finally managed to switch it on there was an almighty screech of feedback.

It's happening again, she thought, as she began to feel light-headed.

'So, you're Mike Church's daughter?' She tried to focus on the judges but the room started to close in on her.

'Yeah,' she managed, plucking at the strings on her guitar as best she could to test the sound.

'I've worked a bit with your father.' It was Tom speaking. 'He's really great. It's awesome to see you play. Good luck!'

Amelie was trying desperately not to throw up. She could taste the bile at the back of her throat. She tried to clear it, swallowing, but it was dry and scratchy. She hoisted the guitar strap up over her shoulder and tried to hold down the strings to make a chord but her fingers felt like sausages, big and clumsy.

'Well, Amelie, let's have your song then?' Trinx said gently.

Amelie wasn't sure how long they had been waiting, but she knew the room was silent.

'I need some water,' Amelie coughed, still looking down, her face and ears burning red.

'Here,' one of the volunteers threw a bottle of water up towards her, which Amelie tried to catch but it fell to the floor with a thump, then rolled along the stage and, with another thump, onto the floor. There was a giggle, and then a 'shush', and then silence again.

'Sorry.' She stepped to edge of the stage and the volunteer loosened the lid and passed the bottle to her. Amelie gulped down half of it. Water trickled down her arms and face and she gasped, the room came momentarily into focus, so she quickly put the bottle down and strummed her opening chord.

'Um, this is a song. Well, I wrote . . . ' She started to pick the strings on her guitar, it sounded clumsy, and she couldn't get the rhythm. She closed her eyes and focused with everything she had, and opened her mouth.

All that mattered was getting to the end, that's all she could focus on. She sang and played, unable to play her guitar properly, her voice cracked on the high notes, and the timing fell apart. When she strummed the final chord, she looked up at the judges, too breathless for tears.

The Hackney Council lady looked pitying. 'Thanks, love,' she said with a warm smile, writing something on a piece of paper in front of her.

'Is that your track?' Tom said. 'I'm sure I've heard it before?'

'Yes,' she squeaked.

'Thanks, Amelie. And well done for writing your own music,' Trinx said without condescension.

'Tell your dad hello from me,' Tom said kindly.

Her legs were like jelly as she walked back off stage. She stumbled on the stairs, steadied herself and kept walking towards the double doors. When they were safely closed behind her, she collapsed onto the grass outside.

And burst into tears.

All the work and effort Amelie had put in had been wasted. She couldn't get the better of her nerves, despite the practice. She'd felt different this year. Stronger. She had played that song a thousand times, each note was seared into her brain, she could play it literally blindfolded (she did this on more than one occasion). *'I'll never be able to do this,'* she fumed.

Sobbing into her hands, she fumbled for her phone and rang her dad.

'It was ... oh, Dad, I can't do it!' She could hardly speak. She broke down completely, gasping for breath, she felt five years old.

'Amelie, honey, what happened?'

'I couldn't play! It was terrible.'

'Oh, Amelie.'

'Can you pick me up?'

'Sure, sweetheart. Is Maisie with you?'

'No. I told her not to come,' she sniffed.

'I'll be there in five minutes. Can you get yourself to the front gate?'

'Yes. I just have to get my guitar case and my bag.'

She hung up and pulled herself off the ground, sneaking in the back to pick up her things while a rockabilly band played a cover of Elvis's 'Heartbreak Hotel'. Amelie felt the world was against her.

Her eyes red and puffy, she stood at the gate waiting for her dad. She looked around, checked she couldn't see anyone and picked up her guitar. She smashed it three times on the school fence until the body broke free from the neck and it lay in a heap on the ground.

# CHAPTER 16

# Red-Eyed and Blue

Mike leaned in and pressed the talkback button on his mixing desk so that Maxx could hear him through his headphones. 'I need to pick up my daughter. Can you give me half an hour or so?'

Maxx gave him a nod through the glass screen.

Maxx needed to run through a few things anyway. He pulled out his notebook and pencil and scribbled down a few more lyric ideas, and then flicked back to the duet he'd started writing. It was a pared-back song, sugary-titled 'Sweet Something', and so far it totally sucked. It was not the new sound he was looking for – it was a slightly less pop version of one of the sixty-eight songs he'd recorded with The Keep.

Inspiration was not forthcoming. And neither was Dee. Since London she had become difficult to pin down; they were all so busy, busier than ever this tour – with press engagements, photo shoots and everything else. Dee had to shoot the video for her new single in Paris, so that took her totally out of action. But Maxx couldn't shake the niggling feeling that she had altogether lost interest in recording with him.

She had managed one forty-five minute writing session with him, but it was awkward – thematically they wanted different things. Dee wanted an upbeat song about redemption, moving on – and Maxx something sad, and more lingering.

It had quickly become clear that he was going to have to do the lion's share on his own if he wanted to take advantage of his short time in the studio with Mike. The three of them had managed to have some brief discussions about the track during the tour, but they'd obviously had to be very discreet. Maxx had one week at the studio and though Dee was only two hours away in Paris, it had so far proved impossible to get her to commit to a day and time she would come to record with him, let alone write.

Mike had suggested getting her to lay her vocals down at a studio in the States, but Maxx was really hoping to get her input into the production as well as just the vocal. But, at this rate, he couldn't really even consider it *their* song. If she was coming on board, it was as a passenger.

After their final gig in Paris a few days before, Maxx found her in the downstairs bar of the Maison Souquet having a cocktail with Lee and Charlie.

'Dee, hey. I've been trying to call you.'

'Maxx, hi.' She'd definitely looked guilty, no doubt for ignoring his messages.

'Um, well, I wondered. Did you want to get together to, um, do that, look into that music we talked about,' he'd said clumsily.

Out of the corner of his eye, he'd caught a hint of a smirk from Charlie, but Dee appeared embarrassed. Lee made a lame excuse and had gone to show the hot bartender a trick he could do with an olive and a martini glass.

'Sorry, I've been really busy. Maybe another time?' she'd offered, with a genuinely apologetic smile. Charlie had pretended to do something on his phone, which was clearly upside down.

'Okay. Maybe see you in London?'

'Let's talk later,' she'd said quickly, clearly keen not to discuss anything in front of Charlie.

Feeling frustrated, he'd left the hotel and taken the first Eurostar to London, determined to try her one more time when he was settled in at the studio. If it really came to it, he could do this track with any number of up and coming singers who would jump at the opportunity.

He put down his notebook, tucked his guitar into its place on the rack and hung his headphones over the music stand, before heading out into the reception area to try to figure out the coffee machine.

Mike had an assistant called Julian – a tall, built, black-haired, tattooed guy who was as handsome as he was flamboyantly camp. He hung about in the control area working with the electrics, and he was the *best* at his job.

'You wanna coffee ... or, an *English breakfast tea*?' Maxx asked in his best posh English accent.

'Oh please! No, don't worry yourself.' Julian put his things down and squeezed out from behind the rack. 'I'll get it for you. What do you want?'

Despite his quite arresting appearance, he was the sweetest, kindest and most helpful guy Maxx had ever met.

'No, I fancy the walk. What would you like?'

'Really, let me.' Julian opened the petty cash tin from under the reception desk. 'I've got the ca-ash!' he sang.

Maxx grinned, realising he only had euros. He was forever working in the wrong currency.

'Okay, then. I'd love a coffee from that place on the corner, the New Zealand one. Mike got me a flat white from there this morning. Is that okay?'

'Sounds very east London. Can I tempt you with a brownie?'

'No, thanks.'

'But they're the 2015 Taste Award-winning salted caramel brownies! Your pancreas will explode with delight! You must!' Julian squealed, clasping his hands together in delight.

'Ha, okay. This is pretty much *afternoon tea* now, isn't it?' Maxx laughed, looking at his watch.

Just after Julian left, Maxx settled down on the reception couch to flick through a hot-off-the-press trashy magazine. There on the third page was a shot of Kyle, Art, Lee, Charlie and Dee from the other night in Paris, presumably on their way out for the end of tour party that he missed. There was a picture of him in a circle next to the headline: 'MAXXED OUT'.

*Has The Keep's favourite singer moved on? With the absence of Maxx on The Keep's end of tour night out, rumours were circulating that he is suffering from exhaustion, following their most intensive schedule to date. Girlfriend Dee looked relaxed in the company of the rest of the boys as they ran up a €10,000 tab at the exclusive Paris House restaurant and club.*

Dee was certainly smiling and looking relaxed, as the rest of the boys strutted along the pavement in their expensive suits. He felt a pang of sadness. Five years of his life was a long time to spend with these guys, and despite the rows they were a kind of family.

Splashed across the side of the article under the title 'HOT GOSS', there was more.

*Is it the end for Dee & Maxx? Go to TheBuzzOnline.com for an in-depth exclusive.*

Just as he tossed the magazine into the recycle bin, Amelie Ayres came storming through the door.

She stood there holding a smashed guitar and stared right at him, her usually sharp eyes all red and puffy and her face filled with sadness and embarrassment. Before he had a moment to register she was there, she was gone.

'Sorry for being here,' she said as she walked past him and into Mike's office, slamming the door behind her.

'Are you okay?' he replied after she was gone. The question hung in the empty air and he stood still for a moment trying to take in what had just happened.

Mike came rushing through next, rubbing his hands through his hair. He tossed his keys into the tray on the coffee table.

'Maxx, I'm sorry but Amelie has had, um, a bad day, and she's going to hang around here for a bit if you don't mind. She won't come into the studio, I told her not to, but she doesn't want to go home. Her mum is in Paris. Bloody hell. I'm really sorry. Julian will look after her.'

'It's really no problem.' Maxx looked at Mike, who was distracted with worry about his daughter. 'Anything I can do?'

'No, it's fine. If you can just bear with me a bit?'

'Of course. Julian's just gone out to get me a coffee. I can go and meet him at the café, if you like? Give you some time?'

'It's okay for now,' Mike said, just as the sound of broken strings being violently liberated from a guitar came from his office.

'You know what? I actually need to get some fresh air. I'll be back in fifteen, okay?' Maxx didn't wait for Mike to protest.

He hadn't really ventured out into the surrounding area since arriving. It was their first full day in the studio and it was a good excuse to get the lay of the land. The clouds were thick and the drizzle was incessant, London was true to its reputation for terrible weather, but after the heat of the continent and in particular their last few dates in Rome, Madrid and Paris, he welcomed the cooler air.

As he walked the short distance to the café, he realised that for the first time in longer than he could remember he was walking in a city, without security, or an entourage, or even an assistant like Alexia. His hair had grown long around his ears and in his low-slung jeans, sneakers and T-shirt he could have been any other Londoner taking a walk in Hackney. And it felt amazing.

Nobody was looking at him. No young fans were around pestering him for autographs and photos, no press to bother him; none of those *'don't I know you from somewhere?'* second glances from anyone because there was nobody who cared – only Mike and Julian, oh and maybe Amelie.

He was surprised by his reaction to seeing her again. There was that spark behind her eyes, something he felt drawn to. Even in her stressed state, standing there with her broken guitar and red eyes, she looked quite beautiful. He quietly hoped she might be around a bit more this week.

He pushed the café door open and Julian was sat on a bench seat waiting for the takeaway coffees.

'Can we get these to have in?' Maxx smiled.

'Hey, sorry, has it taken too long?' he looked so sincerely apologetic, Maxx patted him on the shoulder.

'No, no, no, I just . . . ' He started chuckling.

'JULIAN!' the barista shouted as if there was a large

queue, when there was only the two of them in the entire café.

'Thanks.' Julian jumped up and grabbed the two takeaway cups. 'We're going to sit in, if that's cool?'

The barista shrugged so nonchalantly that it could have been considered rude. Not that Maxx cared, the lack of helpfulness was refreshing after being waited on hand and foot for weeks on end.

They took a seat in the window as Maxx stirred a huge teaspoon of sugar into his coffee and flicked through a free *Hackney Art & Live Music* magazine.

'Jeez, there's so much to do in this town.'

'I know, and that's just Hackney!'

'Wow. I'd love a few nights out while I'm here.'

'A bit early for a break. Have you even laid down a track yet?' Julian joked.

'Mike's daughter is there, and I think, well I'm not sure what's happened but I am just giving them some space,' Maxx explained.

'Oh, Amelie? What? She's at the studio? Now?'

'Yeah,' he said, remembering her haunted look as she stormed past him.

'Oh, she's great. Love the wee Amelie, the little sweet pea, did you meet her?'

'The little sweet pea?' Maxx was sceptical. 'No, well, yes, I've met her briefly a couple of times. She knows my bandmate, Charlie, a bit better I think.'

'Ah, yes,' Julian grinned. 'That was quite the dramarama!'

Since their argument in Copenhagen, Maxx's relationship with Charlie had further deteriorated. If he was honest, the incident had just been a catalyst for whatever competitive stuff had been brewing between them since the band was first formed. They hardly spoke, unless they absolutely had to, and Charlie had become even more withdrawn and secretive.

'Charlie knows how to cause drama,' grinned Maxx. 'So how long have you worked for Mike?'

'Oh, two years or so, I guess. Since he opened the new studio.'

'Cool, bet you've seen a lot of great bands come through?'

'Well, depends on your taste. Mike's pretty picky about who he works with. Plus, he still does the odd tour or one-off show, so he can't always commit to studio time. He was pretty excited about working with you, though.'

'That's cool. Same here,' Maxx said shyly, feeling honoured in a way he never did with The Keep.

'How does it work, you know, with your band, and the label? Do they mind you going off on your own?'

'Actually, funny you should ask.' Maxx looked out the window wondering how much he could say to Julian. 'They don't really know. It's more of an experiment, really. We'll see if anything comes of it. I'm just happy to be here, in London.'

'Oh, so it's a bit of a naughty secret then, eh!? Excellent.' He nudged Maxx playfully, who was now longingly staring at the gig guide in a *Time Out* magazine. 'You know, if you fancied it, I could take you for a night out?'

'Like a date?' Maxx nudged him back, laughing.

'Yeah, exactly like a date, except that I would bring my boyfriend.' Julian smiled, pausing for dramatic effect. 'He worked on your tour actually. I met him through Mike.'

'Oh really? Would I know him, I mean, was he one of the regulars?'

'Sure was. It's Clint? He does your filming?'

'Oh, wow! Yeah I know Clint, he's hilarious. He's your boyfriend?'

'Yes. The straightest gay man in London. Hands off,' Julian teased.

'Oh, wow, that's cool.'

'Yes, and I think we should all go to a gig.'

Maxx looked at Julian with uncertainty. 'Will it, I mean, do you think I could ...'

'I promise you, no one will bother you,' Julian laughed. 'I mean, don't get me wrong, you're more famous than anyone I've ever met, but where we'll go, no one will care. And anyway, out of your boyband uniform even *I* hardly recognised you, and I was a bit of a fan once.'

Maxx felt a rush of excitement at going out in London with some locals – to a regular old pub to watch some live music and just hang. It sounded like bliss.

'Okay. Fuck it. I'm in.' He raised his coffee cup. 'To a night out being a regular dick.'

'Oh, believe me, I've seen regular dick, and you're not that,' Julian laughed.

They touched their cups together. Maxx sipped his flat white and watched the rain fall, the black cabs roll past, and the red buses kick puddles up onto the pavement. He felt the wonderful promise of new beginnings.

# CHAPTER 17

# Please Wake Me Up

When they got back from the coffee shop, Mike was in the studio and Amelie, as promised, was nowhere to be seen. Maxx pushed the studio door open to find Mike fiddling around with some cables and an old vintage amplifier on the floor.

'Everything okay?' he asked.

'Yeah, no worries here, she's a beautiful thing but sometimes needs a little TLC.'

'Ha!' Maxx grinned. 'No, I didn't mean the amp.'

'Oh! Ahh, Amelie. Well. Not really.' Mike looked grim. 'She's had an audition today and it didn't go so well.'

'Oh.' He didn't want to pry further, but Mike seemed to want to talk. 'What happened? Can I ask? I don't want to intrude.'

Mike put his screwdriver down and looked at Maxx gratefully. 'I think she simply has stage fright. Well, not simply, I guess, it's massive to her. I just don't know what to do to help, basically she won't accept any help.'

'Ahh, that sucks. I mean, I understand of course.' Although he'd never had stage fright, Maxx had completely humiliated himself on *American Stars*, which was surely worse.

'No, it's fine. She'll be okay. I think she's going to take some time out and go to Paris to see her mum at the end of the week. But I wondered – and you are more than welcome to say no – but ... '

'Anything, Mike. What can I do?'

'Can she come and watch or even assist me a bit?'

'What? Us record? Sure,' Maxx said without hesitation.

'If you're really sure? I mean she won't get in the way or anything, I'll make sure of that. She's desperate to learn more about recording – I mean, she kinda grew up tinkering – hard not to with me as a dad. But I've never let her in here when there's been a session on before. I promised her this summer ... You know she built her own recording studio in her bedroom?'

'Really? Wow. That must be some damn bedroom!'

'It's pretty basic, but as I said, she built the thing all by herself. It's not just some mic plugged into Pro Tools either.'

'Absolutely, Mike. I'm happy for her to be here. Only ... one thing.' Maxx suddenly grew worried. 'Remember that I'm not supposed to be here.'

'Okay,' Mike replied, 'I know. Don't worry; we're totally confidential here. You're booked under an alias, and Julian is totally trustworthy. There's not exactly anyone Amelie could tell. I've already spoken to her and she knows that whoever is in here recording must have complete anonymity. And ... well I think she's learned her lesson about social media and so forth.'

Maxx considered this answer. Despite the dire warnings from Geoff, Charlie had smugly confided in Maxx that he and Amelie were still secretly in contact, albeit through private messages. In fact, Charlie had presented it as a kind of fledgling romance. Maxx chose his words carefully, not wanting to stir up any trouble.

'Okay, well, could you just remind her that it's important not to mention it to anyone, particularly in my band.'

Mike looked perplexed. 'Okay. I'll make sure.'

'Just being extra careful.' Maxx tried to make light of the request.

'No worries, I understand. I'm just about there. Shall we lay something down? Sometimes just getting something down helps us step back and get perspective,' Mike said as he stood up and wiped the grease off his hands.

'Okay.'

'Most sessions start slow,' Mike said reassuringly, flicking a bunch of switches on his desk so everything lit up.

Amelie sat next door in her dad's office, leaning way back in his chair, inspecting the stark white ceiling and trying to think of anything but the audition.

She opened her dad's computer and logged onto her

SoundCloud, thinking she might cheer herself up by reading some of the kind comments from her followers. But through the prism of self-loathing she read nothing but lies and fantasy.

Excruciating recollections stole her small moments of peace, creeping in like a slide show of horrors. A bemused face in the crowd, a judge's pitying smile, the warm glow of Tara's face as she floated off the stage, high on triumph. She shook her head. There was nothing to do but bask in the pain.

# CHAPTER 18

# No Diggity

Amelie was feeling too low to fight her father, who had stood still with his arms crossed in the doorway for the last eight minutes, refusing to come any further in.

'Okay, okay, I'm coming! Jeez. I don't like this new bossy father.'

'You hassle me for years to help out on a session, and now you're dragging your heels?' he said, standing firm.

Amelie was lying on the floor of her mother's living room, showered and dressed but dragging her feet over going to the studio. If she didn't hate music so much at that moment, she would have jumped at the chance.

He had sold it in as work – she would be paid £5 an hour to assist Julian and him on anything they needed. Trips to the shop, tidying up, helping with the rigging – anything that was required, and it was going to be a great way to pass the school holidays.

'Remember, no one knows he's recording,' her dad reminded her. 'So don't even tell Maisie, okay?'

'I know! You've said that like a thousand times, it's not like I've got any other friends to tell,' she said dramatically.

Mike picked up her leather satchel and walked to the door. 'I think it would be good for you to see what he's doing. I live in hope you'll let me record you too one day?'

'I already record myself, remember?' she said glumly, nodding towards her bedroom. 'It's amazing what I can do without an audience.'

'Well. I want to hear more of your stuff when you're ready. Because, regardless what you can or can't do on stage right now, the recording was very, very good.'

In what she called an immediate self-esteem intervention, Maisie had picked Amelie up from the studio the previous night with her enormous make-up bag and spent the night trying to cheer her up with an Appletini and Seafoam Splendour pedicure. Since she turned sixteen last year, Amelie's mum had let her stay home alone when she worked short stints in kitchens in Paris or anywhere else, and it was fun having the house to themselves. Amelie was so drained from the adrenaline of the audition and the comedown afterwards she was happy to be steamrolled by Maisie.

They painted her nails and her toes, she shaved her legs and soaked in a bubble bath. She had a full facial from Maisie using all her mother's homemade, organic, raw products – an oatmeal cleansing mask, a cucumber and lemon peel and a deep moisturising mask made from coconut oil. Maisie then blow-dried her hair (something Amelie NEVER bothered with usually) and gave her ends a little snip to tidy them up, before forcing her to have a disgusting green smoothie for dinner. She also left behind another in the fridge for breakfast, which Amelie had obligingly drank, although it had started to turn brown and split into a watery liquid topped with a thick, gooey foam.

That morning, after a surprisingly long sleep, she checked herself in the mirror and was glad to see she didn't look completely like death. She pulled on her oldest, most faded black jeans and, deciding against an ironic Backstreet Boys T-shirt, she pulled on a grey T-shirt and plaid bomber.

'You need to move, Amelie.' Her dad pushed as she slyly checked her look in the mirror. 'You look very nice. Now come on – we're going to work, remember.'

'All right already!' She pulled on her white Chuck Taylors and brushed her hair one more time before heading to the door.

She definitely looked a damn sight better than the day before. Maxx had stood there gawping at her with her broken guitar and her face red and blotchy from crying. She couldn't believe she'd been terribly rude to him AGAIN, but was determined to make a super good impression this morning.

Her dad's baby – a vintage silver Mercedes – was parked

right outside, and as she hopped into the passenger seat, her mother called. Again.

'Arghhh,' groaned Amelie sending the call to answer phone. 'I wish she would stop calling. She wants to know how the audition went.'

'Amelie.' Her father took a stern tone with her. 'You need to speak with her. She's worried about you.'

'I'll call her back, I promise.'

Amelie strode into the side entrance of the studio with her father and went straight into the control room. She took a seat at the back of the room on a long blue sofa, kicking her feet up and laying back to play with her phone. The studio was only two years old and although it was small, it was fitted out beautifully. Mike's taste was clean and modern, with dark masculine blues and greys. Practically the opposite of her mother.

Maxx slipped in just after ten, and again Amelie expected the boy in the glossy press shots – but once again he looked like he could have been anyone; a boy at her school, almost. There wasn't a boy at her school anywhere near that attractive, though. His hair, his shoulders thick under those rolled up T-shirt sleeves, and his deep green eyes.

Maxx hadn't noticed she was there as he began chatting to her dad. He was confident and self-assured, though there was something about his face, the way he spoke, his accent, the way that the corners of his eyes moved when he smiled, that made him seem gentle.

'So, damn it,' he sighed. 'I can't get hold of Dee. I'm wondering if I should just go ahead and record the song this week, and lay down her vocals in the US as you suggested.'

'It's an okay idea, but let's try to hold out hope. It will really sound a lot better if you both record here. Chemistry and all that.'

Amelie watched with fascination as Maxx waved away her father's comment.

'I can't really do a *duet* without her.'

'Do you think you'll be able to get her to come?' Mike asked. 'We could put the word out for a UK artist? Confidentially of course ... I could speak to some people at Universal?'

'Let's wait a bit more. I've left her a final final final message now, if we don't hear back she's either dead or REALLY doesn't want to do it.' Maxx half-heartedly laughed.

'Oh, I forgot.' Mike spun round in his chair. 'Amelie is here.'

'Hi. I'm sorry about yesterday. Bad Day!' Amelie pulled herself up from the couch and held out her hand timidly, unable to meet Maxx's gaze.

'Looked like your guitar had a bad day too,' Maxx joked, shaking her hand.

'I'm just very punk rock,' Amelie grumbled.

'Well, I'm glad to have you around. Be great to have your input. What I heard the other week wasn't half bad.' When he spoke he seemed so adult. There was a polish and a confidence in his voice, with none of that flat, snarky undertone that most boys at her school had.

Unable to hold eye contact for more than a short moment, Amelie looked away, pulling her hand back and placing it quickly in her pocket.

'Thanks,' she said dryly. Suddenly worried she was coming across as rude again, she quickly added, 'Thanks for letting me work for you.'

'It's cool. It's gonna be fun.' He smiled broadly. 'Not that I know what the hell I'm doing.'

He was so different to the guy she had seen at the gig. He was relaxed for one, and there was a playfulness about him that she found natural and genuine. His accent was really something – it had a thick, warm southern twang to it, and though it was deep, it was soft.

'Shall we get cracking?' Mike was busying himself with preparing the mixing desk. 'Amelie, come and sit here.'

He mouthed 'thanks' to Maxx with a thumbs up, as he made his way into the studio area.

Amelie sat forward, captivated by the effortlessness with which Maxx worked, the way his fingers moved across the strings on his guitar, and the way the sweat formed on his forehead as he played. She was fascinated by the difference between this guy and the one she'd seen on stage, sashaying five-astride in matching bright sequined suits just a few weeks back. It was extraordinary.

'Mike, let's put down a rough guide track, okay?' Maxx looked up and caught Amelie's eye, he threw her a smile.

'Yep. Just pull that side mic about one inch closer to the guitar,' her dad said.

So Maxx played his song, a pop song – much to Amelie's disappointment – but her dad captured it in all its beautiful simplicity. It was kinda sweet, a song about love and loss of course, and Amelie found her mind wandering as she imagined being the subject of his obvious infatuation.

'*Everything is gone. And everything is forgotten. Just. Come. Back. To. Me,*' he sang, his strong voice cracking slightly at the end of each phrase. His voice was deeper and raspier than when he sang with The Keep, and his southern accent was gently present, giving it a new depth of personality. And believability.

She glanced over at the desk to look at the lyric sheet.

'Can I?' she whispered to her father, who tossed it back to her.

As she read the female part, she tried to imagine the harmony vocal entwining itself around the melody. She could visualise it. It was a good, solid piece of songwriting. But, it *was* lacking something, thought Amelie. Sweet, yes, but it was very simple. Like the first draft. The one you don't show anyone. Even with Maxx's incredible vocal it needed something more.

For the next two hours Maxx and Mike worked on the spine of the song – redoing the chorus, adding in a bridge, figuring the finish, until finally there was a framework with which to lay a drum track, which, to Amelie's amazement, Maxx played himself.

'Didn't I tell you? He can play!' her dad whispered while a very hot and sweaty Maxx wiped his brow with the bottom of his T-shirt. A very wide-eyed Amelie managed only to nod and cough in response.

Each time they stopped, Maxx would come back into the control room, put his feet up and listen back, while Julian scampered about with Amelie setting up for the next instrument.

'We patch this through here,' Julian would whisper, making sense of the myriad of cables and cords twisting across the floor and into the mixing desk.

Each decision, from the type of microphone, to the twist of the mic stand and the position of the musician, produced a different sound. Amelie had spent years learning about engineering – but working in a live session, recording some-one other than herself in her bedroom, was something else altogether.

Before long Amelie was utterly engrossed.

Next they laid down a bass track, which once again Maxx played. It was fascinating to watch him work, and as he and her father bounced back and forth with each other, Amelie found herself starting to buzz with ideas for composition and arrangement. She felt too shy to voice them, but hoped she might be asked, or might grow confident enough to offer her thoughts over the week.

'I'm just not sure if it's too heavy-handed?' Something was really bugging Maxx. He was shaking his head.

'Sounds good with the guide track?' her father offered.

Maxx shook his head. 'I don't know. It's hard to know without the second part. I'm not digging it.'

'Look, let's push on,' Mike insisted. 'I think it's worth getting the parts down, everything is individually tracked so we can tinker around as we like later. But it's a different thing, of course, if you're unsure of the composition?'

'No. Let's keep on as you say,' Maxx said, his brow furrowed.

Amelie sat with her father, shadowing his every move, asking a hundred questions.

'I'm proud of you, Amelie,' her dad said between takes. 'You are a natural engineer. I should have taken a bit more notice when you started stealing my old gear from storage. Oh, don't look so shocked. Of course I knew.'

Amelie smiled, secretly bursting with pride and blushing wildly in front of Julian and Maxx.

By two p.m. everyone was ready for lunch.

'A big fat greasy burger,' Maxx insisted. 'I don't demand much but that was a busy session and I'm starving. My arms hurt. My fingers ache.' He laughed.

'Amelie?'

'I'm up for that.'

'Great, I'll send Julian out. Give me a sec.'

Her dad popped out, leaving Maxx and Amelie alone. Amelie kept herself busy by winding up cables and clearing away the mess her dad had left around the mixing desk.

'So, what do you play then? Just guitar? Or are you multi-talented like your old man?' Maxx asked, filling the silence.

'Some piano and a bit of saxophone, though I don't do that so much any more. I discovered guitar and the sax suddenly seemed totally uncool.' Amelie sighed. She had this horrible feeling that she would never be a proper musician. If she still couldn't play a chord in a room full of people after all this time, maybe it was never going to happen for her. Not like Maxx, or Dee or even bloody Tara. She caught his reflection in the glass as he changed out of his T-shirt into a fresh sweatshirt and plonked down on the sofa. He was fit. Not Instagram-my-abs-fit, softer than that.

'Can you sing?' Maxx asked. 'I mean, can you harmonise?'

'Debatable.' Amelie brushed the question off.

'Why don't you lay down the female vocal for me?' he said nonchalantly.

For a moment Amelie thought she had misheard. She looked at Maxx, who had thrown the question out so casually she didn't know how to respond. Did he realise what she'd just been through? Was this some misguided attempt to somehow help her? Had her dad put him up to it? He looked sincere, but she was completely unnerved by the question.

'Well I need the vocal track, and since Dee's not here yet you could really help me out if you would. I need to hear it properly with the female voice.'

He was looking at her now, searching her face for some kind

of response, but she did not want to open up this door. 'Um . . . I don't know, I don't think so . . . thanks, though.'

In fact, Amelie was terrified of doing it. She wished her dad would come back to interrupt the conversation, which was now making her extremely uncomfortable.

'Oh, go on! Don't thank me, you would be really helping.'

'I'll have think about it.' Amelie tried to put him off.

'Come on! Why don't we try? I mean, I don't have to be here if you're uncomfortable?' Maxx offered, undeterred.

'Um, I guess I could. Please can I think about it?' Amelie finally looked him square in the eye and confessed. 'Honestly, after yesterday, I don't know if my nerves can take it.'

Maxx's face softened, and it was clear her dad had filled him in on the audition.

'Okay, well, you gotta get back on the horse and all that.'

'I know. I just . . . You have to put everything out there to do it. I don't have much left in the tank.' Amelie's voice wavered.

'It's just acting, you know. You just have to pretend. You don't have to give your soul away, every time. But I'll leave it with you to decide,' he said gently.

Although he didn't push it, Amelie could tell he was used to getting what he wanted and this conversation was surely not over until it went his way. She had to admit the idea was extremely enticing, but she just felt way too uncomfortable with it.

She could find nothing else to clean or tidy, so she sat back in her father's chair thinking of a way to change the subject.

'How long are you here for? In London, I mean,' she asked.

'I'll leave at the end of this week, after we finish recording the track. Shame it can't be longer really, but I need to spend some time with my folks before they forget who I am.'

'All week for just this one simple track?' she said, before adding quickly, 'I mean, it's pretty straightforward.'

'Well, four tracks. I want to do an EP if I can manage it.' He sighed, shaking his head. 'So, what do you do around here in the East End? Are you, you know, sneaking into gigs and stuff yet?'

'Ha!' Amelie laughed. 'Starting to.'

They were interrupted by the vibration of Maxx's phone, which he hurriedly picked up, almost dropping it in the rush to catch the call.

'Hang on a sec,' he said to Amelie. 'Dee. DEE, is that you?'

Amelie discreetly picked up a music mixing magazine that was sitting on her father's desk and pretended to be absorbed in an article.

'Yeah, I can hear you. I'm in the studio now – I've been trying to call you. What have you been doing?'

Amelie could hear the tenderness in his voice, but it was mixed with an unmistakable air of exasperation.

'Oh really? You can? That's great news. Well, Friday would work. It's the last day though so you won't be able to help with the production or the writing, which is a shame ...

'Yep, I'm glad you can come at all, we can work with that.

I guess, it's just not going to be really your song. More of a guest vocal? Does that matter to you? Shall I send you the rough track? . . . Okay, great. See you Friday!'

He hung up and breathed a big sigh of relief, shaking his head.

'Well, thank god for that!' he said. 'She's been driving me crazy! Impossible to pin down, that girl.'

'What's happening?'

'She's coming. But not until Friday. So she says anyway.' Maxx nodded, looking relieved but uncertain. 'But at least she's coming. I'm DEFINITELY going to need you to lay down a rough track now,' he said, grinning.

He looked across at Amelie. 'So then, Amelie Ayres. What can I do to convince you? Money? Foot massage? New guitar? You do really need a new guitar by the way.'

Amelie finally laughed. 'I said I'd think about it. Sheesh! You're so bloody pushy!'

At that moment Julian and Mike bowled in, their arms laden with burgers, cokes, fries and a huge tiramisu picked up from the Italian deli across the street for their dessert. Amelie could feel herself starting to relax and feel at home at the studio, and her dad looked like he'd relaxed about her being there. Julian perched down next to her and threaded his arm through hers and was pressing her for all sorts of information on her night at The Keep gig.

'And so you had a great time then, despite the *incident*,' he whispered jokingly.

Amelie rolled her eyes. 'Sorry to say it, but Charlie is a bit of a nob.'

'But the most handsome dick in the line-up,' Julian giggled. 'PRESENT COMPANY EXCLUDED!' he nodded to Maxx.

'Huh? What are you talking about?' Maxx piped up, looking confused as Amelie elbowed Julian in the ribs.

'Well, yes, anyway, apart from the *incident*, it was really great fun, the whole night,' Amelie continued. 'I actually really enjoyed myself.' She glanced at Maxx awkwardly, who was now listening in.

'But isn't she just divine!?' Julian cooed to Maxx cuddling Amelie in closer.

'She's pretty cool.' Maxx smiled at Amelie, who was unprepared for the charge of electricity his look sent through her.

'Oh hey, so what was your favourite city? Who are the best fans?' Julian asked.

'Oh, well I liked Madrid. That was cool. And Vienna – Vienna is amazing.'

'Oh I really want to go to Vienna. Great outdoor classical music concerts. Looks super magical,' Amelie said enthusiastically.

'Vienna has incredible cake too,' Maxx said earnestly. 'And coffee.'

'And Prague is really beautiful, isn't it?' Amelie piped in. 'Oh, didn't your stage collapse there or something?'

'Yeah. Yeah it did. We were lucky it happened in rehearsals.

But how did you . . . ' He stopped suddenly, and a look of curiosity, then an awkward silence. 'Oh. Yeah.'

He quickly turned to her dad. 'We ought to think about getting back to it?'

Amelie and Julian cleared away the food as she watched Maxx walk back into the studio. He was this hugely famous superstar, a god to thirteen-year-old girls everywhere, who was in literally the WORST band she'd ever heard of, and yet she had to admit, he was a nice guy. And fit. Quite fit.

By the time things began to wind up, the place looked and felt well-worn. There were sweet wrappers everywhere, empty cans, and half a hamburger on the table. In the studio itself there were several guitars out, upturned drums, amps stacked upon amps, the grand piano was uncovered, used and then discarded, and paper with Maxx's scribbled notes lay strewn all across the floor.

They had worked and worked the song so much, but still Maxx and her father were unhappy. And the female vocal track, which Maxx had sung to help with the composition, sounded too old fashioned on top of a pretty lacklustre guitar/bass/drums combination.

Amelie knew what it was. It lacked soul.

'It's early days,' Mike had reminded Maxx on more than one occasion.

'Well, I really don't understand why it's not working. A guy singing a love song to himself – it's genius,' he'd joked.

Although it was only the second full day in the studio,

they really needed to be further along since they had another three songs to lay down to make that debut EP that Maxx was hoping for.

After nine hours straight of recording, it was hot in there, and Maxx had worked hard. He came out smelly and sweaty and desperately needing a shower, and a cold drink. 'God, why do I feel so frustrated!' he winced, sniffing his armpits. 'And how do I smell this bad?'

'Well, we're all just warming up,' Mike said, tossing him a hand towel.

'All right, Mike.' Maxx coughed, his voice sounding a little hoarse. 'I think it's time to call it a day.'

'You got it, mate!' Mike switched off the desk and stretched, spinning in his chair. 'Well, Amelie, what did you think?'

'It was amazing. Just amazing. I learned so much.'

'Well, I'm glad you liked it, Amelie, but I'm just not happy with it,' said Maxx, stretching. 'I feel like I need another whole day on it.'

'We've got to move on,' Mike said gently. 'We've only got the week. But, I know.' Mike looked at the computer screen and made a few last adjustments. 'I know what you mean. There's something missing for sure.'

'No heart. No soul.' Maxx sighed.

Mike turned, and Amelie recognised the solemn fatherly expression. 'I can help with engineering, with the sound, even the composition – but, the soul of the track, that's for you to find, Maxx.'

'Yeah.' He looked grim. 'Can you mail me the track tonight, actually? I'll send it to Dee. And see if she can have a listen and offer some feedback before Friday at least.'

'Good idea. I think we should park this track for now.'

'Just what I was thinking,' Maxx agreed.

'And I have an idea. How do you feel about coming out with me to see a show here in Hackney?'

'Ah, Mike, I'd love to.' Maxx smiled for the first time in a few hours.

'Huh?' Amelie said, sitting up. 'Yes, please.'

Her dad smiled at her. 'Would you mind if Amelie comes?'

'Of course not.'

'It's nearly eight. There's a guy on at the Moth Club I think might, well, I don't want to say inspire, but just give you something to think about.' He looked over at Amelie. 'I'll even buy you both a beer if you're lucky.'

'Is it okay?' Amelie said, feeling a mixture of nerves and excitement. 'I mean, will you be okay? What if people recognise you ...'

'Not at the Moth Club,' her dad laughed. 'They're far too self-absorbed and, dare I say it, pretentious to notice a global popstar in their mists.'

'Come on.' Maxx smiled, sensing her apprehension. 'It'll be fun.'

# CHAPTER 19

# Good Vibrations

At the back of the cramped stage, a cascade of gold tinsel fringe glittered under the meagre stage lights. The venue was brightly lit when they arrived, but as an unremarkable looking trio among the Hackney artists and musicians, they were able to slip into an empty booth near the back, relatively unnoticed. Amelie sat alone, opposite her dad and Maxx, who wore a new baseball cap pulled tightly down over his face.

'I think that makes it look more obvious,' Amelie remarked.

'What?'

'Your disguise.'

'I'm not in disguise,' Maxx insisted, pulling the hat off and inspecting the emblem on the front. 'Is it that bad?'

'Not if you like Limp Bizkit,' she smirked.

'How the heck do you know about Limp Bizkit?' Maxx asked, incredulous.

'Amelie is an encyclopaedia of late twentieth century rock. Don't get drawn in, you'll lose.' Mike pulled a £20 note out of his wallet. 'Beer, Maxx? You guys all right for a minute?'

'Dad, that's not true. I know this century too.'

'Oh yeah?' Maxx raised his eyebrows.

Amelie played with a coaster and Maxx sat with his arm up on the back of the booth, taking in the room. He seemed unbelievably at ease, where as she was finding herself increasingly uncomfortable with such an extraordinary situation. Her eyes darted back to him over and over and she tried to take stock of the situation. *I'm actually at a gig with Maxx from The Keep.*

'So, about the other day. I just wanted to say, I'm a bit embarrassed.'

'Oh, don't worry,' Maxx smiled gently. 'We've all been there.'

Amelie looked out across the room, curling her lip slightly. Maxx had been there? She doubted it very much.

'So, you're a real musician?' Amelie smiled. 'I didn't know you played so *many* instruments.'

'Why would you? I've not exactly been exercising my skills lately.' He laughed, pulling his phone and wallet out of his back pocket and sitting back down. 'What was this place? Looks like an old army bar or something?'

'I think it is a servicemen's club.' Amelie eyed his beautiful leather wallet and brand new iPhone and wondered if Maxx had ever stepped foot in such a place.

'Reminds me of a lot of places back home,' he said with a grin.

'Memphis, Tennessee. The South.'

'Yeah, I know where Memphis is,' Amelie said.

'You an Elvis fan, then?' he smiled.

'Well, yeah. I mean, of course. But I'm really a Sun Studios fan,' she said coolly, looking towards the stage before adding dramatically, 'It's my Mecca.'

'"Sun Studios is my Mecca"?' Maxx looked bemused. 'I don't think I've ever heard someone say that.'

'No way! Have you been? It's my dream. My. Life. Long. Dream.'

'Been? I've recorded there.'

'The Keep recorded at Sun Studios?' Amelie said, unable to hide her look of shock. Her dad arrived back with two pints for him and Maxx and a half of shandy for her, much to Amelie's disappointment. 'I mean, well, I kind of saw you guys working in some kind of vast private studio in the LA hills.'

'No, no. I recorded there when I was fourteen with a couple of the guys from my dad's church for a charity. Anyway, these days it's mostly for tourists. You should go.'

'You've recorded in a lot of places,' Mike said, gazing across at a woman in a long fur coat and vintage maxi dress, standing by the sound desk. 'I was looking into your background – over twenty-two producers!'

'Yep.'

'And not one got you to play guitar? That's a sin.' Her dad

laughed, looking across again at the woman who was smiling, clearly surprised at seeing her dad. 'Oh, sorry you guys, I feel bad but there's an old friend on sound tonight. Will you excuse me again?'

He got up and Maxx smiled warmly at Amelie. 'So, encyclopaedic knowledge then, huh?'

'No one has better taste than me,' she said proudly.

'Oh yeah?' He grinned. 'Gimme your top five albums.'

'Impossible.'

'Correct answer,' he laughed. 'Okay. What's the last record you bought?'

'Hard to answer. Physical? Digital? Bought or streamed?'

'Bought. Physical.'

'Vinyl, then,' she said smugly, before remembering it was an Oasis album she picked up for £2 on record store day. '*Pet Sounds.*'

'You bought *Pet Sounds* at seventeen? What took you so long?' He grinned. 'Anyway, that's too obvious to be true.'

The immediate red flush that filled her cheeks betrayed her. 'What about you then?' she snapped. 'NSYNC? One Direction? The Wanted?'

'The who?'

'Yeah, I know The Who.'

'No, I mean, *who*?' he laughed.

They both looked at each other confused, until Amelie twigged. 'Oh, who are The Wanted? They were a British boyband. I take it they didn't break the States then,' she giggled.

'Actually, the last physical record ... I think it was *The Great Adventures of Slick Rick*,' he laughed.

'I LOVE that album,' Amelie blurted out. 'I don't know anyone else who owns it. What's with the eighties and nineties obsession?'

'Dunno. That's why I love your dad. His band, Ash Fault, was great.'

'One hit though,' she raised an eyebrow. 'I'm kidding. I love his band. They were rather ahead of their time, I think ...'

'You talk about music like some old timer at Lafayette's.'

'What?'

Suddenly, the lights went down and a guitar sounded.

'Do you know who's playing?' Maxx shouted.

'No idea,' she yelled back.

A thinly bearded, baby-faced guy – he couldn't have been more than twenty – in a leather waistcoat and pinstriped trousers with a heavily tattooed right arm swaggered onstage. He had a Gretch, the king of country guitars, and his eyes were mostly on the floor.

'Hi, I'm Ezra Change,' he said in the faintest of voices into the microphone.

'What did he say?!' Amelie looked at Maxx. 'He needs to speak up!'

Mike slipped into the booth, this time next to Amelie.

'This is who I wanted you to see.' He smiled. 'Maxx – watch his lightness of touch, and his compositions, but mostly, I want you to listen to his lyrics. It's the stories.'

Ezra began to play and immediately Amelie and Maxx were spellbound. His voice was deep as Johnny Cash, but smooth and rich. His sound was vintage country with a modern cabaret feel, inspired and exquisite storytelling over timeless melodies.

'Ezra Change. I just recorded him,' whispered her father. 'Do you hear it? This isn't songwriting for money, for fame, even for the audience's entertainment.'

'Reminds me of Marlon Williams,' Maxx said, and Mike nodded.

Amelie was transfixed. 'He doesn't look up,' she said, wondering if she could adopt a similar measure.

'He will. He's just uncomfortable playing live,' Mike remarked. 'When I first saw him, he played sitting down with his back to the stage.'

The comparison was not lost on Amelie, she closed her eyes and let the music fill her, noting the chords, the changes, the tempo. When she opened her eyes her father smiled at her. 'You should try not to pull it apart, and just listen sometimes.

'Maxx,' he continued. 'There's no po-faced lackey holding a recording contract over a fire here. You can do what you want this week. Tell your stories.'

Amelie bit her lip, feeling for Maxx. She'd knew her father well enough to read the subtext: Maxx, your writing sucks.

'You don't think I'm ready?'

'I'm not saying that *exactly*,' her father said. 'Just, you've been playing the same pop nonsense for five years and at the moment it's showing in your music.'

'Don't hold back, Mike.'

'Did you write any music for The Keep?' Amelie asked.

'God, no.' Maxx smirked.

Amelie looked into his calm, kind and confident eyes and wondered how he seemingly took everything in his stride.

'Well, that's a start,' she smiled.

'Hey, I just know you can do this. I wouldn't have said yes if I didn't think so.' Mike smiled, taking another swig of his beer. 'Find out your story, and tell it.'

'I don't know what my story is.' Maxx sat back in his seat, finally looking defeated. 'I'm trying to move forward from The Keep but I keep looking back.'

'Quickest way to fall.' Mike raised his eyebrows.

Amelie sat watching them both, her mind buzzing with feedback of her own. She tried to imagine telling Maxx, *'The harmonies are wrong and the beat and percussion is off. I also think the track could use a bit of bluesy brass – saxophone, trumpet, to give it a cool retro vibe. Back to your Memphis roots.'* But she couldn't say it. Her mind was racing with ideas too numerous to vocalise, and she felt too unsure of herself to try.

She watched him; deep in thought, slightly hunched, eyes fixed and serious, and she recognised the Maxx she saw backstage at Dee's set. What she now recognised not as a desire for her, but a desire to be like her. On stage. Solo. Playing his own music.

'Well, *you* look a lot happier.' Her dad gave her a squeeze, causing her to blush wildly, as Maxx rubbed his eyes and stretched.

'Da-ad . . . ' she tried to wriggle free of him.

'I love that I can embarrass you, it just encourages me further!' he said, pulling her in tighter. Ezra Change was finished, and popped his guitar back in its case as three girls took to the stage.

The Grumpettes were a trio of ice-blonde punk girls who played screaming, squealing guitars over utterly incoherent lyrics. It was almost ten now, and despite being a Sunday night, there was a decent crowd forming near the stage.

'Ahh. Some punk rock now, as much as I'd like to stay . . . ' Her dad nodded as the lead singer plugged in her lipstick pink guitar and muttered into the microphone, so close that whatever she said came out as a distorted growl.

'Mike, if it's cool I'm going to have to get to bed and collapse,' Maxx interrupted.

Amelie felt momentarily disappointed as he stood up and called his driver to come and get him.

'It's the Moth Club? Right? You back at the studio tomorrow, Amelie, or school? I don't even know when school is these days.' He shrugged his shoulders.

'Yeah, I am . . . it's school holidays,' Amelie said, her mind racing with thoughts too numerous to settle. 'I guess no punk tonight? You guys are basic.'

'Thanks for the thoughts, Mike.' Maxx nodded at her father. 'See y'all tomorrow.' And with that he was gone.

As she watched the girls set up, Amelie got an idea. There was one simple way to channel her thoughts, but she couldn't do it, could she? She glanced over at her dad and weighed up the consequences. Would she get in trouble? Was this stupid?

'Dad,' she was nervous, 'I left my computer at the studio and I need it. I'm going to go pick it up and head home.'

'Okay . . . ' He looked unsure.

'I have the keys.'

Her dad looked at her. 'How will you get home?'

'Uber?'

'I'm not sure, Amelie. Your mother is still out of town. Hey, did you call her back?'

She wasn't going to be sidetracked. 'Yeah. I called her earlier. Everything's fine.'

'Okay, well, text me when you're home, okay?'

'You got it!'

'Why do I think you're up to something?' he said, slipping her a £20 note to cover a taxi home.

'I'm not. I promise,' she lied with a big grin. 'Not any more than usual, anyway.'

## CHAPTER 20

# Heavenly Pop Hit

'Helllooooo,' Amelie kept trying to answer her phone but it was still ringing. 'Hello,' she shouted again as her phone fell away from her and she found she was in the recording studio but her mic was turned off. It was her mother at the mixing desk but she couldn't hear her. 'Helllooooo!' she shouted again. 'Mum! Hellloooo!' She started to panic.

Roused suddenly from sleep, she slowly realised her phone was ringing from the other side of the room, she tumbled out of bed and crawled over to her jeans. It was Julian. She looked at her watch. AND IT WAS NEARLY MIDDAY!

'Julian!' she said, trying to sound as awake as she could on so little sleep.

'We're on our way to get you. Your dad isn't in yet. Girlfriend, you need to learn how to be punctual! He's not going to forgive this forever!'

'I stayed late.'

'Yep. I know you did,' he said sternly. 'I hid the evidence this morning. Does your dad know what you're doing? MAXXXXXXX! Hang on a sec, Amelie, just picking up another late-comer.'

Amelie put the phone on speaker and hurried through into the bathroom. She ignored the bird's nest on her head and ran the tap. 'Just washing my hands!' she shouted.

'No, you're not.' Julian laughed. 'Hello you!'

'Hey, Jules. Thanks, I was going to walk but realised I have no idea where I am, and this damn phone isn't working.' Amelie could hear Maxx's deep voice and the car door slam as he jumped inside. She felt an unexpected little flutter in her stomach and in surprise she flushed the toilet.

'TOLD YOU!' Julian laughed. 'YOU'RE HAVING A WEE! Maxx is in the car, we're on our way to get you.'

'We? You're not coming with Maxx, too?'

'We're on our way. You're on speaker by the way.' She could hear them both laughing in the background.

'So are you,' was all she could say in return.

*No no no no.* She was not ready at all, and they would easily be less than five minutes away. She jumped into the shower and was out before the water had a chance to warm up. As she shut the door to the flat she heard the car pull up, Foals playing loudly on the car stereo.

'Amelie, Amelie, Amelie,' Julian said. 'Always late. Always great.'

'What the hell are you on about, Julian?' she croaked, as Maxx jumped out of the car to offer up the front seat.

'Just been talking about you,' Julian laughed. 'How you're always late, but always great. Well, Maxx said you were great. I said the late bit. Basically, we both need coffee if you want the conversation to improve.'

Amelie slid into the front seat, her hair wet from the shower, but not washed and hanging in lank rat tails. She glanced up in the rear view mirror at Maxx, who was smirking at her. 'I know I look like shit.'

'Not at all, actually,' Maxx said casually. 'Up late then?'

'Yeah. Just playing about,' she said dismissively.

'Yes, you were,' Julian said, pulling out of her street and down towards the studio. 'You're *definitely* his daughter.'

Maxx laughed. 'Was there a question?'

'Oh god, no!' Julian interrupted quickly. 'I meant because she's a total natural in the studio!'

'My parents aren't together,' Amelie interrupted. 'I'm the bastard child of a one-night stand.'

'Oh, stop it. It was a summer romance ... it was totally romantic!' Julian chimed in. 'I'd swap parents with you any day. Ella is divine.'

Amelie rolled her eyes and stared out of the window, slipping her sunglasses on. Her mother. Whom she still hadn't called.

Ella had been in Paris for a couple of days now, and without doubt had secured the job and was arranging to move her whole life over to there and leave Amelie behind. Amelie couldn't think about it.

She was loving the studio. And she was loving being finally invited into her father's world. It was the first hot-ish day of the year, and finally it felt like summer might come to London.

'So Amelie and I went out last night with Mike.'

'Ohh, boo! I wanted to show you off,' Julian huffed. 'I mean, around.'

'We saw Ezra Change,' Amelie said. 'He was great.'

'Yeah, Mike just did his EP. Might be getting signed to Transgressive Records, is the rumour.'

'Was so good,' Amelie enthused.

'I'd still love to hear some more of *your* music,' Maxx said genuinely. 'That day I had the pre-production meeting with your dad – that was you, right? What I heard of it was pretty cool.'

'Well, considering The Keep, your music isn't as bad as I thought it would be,' she said impulsively, regretting it immediately.

Julian and Maxx both burst out laughing.

'Don't worry. The Keep *were* terrible. I can take it,' Maxx laughed. 'And is that my first review, Amelie? *It's not as bad as you thought it would be.* Okay. I'll take that.' He grinned.

The car turned down Mare Street, and Julian pulled in to pick up some coffees. 'Why don't you two go ahead and get settled in before the boss arrives?' he suggested.

'Good idea.' Maxx jumped out, opening Amelie's door. 'Out you get then, Amelie.' He held out his hand to help her out.

'You're *so* well mannered. It's totally weird,' she remarked, taking his hand and allowing him to close the car door behind her.

'I'm a good southern boy.' He grinned, his thumb sliding across the back of her fingers. She pulled away quickly, surprised by how awkward his touch made her feel.

They wandered along Mare Street and Amelie found herself increasingly nervous. She pushed her sunglasses back so she could study him as they walked.

'So, my parents are pretty traditional. I mean, we have a flag in the front lawn and everything,' he laughed. 'But it sounds as if your mom, like your dad, is pretty liberal. Well, cool.'

'Everyone loves Mum. I mean, we're really close but she sometimes drives me crazy.'

'Well, that's their job.'

'She's not really into music. She's more into food. And men,' she added wearily, wondering if it was a man behind this whole Paris business.

'Do you have a step-dad?'

'Oh, god no. That would require a long-term commitment from my mother.' She laughed.

'What about your dad?'

'You know, I have no idea.' She looked at her feet. 'I don't know that much about his private life, really.'

'Probably a good thing,' he said. 'You know how these sound guys are. Never check his browser history. Never.'

'Cheeky!' Amelie punched him in the shoulder and they both laughed.

He had dark brown eyes. Almost black, and with his dark overgrown hair, there was a slightly gothic feeling about him. His face was in a constant state of stubble, and his jaw was thick and manly, unlike the boys at Amelie's school. He wore a chain around his neck with a key (to his parents' house – he explained) and his clothes, while clearly expensive, were always in want of a wash. He must have been about half a foot taller than her, which made the age difference of four years feel a lot larger. There was no doubt she was feeling a connection with him – so far his taste in music had been surprisingly acceptable – but every time she started to feel something ... *more* ... the image of Maxx the Popstar with the famous, accomplished musician girlfriend came flooding back.

'Why did you join The Keep, Maxx?' It came tumbling out, abruptly.

'Well,' he smiled. 'You know, I guess they needed someone to add a touch of cool to the line-up.'

'You joke a lot,' she countered.

Maxx stopped at the lights and for a moment fell silent. Peering down on them from the railway arches was a huge Keep billboard, which someone had defaced with two enormous penises coming out of Art's nose, and changed Keep to Sheep.

'Whoever hung a Keep poster in east London needs to be fired,' said Amelie, smirking.

'You wanna know why I joined? Because I felt I had no choice. I was fifteen years old and a smart guy in a suit told me this was the only way to the top. And I thought I wanted "the top". I didn't know what was happening until they told me to put down my guitar at the audition.' His voice was tense.

'Green man,' said Amelie meekly, grabbing his hand to gently guide him across the road and out of view of the billboard. When they were across he pulled his hand away and put it in his pocket.

'It's hard to find a way back,' Maxx said. 'And, I'll miss the guys, and Dee and that family away from my family. But I need to do this.

'Pretty scary though. When it's just me. On my own. I can't blame someone else for the crap music, can I?' He gently laughed before turning to her. 'But I have to try, right?'

Amelie was taken aback by the frank admission. She walked in silence next to him, unsure what to say. Ahead, she spotted some girls from her school hanging outside the charity shop and there was no way past without saying hello. In a panic, she pulled Maxx down a side street. 'Short cut,' she explained quickly.

'Are you saving me from those girls, or saving yourself from being seen with me?' he laughed.

'A bit of both.' She shrugged and they both laughed, the tension dissipating a little. 'The pressure you're under. I didn't think of it,' Amelie said. 'I just imagined it was easy for you to go from global megastar to this. To do what you want.'

'Well. I'm looking at myself in the mirror for the first time since I was fifteen, and unfortunately – as you can tell by the crap I produced yesterday – I'm finding I have nothing to say.' He slapped his forehead, and let out an exaggerated howl, laughing. 'I'm an empty shell!'

'That's not true,' Amelie said, finding herself hopelessly unable to offer any advice.

'And you? What's your dream, Amelie?'

'Play three chords in a row in public without puking,' she said wryly.

He frowned. 'We all got our problems.'

As they arrived back at the studio which she'd left just hours before, her dad was pulling up behind them as she pushed the door open.

'We've got to produce an awesome EP, don't we?'

'Yep,' Maxx smiled. 'But first I have to work on these damn songs.'

'Got to get your head back to Memphis,' she smiled. 'Back to your roots. Pretend this whole boyband thing never happened.'

# CHAPTER 21

# The Weight

Once again, Amelie had hardly slept. She pulled herself out of bed and tugged a comb through her tangled hair. Where's Maisie for a makeover when I really need it, she thought wearily as the comb snapped and became lodged in the matted mess at her neck. She pulled on the clothes she was wearing the day before, stretched and, feeling bone-tired, tried to get out and face the day.

When her mum was away, things tended to go to pot around the house.

She wandered into the kitchen and opened the fridge. Something really stank in there but she was too tired to fish about and find the offending item. She tipped some cereal into a bowl and sniffed the milk, which had now turned to yogurt. She tossed it into the overflowing bin and, yawning, she wandered over to the radiator on the wall and huddled up close to it, eating her cereal dry. Despite some promising moments, the summer had still not shown up and the mornings were chilly.

She felt good, though. The memories of Saturday's audition were easy to ignore if she focused on the last amazing three days in the studio with her dad. And with Maxx. She was so glad she'd stayed late again – although she didn't mean for time to get so far away from her. It was four a.m. when she crawled into bed this morning. She was exhausted but exhilarated.

She decided to finally call her mother. She switched her phone on and without first listening to the voicemails, she dialled her number. The phone was picked up almost instantly.

'Amelie!'

'Hi, Mum.'

'Jesus, Amelie. I've been worried bloody sick. What's been going on?'

'Oh, I'm sorry. I've been with Dad at the studio.'

'I know, I know. Did you not get my messages? I really needed to talk to you, like two days ago, but it's too late now. Amelie, I have some news.'

Amelie closed her eyes and waited for the inevitable.

'I've been formally offered the new job. Here in Paris.'

Amelie sighed. 'Okay.'

'I wanted to speak to you before I accepted it, but I had to make the decision yesterday.'

'Right.'

'So, Amelie, I said yes. I took the offer. It's a really good salary and they will put me up in a little apartment for the summer. It's not really big enough for both of us. Well, you could come for a few weeks, but you'll really need to stay in London like we discussed.'

Amelie held the phone to her ear, but she was no longer listening to her mum. She didn't want to go to Paris, not even for a few weeks. She wanted to spend the summer in London and work at her dad's studio and hang out with Maisie on the weekends. She waited for her mum to finish.

'I know it isn't ideal. I really wanted to speak with you first, but, Amelie darling, it will be wonderful! You loved Paris when we used to come here when you were little. And this job is a real break for me. Me! Cooking in a top French restaurant. That's totally making it, Amelie.'

Amelie looked around the tiny, pokey lounge room that her mum had decorated with care and passion and with virtually no budget, and felt a surge of love and great affection for her mother.

'But I thought you wanted your own thing, the stall on Roman Road market?'

'Don't you see? This is going to totally help! I feel so terrible, Amelie, but I need to do this. For me. For us. Amelie, are you there?'

'Yes.' She couldn't hide the misery in her voice. 'Mum, I just hope this is only for the summer.'

There was silence. 'Oh, Amelie,' Ella sighed. 'Of course it is. I wouldn't pull you out of final year. I promise.'

'Okay,' Amelie said, unconvinced.

'Can you come over though? Friday morning, and just take a look around?'

'I've been to Paris, Mum.'

'But come and spend the weekend and take a look around with me? Bring me some stuff from the house?'

'Sure, I'll come and look, Mum. Not for long though, I'm enjoying being at the studio with Dad.'

'Oh, that's great. He's let you stay on? Great. Just great. I'm so pleased you two can connect through music. Oh god! Amelie. How did the audition go?'

'I bombed.'

'Sweetheart.'

'It's okay, Mum, I'm over it.'

Amelie sat with this thought for a moment and realised that it wasn't true – she was managing to distract herself, but if she faced the reality of the loss fully she knew she would fall apart. The last few days in the studio had exhausted and exhilarated her and she had managed to forget just a little bit. She intended to keep it that way.

'I just need to keep busy,' Amelie continued.

'Baby, I need to get on the metro in a moment as I'm late for a meeting with the maître d'.'

'Mum, can I talk to you later about this?'

'Of course you can. But you'll come, Friday?'

'Yeah.'

'Of course.'

'Mum, I'm happy for you. With the job. That's great news.'

'Thanks, darling. Please, please, please call me back as soon as you can, okay? I'm going to get your Eurostar tickets for Friday morning, I hope that works for you.'

'Sounds good, Mum.'

'Thank you, darling. I love you so much. You're my best friend, darling, and I hope you understand. It will be a new adventure for me!'

Amelie slowly pulled her things together and got herself ready for the studio. She pulled a £20 note out of the grocery jar that her mum left for her when she went away, grabbed her Eiffel Tower key ring and left the house.

TO DAD: I'll be in late (again), need to stop by and give Maisie her birthday card.

As she wandered towards Maisie's house she mused over everything that had happened over the month since she turned seventeen. She felt like something had changed in her, that she'd grown beyond her years.

'So! How are you feeling?' said Maisie, glowing from a morning Bikram yoga class. 'I have been thinking about you every minute. Even when I was trying to meditate, your little face kept popping up and I just wanted to hug you.'

'Oh.' Amelie looked at her with half a grin. 'I feel better. Being busy has helped. You look frickin' amazing though.'

'Thank you. I'm doing a post-school-term yoga detox thing with my mum. Dad is hysterical because we're off meat again. He thinks we're rejecting him just because we've gone plant-based. Honestly!' She laughed, pulling a jacket over her yoga outfit. 'It's still not warming up here though – looks like rain?'

'I know. Again.'

'Well, tell me. What's been happening? I didn't want to push it on Saturday but have you decided what's next? After the audition I mean? You need a plan B.' Maisie stared at her friend.

'Well, mostly I've been working at the studio with Dad. It's pretty hectic so I'm kind of not thinking about much else right now.'

'Well, there's always next time?' Maisie said meekly.

'Here's your birthday card by the way.' She ignored the suggestion, knowing that there would not be a next time. Maisie peeled open the envelope and pulled out the card, which read: *YOGANA HAVE A GREAT DAY!*

'That's the worst one yet!' Maisie burst out laughing. 'I love it!'

She flicked it open and quietly read the short but sweet message Amelie had written inside. 'Oh, Amelie. I love you too. We should try to do something one night this week – dinner or something? Would your mum let you?'

'Sure. She's still in Paris.' Amelie did the thumbs up. 'Maybe forever!'

'Oh god.'

'Yeah. At least the summer. She's got the job and she's starting straight away. But I can stay here. I think maybe at the house but I'm not sure yet.'

'On your own?' Maisie raised her eyebrows up and down with a huge grin.

'I guess. But I'll be working with Dad most days so I'll be busy. It's really long days working at the studio!'

'Ooohhh, I can't believe I didn't ask ... tell me, is anyone interesting recording there?'

'I'm not allowed to say,' Amelie said with a grin, knowing she would confide eventually. But for now she would keep the secret. 'But yeah. You could say that.'

'Oh WHAT? Who is it? You have to tell me now!'

'I really can't. Oh my god, I really want to. And anyway, that's not the point. The point is that I'm having a brilliant time and I've forgotten all about that awful audition. Almost.'

Maisie eyeballed Amelie with suspicion. 'Well, can I at least walk you there so we can keep chatting? I mean, your dad can't stop me from being in the same area, can he?'

'Of course not! Let's go through the park, it's quicker – and it really looks like rain!' Amelie led the way, turning back down the canal as the dark storm clouds gathered overhead.

## Chapter 22

# The Tide is High

Huddling under the awnings outside the 'Best Fried Chicken' shop on Mare Street, Julian and Maxx clutched their usual flat whites as the rain pelted the footpath, and the gutters, stuffed with debris, overflowed into the streets. Amelie and Maisie appeared, squealing and giggling, huddled under Maisie's coat and running towards the safety of the same awning.

'The rain! My god, it's relentless!' shouted Maxx over the deafening noise.

'We actually had a really dry summer back in 1986,' Julian insisted, shouting back at him. 'It won't last, don't worry!'

'Arghhhhhhhhh!' Maisie shrieked. 'Oh my god, it's POURING!'

'Julian! Maxx. Hi!' Amelie was giggling, her hair and clothes soaked through. She and Maxx smiled warmly at each other.

'Oh my god, my hair,' Maisie said as a natural curl started to tighten up with the damp. 'I look like an eighties aerobics instructor.'

'Suits you.' Julian air kissed Maisie. 'Long time no see, lady.'

'Hiya, Julian! And ... ' Maisie looked to Maxx, waiting for an introduction – she obviously didn't recognise him without his usual boyband get-up, much to Amelie and Julian's amusement.

'Maxx.' He held out his hand, smiling, and they shook firmly as Amelie wrung out her T-shirt and tried not to laugh.

'Ooh, American? Now, let me guess where you're from. Say something.'

'Something?' He smirked, playing along.

'No, like, ask for something. Ask for a hotdog. I'm so good at accents.'

'Can I please have a hotdog?'

'Okay, I've got it. Denver,' she said dramatically.

'DENVER?' Maxx said, aghast. 'No. I'm not from Denver.'

'No ... you're Canadian,' Maisie tried.

'Put her out of her misery, please,' Julian insisted, as the rain started to ease.

'I'm from Tennessee. It's nice to meet you ... ?'

'Maisie. Are you recording with the band?' she started to ask, trying to snoop.

'Ohhhh-kay Maisie,' Amelie interrupted, pulling her friend by the arm. 'We need to get to work, so time to bugger off.'

'All right, already. Jeez,' Maisie complained. 'It's nice to meet you anyway. Julian, we need to catch up immediately, I'm getting withdrawals.'

It was impossible not to adore Maisie, looking ridiculous in her lululemon matchy yoga outfit. With her huge, genuine smile and bubbly personality, she was so sweet and full of energy. Maxx peeked out from under the awning at the sky, as the sun broke out through the dark clouds.

'Why don't you both come out with us tomorrow night? Julian and his boyfriend are showing me the sites,' Maxx asked, to the surprise of everyone.

Amelie felt a surge of anxiety. Another night out? With Maxx? In London? But without her dad? She was equally terrified and excited by the prospect. It was one thing to sneak into a booth at the back of the Moth Club on a Sunday night, quite another to hit the town with Maxx from The Keep, a couple of completely indiscreet boys and Maisie.

'OMG. We're so in. It's my birthday actually, so we were just saying we might do something this week, weren't we, Amelie?' Maisie was virtually bursting with excitement.

Amelie froze, trying to telepathically send 'no' signals across to her mate.

'Excellent idea, Maxx.' Julian clapped his hands in delight.

'What are we doing?' Maisie's eyes widened.

'Lexington, some live music? There's some punk rock on, and there's an open mic night down the road as well – if that's your thing.'

'Oooh, great.' Maisie turned to Amelie. 'This is PERFECT. And you're off to Paris the next morning, right?'

'Um, yeah.' Amelie started to get mad at her friend. 'Dad won't really like me going to a bar without him. I need to pack. I should also go to Tesco's.'

'Any other excuses?' Maxx joked. 'Let me speak to your dad.'

'Don't worry about that, you're seventeen now, you're practically legal. Nothing wrong with sneaking in, love,' Julian advised, somewhat less practically.

'Okay, details, details.' As Maisie and Julian began the planning, Amelie watched as her dad parked across the road from the studio.

'Okay, it's REALLY time to go, Maisie! Dad's here,' she said, nodding towards him as he unloaded some boxes and a guitar case from the boot.

'Work time!' Julian agreed, and then added without thinking, 'Let's go record you a record, Maxx. Bye, girls.'

'Nice to meet you, Maisie, see you Thursday,' Maxx said, turning as they crossed the road, leaving Maisie gawping at Amelie.

'What just happened? Hang on? Who is he?'

'You really don't know?'

'No, Amelie. I'm not as cool as you,' she teased. 'Is that who's recording?'

'Yes.' Amelie grinned. 'It's Maxx, from The Keep.'

Maisie clasped her hands across her face. 'OMG, you what?'

'It's true,' Amelie laughed.

'OMG. You would NEVER recognise him; he looks so different. So normal! And the hair! Jesus. He must have been using more hair product than I do, he looks totally different without all the ... ' She waved her hands about.

'All the boybandy stuff,' Amelie finished. 'I know, right?' She watched Maxx and Julian as they greeted her dad at the car, Maxx graciously offering to help with the heavy lifting as the three of them made their way inside.

'But, you see,' she turned back to Maisie, and gravely said, 'we really shouldn't go out with them, what if he DOES get recognised? Remember ... '

'Honestly, I don't think he will. And I'm sure if you ask him he won't get you in any kind of online storm again. And anyway, WHO CARES!!!!' Maisie grinned. 'Oh, Amelie, come on. You need to loosen up. This is FUN. It's what being a teenager is about. You've had your nose in your music all year, practising, playing, more practising. I mean we NEVER do anything like this together. PLEEEEEEASE.'

Maisie clasped her hands in a prayer and held the high-pitched 'please' for as long as she could. When she ran out of breath, she sucked in as much air as she could and started again, in a slightly higher pitch. 'PLEEEEEEEEEEASE ... '

Amelie put her face in her hands. 'Fine,' she said, sighing dramatically with her fingers in her ears. 'Fine, fine, fine. Let's go. SHUT UP! AND DON'T TELL ANYONE HE'S HERE!'

They hugged goodbye and Maisie took off down the street, stopping to do some lunges and a squat at a bike rail. Amelie shook her head at her crazy friend, and took a moment to compose herself before she headed inside. It was time to share what she'd been up to in the studio at night, and she was dreading the reaction.

She whipped the rain out of her hair, marched forward, and, summoning all her confidence, walked in to tell her dad and Maxx what she'd done.

But it was too late for a big reveal.

Her dad, sat at the desk with his computer open on her recording session, was shaking his head – he looked angry, confused and disappointed. It was the naughty daughter trifecta. He looked up at her, and she began to squirm.

'I know what you're going to say, Dad, but in a way Maxx *did* ask me to do it.' She looked over at Maxx with pleading eyes.

'I did,' Maxx said quickly, looking at her, puzzled.

'You did?' her dad said disbelievingly. Amelie chewed her fingernails, nodding at Maxx desperately.

After a moment's silence, Maxx broke the stand-off. 'Um, what did I ask you to do?'

Mike leaned back in his seat, his voice steady but stern. 'Amelie, it seems, has been staying back at night and has decided it was appropriate to do some recording on your track. I'm speechless, Amelie.'

Amelie bit her bottom lip. 'Look, you can just delete it, I made a duplicate session so I didn't wreck anything.'

'It's just so highly unprofessional. Maxx, I'm just, well ... shocked, and very sorry indeed.'

'You recorded the female vocal?' Maxx said excitedly, tossing his bag on the couch. He took a seat next to her dad. 'Awesome. Let's hear it then! I did ask her! I didn't know that was what you'd been sneaking off at night to do!' Maxx nodded to her dad, who was still shaking his head at Amelie.

'It's not just the vocal she recorded,' he said quietly, looking at the screen.

'Can you just play it and then tell me off later?' Amelie asked. 'I think it's okay. I mean, quite good in places.'

'The suspense is killing me!' Maxx laughed. 'Let's hear it. Honestly, don't worry, Mike.'

His finger lingered over the keyboard as he sat back, sighing loudly at the ceiling. Amelie curled up as tight as she could on the couch, covering her eyes with her hands.

'Have a little faith, Dad,' Amelie pleaded through her fingers as he hit play.

The record started, but instead of Maxx's guitar, there was a piano introduction. The timing was changed and the vocal came in on the offbeat, which gave the track a more laid-back cool than the earnest arrangement they'd been working on the day before. And then Amelie's voice came in.

Maxx was totally engrossed, and Amelie felt a faint glimmer of hope that he might like what she'd done.

She watched closely to see if there was a reaction to the

tweaked lyrics, or the new bridge, or the slight rearrangement of the chord structure in the chorus.

The track played through, and when it finished he didn't smile, he just said very steadily, 'Can you play it again?'

Three more minutes of torture as the track played through a second time. Amelie cringed as her voice came in again. This time around she could hear every waver, ever imprecise beat, every questionable decision. Maxx whispered a couple of times to her father, who shook his head. Amelie, unable to hear their exchange, began to quiver. Had she made a terrible mistake?

But, as the track finished, to her immense relief Maxx swung around with a broad smile and clap of his hands.

'I love it,' he said simply. 'I was just asking if your dad knew you were such a good pianist?'

Her dad looked only slightly relieved, the anger behind the eyes still evident.

'You like it? Really?' Amelie said meekly.

'It's cool. Really. So great, so many clever ideas in there.'

'Oh, thank god!' Amelie was so relieved and delighted she wanted to run across the room and wrap her arms around Maxx.

'And you can sing! What a voice! Bluesy, husky – it's very warm and unique. Who knew?' He was totally gushing. 'Play it again, Mike, let's go through it and decide what to keep.'

'What to keep?' Amelie piped up, finally feeling confident enough to join the two at the desk.

Maxx laughed. 'It's not perfect. But it will be.' He banged the desk in delight.

As her dad hit play on the track again, Amelie caught his glance that said 'we will be talking about this later, young lady'.

But as the morning wore on, it was clear that Maxx had come alive. He was animated and excited and speaking a hundred miles an hour.

'Isolate that part,' he said to Mike. 'Yeah, drop that. I'll do a new bass line there, the old one doesn't work.' Mike worked fast to keep up. 'Lose the snare. Okay, mark that down – it needs a harmony.'

'Amelie,' Maxx turned to her, 'what do you think about this part – the middle eight? I want to lose the snare and pare it right back – thoughts?'

'Yes. Yes, that could work. But . . . ' Amelie looked nervously at her father and then back to Maxx.

'Go on.' Maxx wasn't going to let her shy away.

'Well, story-wise, I think it needs building rather than paring back, but softly. I'm not sure how – maybe bring the acoustic guitar back? Or a second one? Or—'

'No, I've got it,' her dad interrupted. 'We need strings.'

Maxx and Amelie both nodded. There was an incredible sense of teamwork emerging and everyone felt the excitement.

As the day slipped into evening, the track was worked and reworked until, at 9.30, the team cracked open a beer and sat back to listen to the finished track.

Maxx sat down next to Amelie and put a hand gently on her shoulder. 'I could kiss you!' he said, delighted.

Her dad smiled, shaking his head at Amelie. 'That was a good day.' He nodded, before adding, 'Don't ever do that again. At least, without asking me first.'

It was nearly midnight when Maxx got back to the Town Hall Hotel in Bethnal Green, and he stopped by the bar for a whiskey on the way to his room. He wouldn't normally, but he was buzzing and needed something to steady himself before he crawled into bed and tried to sleep – he was too excited from the day's events.

If he was astounded by the talent of Mike, he was totally floored by what his daughter had achieved. She was a real talent, and had transformed the track. And, he had to admit, a rare and intriguing beauty. But, as tipsy thoughts of kissing her sulky lips came into his head, he dismissed them. He was sure she had a crush on Charlie, and if she knew about the stage collapse – which was not publicised – she was definitely in touch with him. It was difficult to swallow, but facts were facts.

After switching on the TV set in his room and trying to make sense of the different British channels, he decided to try to call home. Unfortunately, or fortunately considering his slightly inebriated state, his parents weren't home. He checked his watch – then, tossing back the last of his whiskey, and wanting a friend to talk to, he decided against his better judgment to FaceTime Dee.

He was surprised when she finally picked up.

'Hey!' he said, delighted, high from the whiskey and the excitement of his day.

'Hey, babe. Is there something wrong?' She fumbled with the phone, turned a light on and squinted. She ran her fingers through her hair and rubbed her eyes. He'd just woken her up. Maxx could see the lace of her nightie and what looked like a half drunk glass of champagne sitting on the bedside table.

'What's going on? How's Paris?'

'Good. Maxx, is something wrong? It's after one a.m.,' she yawned.

Maxx had forgotten the time difference.

'Oh no, I just wanted to tell you how awesome the recording was, but I forgot how busy you've been.' He tried to sound cool and hide his irritation, but Dee had clearly not been 'busy', rather she'd been having a nice time in Paris.

'Oh yeah?' She sounded relieved, her eyes darting to the side of the room – was she looking at someone? 'That's great. I *have* been busy, though.'

'Yeah? Well, the single is great, did you listen to it?' Maxx began, then, realising she had only been sent the first, inferior, version without Amelie's input, added, 'Oh, you haven't heard the new version. You'd never believe who reworked it, transformed it really. We've got a guide track now. And a new title. It's called "The Ballad of Beginnings". Let me play it for you!'

'I didn't get a chance to hear the other version; it's on my Mac though. But are you saying don't listen to it now?' She sounded disengaged.

At that moment there was the sound of a door opening in Dee's room – and she waved up at someone off-screen.

'Someone there with you?'

'Um, yeah.'

'Okay. Well now probably isn't the time to play the track, anyway,' Maxx snapped, trying to be nonchalant but feeling like a total dick.

'Maxx, let's catch up later. Get yourself to bed. You're a bit drunk,' Dee said gently.

'Well, I'll see you Friday. Are you still coming?'

'Yeah, I'll see you Friday. I'm flying back home from Heathrow, so I've got the whole day there. I'll lay down the vocal.'

'Cool. Well, see ya,' Maxx said. 'Have fun,' he added dismally.

He closed his computer and pushed it off his bed, and it crashed onto the floor.

Making his way into the bathroom, he tore the plastic wrapping off the hotel's complimentary mini toothbrush and toothpaste, and brushed his teeth clean of the taste of whiskey and pizza. He pulled his jeans and stinking T-shirt off and tossed them on the floor, before forcing himself into a nice hot shower to help him sleep. He washed his hair with his single serving of shampoo and conditioner, and rubbed the pleasant, unisex-scented hand cream into his overworked, dry cracked fingers and hands.

At just before one a.m. he pulled back the duvet, suddenly hating that freshly laundered smell of his 600-count Indian-cotton sheets – and as he closed his exhausted eyes he longed to feel like something in his life was lived in. He was lonely, but happy here in London. He missed Dee but was glad she was gone. He was scared of this new life he was trying to forge, but he wasn't looking back.

For a moment he lay there in bed listening to the quickening beat of his heart, then he threw back the covers and picked up his guitar. He had to get it out, the only way he knew how.

# CHAPTER 23

# Summer Friends

Amelie left the studio to pack her things for Paris. She grabbed the old green suitcase from under her bed (a 1960s one with a lockable clip that didn't lock, which her mother had found for 'next to nothing!' at a junk shop). She pulled out an assortment of jeans, T-shirts and jumpers from her wardrobe, and two pairs of trainers, her PJs (which really needed a wash), her hairbrush and some underwear and lay them all out on the bed.

Maisie would be there in twenty minutes and she wanted to be completely ready for her eight a.m. train the next morning so that she didn't have to stress about anything while they were out. She packed all her toiletries and then went through into the kitchen to clean out the virtually empty fridge and take out the rubbish. She had been alone at the house for nearly a week now, but since she'd spent practically the whole time at the studio, the house had been well and truly neglected. She guiltily decided to clean the kitchen a little, and then the floor, and just quickly dust the window sills, rearrange the LPs, and by the time Maisie arrived she was clothed in an apron and marigolds and not at all ready to go out.

'SHIT!' Amelie said, peeling her gloves off and rushing to the door. Maisie stood there looking like she'd stepped off the pages of teen *Tatler*, her long caramel hair was pulled back in a casual chignon, and she wore a three-quarter length bra top in bright florals with a pair of high-waisted jeans and black heels. She held out a pinky-orange juice in a reusable glass eco-thermos.

'Pretox Juice? Don't worry, the container is BPA free,' Maisie offered.

'Is that an STD?' said Amelie, shaking her head.

'Oh, Amelie! You're not even showered. Get in there, now!' Maisie ordered. 'We have to leave in five minutes! UBER EN ROUTE! I'll pick your outfit.' She clapped her hands together with delight and immediately entered full makeover mode.

'Where do you keep your going-out clothes?'

Amelie pointed to the only wardrobe in her room, laughing. 'Like most normal people I keep everything in one wardrobe.'

'Why are you still here? Shower!' Maisie replied.

Amelie gave Maisie a comical salute and slammed the bathroom door, she brushed her teeth in the shower and quickly washed her hair for only the second time that week. She was just about to condition when she heard Maisie banging on the door. 'Two minutes, Amelie, get a move on!'

'No time to dry it, sorry!' Maisie said, holding out an outfit as Amelie emerged with her hair wrapped in a towel.

'Can I at least put some knickers on?' Amelie laughed, pulling a face at the outfit Maisie had chosen – a black halter neck dress with sandals and a red cardigan. She tugged a pair of jeans out of her closet drawer.

'But you can't wear your usual uniform,' sulked Maisie. 'We've got a doorman to convince you're over eighteen, remember? Can I at least do your hair?'

Amelie nodded. She secretly loved it when Maisie did her hair and make-up, but she drew the line at stupid dresses.

Maisie attacked her hair with a comb, and, parting it neatly in the middle, she swept Amelie's fringe across her face and wound it into some waves with her fingers. 'It will dry perfect. Don't touch it. We'll do the make-up in the taxi,' Maisie insisted, checking her phone. 'Please not *that* top.'

'I feel comfortable like this,' Amelie said, pulling on a plain T-shirt. 'I'll wear some jewellery!' she said by way of compromise, and liberated her birthday diamond earrings from their box. She clipped them in and held out her hands. 'Well?'

'Well, they suit you,' Maisie said with her hands on her hips, bemused. 'You look a *little* more like a girl. Actually, you look lovely.'

'Why, thank you.' Amelie did an awkward, exaggerated

curtsy. 'Do you think Maxx likes jewellery? On girls I mean. He wears his parents' key around his neck, you know.'

'That's sweet,' Maisie said, raising her eyebrows. She firmly and clearly added, 'He must like jewellery, his *girlfriend* Dee wears quite a lot, doesn't she?'

Amelie frowned. 'Hmm, yes. Dee's arriving tomorrow.'

Maisie gave Amelie a sympathetic smile. 'You've so got a crush.'

'I do not!' Amelie giggled, feeling embarrassed.

'Are you sure *sure* sure they're still together? Wasn't there a fight or something? All seems a little bit iffy?'

'I think so, well, I mean, they're doing this track together tomorrow.' Amelie felt glum about it, but had decided to just suck it up and enjoy herself tonight.

There was no mistaking the chemistry that had developed between her and Maxx. From a low simmer to a fierce boil, every time their hands touched, or they found themselves alone in the studio without her dad or Julian, the air was thick with tension. She couldn't be alone in feeling it.

This afternoon in the studio there had been a particularly difficult one, though, as they put the final touches on a new track – a real classic Memphis blues number which Amelie adored, and the only thing left to do was prepare for Dee to come and lay down the vocals for their duet. Amelie had allowed herself to hope that Maxx might keep the track with her singing, but as the day wore on she realised it was nothing but a fantasy. Of course Maxx wanted Dee to sing on his track.

It made commercial sense, as well as practical sense. It was a love song between two real lovers.

But he'd gotten a little under her skin, this handsome, southern guy with his beautiful voice and his gentle, polite charms who could play guitar with the ferocity of a fist fight. It was going to be hard to say goodbye.

'Taxi's here, Amelie!' Maisie squealed, jolting Amelie out of her daydream.

She shoved Amelie out the door, and the two of them took off towards Angel to meet the boys. The plan was to have some food and beers and then head to the venue.

Maisie put the finishing touches on Amelie as the taxi headed down Balls Pond Road and pulled over just outside a dark and pokey but buzzing pub called The Ship, which served 'proper' British food with a cult following. The jukebox was loud, the lights were low, and the atmosphere was pure London – part punk, mildly earnest and a little bit troubadour.

'What makes the food "proper"?' Amelie whispered to Maisie.

'Fat. And sugar,' she replied grimly.

It was chosen as a venue *because* it was dark and pokey, as the most important thing for Maxx was that he could manage a night out without being hassled. They'd booked a back booth with table service for extra privacy.

'Take a look,' Maisie held her mirror up. 'You look delicious, Amelie. Just beautiful!'

Amelie had just the lightest make-up on, but with a little

gloss on her lips. Her natural hair had dried perfectly, falling in waves across her face. She definitely looked older than eighteen, but the result was pretty subtle.

'Wow, Maisie. You should totally do this for a living.'

They squeezed through the tiny entranceway and into the pub, where the music was loud enough to feel happening but not so loud you couldn't hear yourself think. She immediately saw Clint waving from a back booth, a big broad smile across his face.

'AMMMMELIE!' He stood up and squeezed past the queuing customers to give her a hug. 'They're with us!' he nodded to the waiter who gave him a friendly wink. 'That's Johnny. And yes, I've been there. You must be Maisie?'

'Hello!' she smiled.

'I've heard a lot about you!' he said warmly.

Julian and Maxx were both on their second beers when Amelie slid into the booth. She was relieved but also a little disappointed not to be sitting next to Maxx, but found herself directly across from him. He smiled at her, his eyes lighting up when she sat down.

'The lady of the moment,' Maxx smiled.

Amelie blushed, but accepted his gratitude. She did feel she had really made a difference to the record and it felt like an incredible achievement.

'Oh my god, yes, Julian told me!' Clint's eyes were dancing. 'I mean, this is just such exciting news. Good for you! Obviously got your father's rare talent in the studio, then.'

'She sure does. And by the way, you look beautiful,' Maxx said, his eyes wandering all over Amelie, who was starting to feel overwhelmed by the attention.

Maxx looked perfect. He was wearing a brushed cotton navy shirt over a black T-shirt, his usual blue jeans, and his thick dark hair was damp, hanging across his dark eyes. She could smell fresh shampoo and expensive cologne. Two of his fingers had fresh white plasters covering cracked calluses from playing too much guitar.

'I need an alcoholic drink!' Maisie interrupted, waving at the waitress.

'So, Maxx, have you enjoyed your time in London?'

'Oh, so much,' he said slowly, moving his eyes off Amelie as the waitress came across and took their orders. The four others chose beer, while Amelie opted for a red wine.

'See, you're already Parisian!' Maisie declared, before very matter-of-factly updating the table on Amelie's news. 'Amelie is visiting her mum in Paris tomorrow. Amelie lived there when she was little. Her mum's a chef.'

'Well ... more a cook,' Amelie corrected. 'But she just loves Paris. Hence my name. Hence her moving there for the summer without me.'

The beers and wine arrived, along with water and bread, and everyone placed their orders with the pale-eyed, silver-haired waitress, who couldn't keep her eyes off Maxx – not that he seemed to notice. He was spending a lot of time staring at Amelie; she could feel his eyes on her and, in order to avoid completely falling to pieces, she was desperately trying not to look back.

'Excusa moi. May I borrow a pen pour vous?' Clint asked the waitress in his best worst French.

'Oui,' she replied with a smile, handing him a spare one from the pouch around her waist.

'God, what's coming?' groaned Julian, dramatically putting his head in his hands.

'Okay, so since we're hosting our guest Maxx tonight, we need to play a little getting to know each other game,' Clint announced.

Julian rolled his eyes and mouthed 'sorry' to the group as Clint tore up a piece of paper into five and put the pen in the middle of the table.

'I LOVE THESE GAMES!' Maisie grabbed the pen. 'What do I do? I want to go first!'

'Everyone has to write something about themselves on a piece of paper, and then fold it up and put it in this glass. A confession. The more sordid the better. Preferably it includes sex, drugs or rock and roll, someone at the table ... or a celebrity.' He popped an empty water glass into the centre of the table. 'Then we each take one out and have to guess who wrote what.'

'Oooh, dangerous. I love it,' Maisie laughed.

Amelie looked at her piece of paper and wondered what she should write. She thought about something from her childhood, or her interests, and realised her life – despite all its music – was pretty un-rock and roll. Then she remembered one incident, over five years back. 'I smoked a joint when I was 12' she wrote, and slipped it into the glass.

She had. It was a catastrophe, and one of the main reasons she'd never touched the stuff since. When her dad was having a bath, she had found his stash in the kitchen drawer and sparked it up. When her dad walked back in, he furiously made her a chocolate thick shake and told her to watch *South Park* lying down. Unfortunately, she'd spent the next two hours with her head down the loo, suffering what her dad called a *whitey*.

She didn't stay at her father's often after that night.

'I couldn't help but notice ...' The waitress was back to lay down the cutlery, and was trying to spark up conversation with Maxx. 'Only, you look so much like him. Are you Maxx Cooke?'

'Um, yes.' He smiled kindly at her.

The waitress blushed wildly. 'I knew it! Can I get a photo before you go?'

'Well,' Maxx lowered his voice, 'if you don't mind, I'm kind of trying to have a quiet night with my friends. I really don't want to draw any attention. I'm so sorry.'

'Enough said! I hope London shows you a proper good time.' She stopped short of winking at him, but Amelie couldn't help pulling a face as she sashayed off.

'What?' Maxx asked Amelie. 'What's with the face?'

'Jesus! Does that always happen? She's so brazen!'

221

'What?' Maxx looked genuinely puzzled, shaking his head.

Amelie stopped herself, realising she sounded jealous, and waved her hand dismissively, eliciting a raised eyebrow from Maisie. 'Nothing. Don't worry.'

'Okay, is everyone done?' Clint asked.

'I need to do mine again!' Maisie wailed. 'It's too boring.'

When the food arrived – sharing plates of fancy scotch eggs, potatoes, ham hock n' peas, and mini fish and chips – the game was well under way.

'I watched my parents have sex,' Maisie said after unwrapping the first piece of paper. 'Oh my god! That's disgusting!' She looked around the table, eyeballing each of them before settling on Maxx. She waved a finger at him. 'Just because you're from the *south*, I'm guessing it was you,' she grinned.

'Sorry. I've never had that pleasure. What happens if she guesses wrong?' he asked Clint. 'There needs to be punishment!'

Clint laughed. 'Drink?'

Maisie didn't need to be told twice, so she took a swig of her beer.

'Well, it's not me and it's definitely not Amelie. Hmmm . . . It could be either of you, but since Julian can't look me in the eye, I'm going for Julian?'

'Yes! It's me.'

'I hope you weren't, like, seventeen or something!' Amelie laughed.

'No, no. It's a terrible story actually. I was going through my mother's drawers, as you do, and they suddenly arrived home early from some charity dinner thing, and so I did what any young gay boy would do – I hid in the closet. It was awful. Mum did a weird dance. And dad was not at all a performer.'

'Ewwwww.'

'Mum found me asleep there the next morning. We never spoke of it again. And now I'm gay,' he said dramatically. 'Okay who's next?'

Maxx jumped in and pulled out a piece of paper, as the others began to help themselves to the delicious food on the table.

'I once licked Rihanna's Louboutin,' Maxx announced, reading his piece of paper. 'Good grief. Well I'm pretty sure I know who this is,' he said, laughing at Clint and Julian, 'especially since I'm pretty sure we were on the line-up with Rihanna at that festival in Spain. Am I right, Clint?'

'That's gross!' Amelie laughed. 'Although, I think I would probably try to lick her if she were in my vicinity.'

'Yup!' agreed Maisie.

'Yep. It was me. And it was in Spain,' Clint joked. 'But it wasn't actually on her foot.'

'Booo!' said Julian. 'That's a boring confession! Did you know Rihanna is really uninvolved with her music? She literally turns up and lays down her vocal to an MP3. It's extraordinary.'

Amelie waved the waitress back over.

'Hello, please could we have another round of drinks, a red wine and four beers.'

'Sure thing,' she said, then smiled exclusively at Maxx. 'Anything else?'

The fawning was so dire, and this time Maxx did notice. He leaned across the table and took Amelie's hand without losing eye contact with the waitress.

'No thanks,' he said, smiling. After a glass of wine Amelie felt slightly chuffed, but quickly pulled her hand away.

'Jesus, don't do that. What if I end up in the papers again?' Amelie half laughed, looking nervously around. 'They'll think I'm doing the whole band.'

Maxx winced and sat back.

'So, so, so.' Clint looked around the table. 'I hope this topic of conversation is not out of bounds, but I have to ask. Amelie. WTF was up with Charlie? Maxx, I hope you don't mind, but I'm not a big fan.'

'It's okay.' Maxx shook his head diplomatically, while watching Amelie's reaction. 'You don't have to like him, Clint.'

'Oh god.' Amelie waved her fist playfully at Clint. 'It was a total nightmare. I'm just glad it's over.'

'I laughed so hard when I read the headline,' Clint continued. 'I was telling Julian how he was being such a creeparoony at the gig. Guy needs to get laid. My opinion!' he said with his hands in the air.

'He's always getting laid,' Maxx murmured.

'It was the worst,' Maisie piped up. 'She had a photographer outside their front door – who – HER MUM ACTUALLY WENT ON A DATE WITH!'

The table erupted with laughter, even Amelie couldn't help a smirk.

'Well, not quite, Maisie, but yes, they did swap numbers.' She rolled her eyes. 'But seriously, Charlie *has* apologised and he's been quite nice since so I have forgiven him,' Amelie said earnestly, not wishing to create any kind of bad feeling.

'You *are* still in contact then?' Maxx asked.

'Well, kind of. Did he say?' Amelie was surprised by this, and started to feel uncomfortable about where the conversation was heading.

'Um, yeah. He did. To be honest ... ' Maxx paused.

'What? To be honest, what?' Amelie pushed him.

'I thought you kinda had a thing for him,' Maxx said carefully.

'WHAT. THE. ACTUAL?' Maisie burst out laughing, but Amelie was unimpressed.

'Did he give you that impression?'

Maxx shrugged. 'Oh look, I'm not entirely sure, I must have misunderstood.'

'Well, let me clarify.' Amelie felt annoyed at being implicated in some kind of *thing* by Charlie again. 'He contacted me a couple of times. I have been polite. I have NO IDEA why he was messaging me. Maybe he felt bad? Either way, I couldn't be less interested.' Her heart began to race, and she felt her cheeks go red.

Maxx was clearly taken aback by this news, and also Amelie's forthrightness in delivering it – he couldn't hide the whisper of a smile that spread across his face.

'Well, I stand corrected,' Maxx said. 'I have to say, it's not quite the way he told it. But it never is with him.'

'Well, yes. I don't like him like that.' Amelie took a deep breath and a large sip of her wine. 'Or maybe at all, if he's been insinuating something? It's simply not true, I can promise you.'

'He's a strange one. We've never really bonded, I don't think. The rest of the band like him, Dee likes him, but I dunno, we never became close.'

'Very diplomatic,' Julian said, with one eyebrow raised comically high.

Another round of food arrived – heritage tomato salad, sliced beef, stilton – but Amelie was no longer hungry. She watched Maxx as he sat back in his seat, looking back to her every now and then and smiling. There was an unmistakable change in him. He had quickly become more shy and with-drawn with her. She wondered how long he'd thought of her as some fangirl chasing his bandmate via Twitter and it irritated the hell out of her.

'I need the bathroom,' he said, putting his napkin down and slipping out of the booth.

'I hate Paris,' Julian said, reading out the next piece of paper. 'Well that one's simple.' He looked at Amelie and smiled.

'Oh my god! So does my dad!' Amelie shrieked a little too loudly. She was beginning to feel the effects of the wine and realised she had better slow down.

'That wasn't you?' Maisie said, disbelievingly.

'No,' Amelie laughed. 'How weird, I wonder why?' she said, craning her neck to see the disappointing sight of Maxx talking to that bloody waitress.

Clint pointed at his watch. 'Guys, we have to go!'

'Oh my god, yes we do!' Julian knocked back the last of his beer. 'Where's the bill?'

He began waving the awful waitress over, just as Maxx arrived back and held out his hand to help Amelie then Maisie out of the booth.

'Starts at nine? Right?' Maxx asked.

'Yep! We need to scoot,' Amelie smiled, feeling a little unsteady on her feet.

'The perfect gentleman,' Maisie whispered as she stood next to Amelie.

'How shall we split it?'

'It's taken care of guys,' Maxx smiled. 'And I don't want to hear anything. You can buy me a beer at the next place.'

He put his hand on Amelie's lower back, and guided her towards the door. The shockwave was intense, and she squirmed free of his touch. 'I'm ticklish,' she muttered.

'Oh really?' he said, his beautiful eyes dancing with mischief as he touched her again, this time holding her by the arm so she couldn't pull away.

'Stop it,' she giggled, balking at the foolish little girl she could hear in her voice. 'Please.'

'He's a dreamboat,' Amelie heard Julian sighing as they all squeezed through the thickening crowd towards the door. For a few slow steps she sank back into the heat of Maxx's body.

# CHAPTER 24

# Big Time Sensuality

The Lexington was packed to the rafters. There were what felt like hundreds of sweaty young music fans shoulder to shoulder at the bar, ordering their tequila shots and pints of lager in another pub so thoroughly British it could have been fake. Small wooden tables and chairs were scattered among the long leather couches under low wattage pendant lighting. It was loud as hell, and the band hadn't even started yet.

'I better just have a glass of water!' Amelie shouted to Clint. 'I'm not used to drinking! I feel a bit ... drunk,' she smiled, keeping her hand on the back of a chair to steady herself.

'Jesus! It's so busy!' Maisie wasn't totally into it, Amelie could see her friend recoiling from the smell of sweat, piss from the nearby toilets and stale beer stuck to every surface. The five of them were huddled around a table with enough chairs for three, but no room to sit in them. 'It's so busy and so gross!'

'Don't worry, everyone's going to move upstairs soon!' Julian shouted to them as Clint arrived with a tray of drinks and slid them carefully onto the sticky table.

'Do you guys want to go to the very loud, very aggressive rock band upstairs? Or, there's a pub down the road – they have their open mic night for destitutes and debutants.'

Maisie laughed, 'Please let's go to the open mic! I'm so up for some bad emotional music. And a quieter room where we can talk!'

'Well, don't expect it to be any cleaner than this place,' Clint remarked.

'But Maxx – what do you want?' Amelie tried to focus on his face, but realised she was struggling to see straight. 'It's your night.'

'Well, while I love an open mic night, my vote's for some dirty rock and roll.' He grinned. 'I didn't have the energy the other night, but I do now!'

'I'm with Maisie, I'm afraid,' said Clint. 'Why don't we go get a table and see you there? It goes on until three a.m.!'

'I'm just going to catch up with some friends and I'll join you,' Julian nodded to a table of earnest looking uni students. 'They will be discussing Blur and then Arcade Fire, and I'm going to interrupt them with talk of Tay Tay.'

'One hour,' Amelie promised Maisie, who gave her a knowing grin.

'So it's you and me,' Maxx smiled as their little group parted ways.

'And the music,' Amelie laughed.

Maxx reached for her hand and pulled her through the crowd towards the upstairs venue. In the corner of her eye she could see people looking twice at Maxx, good-looking enough to turn heads, and famous enough to invoke gaping stares. She blushed as she looked at their hands, feeling the warmth of his fingers curl around hers, and the hint of a stroke from his thumb. Was it a stroke? Her stomach turned. Suddenly her hands felt sticky with sweat.

The band were already deep into their set when they made it into the crowd, and Amelie, fuelled by wine, pushed her way front and centre. The music was loud, incoherent and raw, and the mosh pit was starting to swell. She grinned at Maxx, whose eyes were on her and not the band. He looked amused and intrigued, and the attention fuelled her. She felt wild and loose. Suddenly, she was tossed sideways into his arms.

'Are you okay?' he said, pulling her up and into him. She felt the heat of his body against hers, and his breath hot on her neck.

'I'm GREAT!' she squealed, pulling away and throwing herself back into the mass of sweaty, heaving bodies before turning to him laughing. 'Come on!' She jumped up and down as the band's jangly guitars and addictive beats lifted the tiny venue.

Amelie felt Maxx slide in right behind her – a protective

move, shielding her from the more raucous guys in the mosh pit.

'Why won't you cut loose!' she yelled at him. 'This is awesome!'

He grinned at her, sliding his arm around her waist, pulling her into him he shouted in her ear, 'I'm enjoying watching you too much.'

Amelie felt everything melt away from her, the thumping groove of the music, the closeness of Maxx's body, the energy of the crowd, and the arm that ran almost possessively around her. She turned to him and looked up into his eyes. For a moment he looked at her, curiously, before understanding her intention. She lifted her head up, and he leaned into her – when she was once again tossed sideways with a huge whack.

'Oh shit!' Amelie said as she hit the floor, landing awkwardly on her arm. Hands were immediately thrust down from all directions to pull her up; she searched desperately for Maxx's. He had been swallowed by the crowd, so she accepted one from a girl with bright red lips and a black slip dress.

'You okay?' she shouted.

'Fine!' Amelie said, shaking off the pain in her right arm and craning her neck to find Maxx.

'He's over there,' the girl pointed to him. 'You better go save him!'

'Thank you!' Amelie said, pushing towards him.

'That's that boyband singer, isn't it?' she heard the girl shouting as Amelie fought through the crowd.

Maxx was pinned to the far wall by a couple of girls who were pushing right up against him – one holding up a phone trying to get a selfie. He looked uncomfortable, ruffled and alarmed, until he saw Amelie.

Amelie pushed through the mob, and this time it was she who grabbed Maxx by the hand, pulling him out of the crowd, down the stairs and through the doors onto the street. As the chilly evening air hit the sweat on her body, she felt immediately cold and alert and pulled her hand away. And then she felt the first drops of rain fall on her arms.

Maxx, sweaty, dishevelled and out of breath, looked achingly hot. He stared at her curiously. 'Are you okay? You fell. I'm sorry, I couldn't find you.'

'Let's go find the others,' she said quickly, her head spinning, her vision blurred. 'I'm a little drunk.'

# CHAPTER 25

# To Hell With Good Intentions

They squeezed through the narrow entranceway, past the smokers huddled round the awnings, and into a large room with a small stage at one end and a bar at the other. It was filling with all types of modern punks: dip-dyed rockabilly girls with huge tattoos running down their arms and flowers in their hair; men with undercuts and facial piercings in white singlets and ripped jeans. Lotharios, bohemians, groupies of all genders. Band T-shirts. Beards. Piercings.

They pushed on through to where Maisie and Clint had found a cosy five seats around a small table.

'Yes!' said Amelie, delighted to get off her feet.

She looked up to see Maisie ever-so-subtly sliding across so that Maxx could slide in next to her. Amelie felt Maxx's thigh up against hers and she picked up her water to try to focus on anything other than his touch. It was quieter in here, and dark, and Amelie felt yet another rush of excitement. In her tipsy haze any thoughts of Dee or Charlie faded away and she decided to just bask in the feeling.

'Your father will kill me if you drink any more,' Maxx whispered.

'Don't worry, I'm not drinking any more now. I'm just going to sit here next to you and listen to some nice music. And try not to fall asleep on you,' Amelie smiled brazenly.

'I wouldn't mind that,' Maxx said, looking at the guy on stage adjusting his amp, and Amelie felt her stomach tighten and her toes curl. She smiled without turning her head to look at him, and felt his thigh press more firmly into hers. Their hands were just a few centimetres apart.

Amelie didn't care that his on–off girlfriend was arriving the next day, didn't care that he was going to re-record their track with her vocals, didn't care that she was leaving tomorrow and might never see him again anyway. She had never felt such a warm and delicious feeling as the one she felt right now, sitting right up next to Maxx, the warmth of his body matched by the warmth in her stomach. Tonight she could believe that he felt the same way as she did, and enjoy it for as long as she could without worry or guilt.

The guy on stage plugged his electro-acoustic guitar in and spoke gently into the mic.

'I'm going to play a song I wrote for my mother,' he said earnestly. 'Who I miss every day.'

'Oh dear,' Clint whispered. 'Interest level plummeting.'

'*Mother, I miss your face, a woman's worth is measured by her grace. You birthed me and dressed me, and fed me and changed me . . .*' he sang, finger picking just two chords, in a piercing, whiney high-pitched voice. It was a completely failed falsetto, though there was no stopping him from wailing away.

'It's a faux-setto,' Amelie laughed.

'A fucked-setto, you mean.' Maxx took a sip from his beer.

'It's gross. Too much information.' Maisie stifled a giggle.

'Dorkward,' giggled Clint.

Amelie took another sip of her water, and leaned down to grab her phone out of her bag, her hand brushing past Maxx's on the way down. She fished around and pulled it out, and unsurprisingly had a text from both her mother and father.

'Gah. I'd better reply,' Amelie moaned, reading through them.

FROM DAD: Have fun tonight, Tell Maxx I will kill him if you get too drunk and/or miss your train. What a great week. Proud of you. Have fun in Paris and let's chat when you get back. Dad. X

TO DAD: At open mic nite. Drunkin' water. ☺ Love you

FROM MUM: Don't miss your train! Mum x

This text was followed by an emoji of a cable car, a 'thumbs up', a glass of beer and a tree. Or was that the Eiffel Tower? Amelie shook her head laughing.

TO MUM: I won't. M packed n ready. X

As the small audience clapped, a young punk bartender in a flannel shirt with a spike through his septum came around to collect the glasses from their table.

'Hey, um . . . excuse me . . .' he said to Maxx. The table went immediately quiet, and Maisie elbowed Amelie.

'Hi,' Maxx was polite, but if you knew him, you would know his voice was a little clipped.

'Have we met? Are you Jean's brother?'

'Joan? No. Sorry.'

'No, Jean.' The barman looked confused. 'I'm sure I—'

'I don't think so. I'm not from London.' Maxx gave a quick smile, trying to wrap things up.

'God, you look familiar,' the barman persisted, shaking his head. 'Sorry, I'm sure we've met before. Oh god!' The penny dropped. 'You're from that boyband. Sorry to intrude, mate, how embarrassing.'

'No worries.' Maxx looked back to the stage and took another sip of his beer. As the bartender turned to walk off, Maxx smiled at the others, whose faces showed a mixture of embarrassment and concern. 'Don't worry, it happens all the time. I'm so used to it. It doesn't bother y'all does it?'

'What?' Amelie looked up at him. 'You don't mind being spotted?'

'Yeah, it's not a big deal. It's not like they know I'm recording – that's the thing I wanted to keep shtum. I'm just a guy from a band on a night out. It can't be much fun for you guys, though. Sorry,' he added quickly.

'No problem for me,' Julian said, while Maisie nodded in agreement and looked at Amelie.

'Anyway, look who's behind the bar,' Clint offered. They all turned to see Pete Doherty pulling a pint and spinning a yarn for a star-dazzled young man, in full Libertine performance mode. 'You can't compete with that, my friend,' Clint laughed.

Amelie shrugged, trying to be nonchalant, while taking another sip of her water. The next performer took to the stage – a white-haired girl with a candy-pink dip dye and long, white flowing dress.

'It's Dee,' she whispered.

Maxx rolled his eyes. 'She has spawned a thousand sound-alikes. You should see the covers of her songs on YouTube.'

Amelie detected a hint of bitterness in his voice, and felt ashamed that it gave her pleasure to hear him talk in a disparaging way about Dee. She watched with fascination as the girl even opened with a cover of Dee's first single.

'You must be looking forward to seeing her tomorrow?'

Amelie was now unashamedly digging. 'You've been apart for a week or so now.'

Maxx laughed. 'Apart? Yeah, I guess so. I'm looking forward to finishing the track. It's going to be so brilliant.'

'So, you *are* still together?' Amelie blurted out.

He turned to her suddenly. 'What? No, no. We broke up months ago. It's not public yet. I always forget people think we're still together.' He smiled reassuringly at her, and there was a moment of pure electricity before Amelie turned quickly back to the stage.

'That reminds me, I need to give you something before I go,' Maxx continued.

'But I won't see you, I'm leaving in the morning.'

'Damn.' He smiled at her. 'You're going. I'll leave it with your dad.'

Amelie felt the room begin to come into sharper focus, and her head was starting to clear. She realised she desperately needed the toilet.

'I'll be back.' She moved to stand.

'Yeah, but I'll be back in Memphis.'

'No! I mean, I need the loo,' Amelie laughed.

'The loo?' Maxx mocked her accent.

Amelie hit him playfully, smiling.

'Get a room, you two,' Clint teased, making Amelie blush as she pushed her way through the sea of tables.

The toilet had a long queue, and she could hear the giggle of a couple of girls inside taking their time, doing god knows what, and the wailing from the Dee-lookalike singer, who had exchanged her guitar for a mandolin.

'Girl needs blisters,' Amelie said to the girl next to her in the queue.

'Sorry?'

'Blisters on her fingers. She needs to practise.'

The girl smiled at Amelie, still not really understanding, and Amelie's thoughts drifted back to Maxx. His eyes on her, his unbelievably warm and comforting smile, his hands brushing hers. Maxx. Who was not in a relationship with Dee.

The toilet door swung open and Amelie rushed to lock the cubicle behind her.

'Gotta go. Literally!' Amelie shouted. She tried to take a deep breath but felt her chest tightening, making her unsteady on her feet, the broken cubicle light occasionally flickering on and off added to her sense of disorientation. She sat on the toilet with the seat down and put her head between her legs, trying to stop herself feeling sick.

She looked up at the walls around her, the graffiti scratched into the paint, stories of who loves who, confessions, and declarations of war. An A4 poster with the venue's gig guide from last month was taped to the back of the door, though it was impossible to read under the flickering light above her head.

She thought about Maxx and Maisie and Clint back in the other room and wondered if it would be possible to slip out and send them a text once she was home. But her bag and phone were still tucked under the little table. She tried to pull herself together, when there was *bang bang bang* on the door!

'Amelie?' Maisie's voice was full of concern. 'Are you being sick?'

'No, for god's sake.' Amelie was relieved to hear her friend's voice.

'What's going on? Mandolin lady is finishing up, if that's what you're hiding from ... '

'I'm coming.' She unlocked the cubicle, and Maisie gave her the *look*.

'Jesus, what's happened. Let me fix your make-up. You look like you've been crying?'

Amelie looked at her friend, feeling doe-eyed and vulnerable. Maxx. She needed to say it out loud. 'I think I really like him. I mean, I'm falling for him.'

Maisie gave her a big hug. 'I think he might feel the same, the way he looks at you. I mean, I don't want to wind you up unnecessarily, but you're like a couple of lovebirds in there. It's super sweet.'

'And he's not with Dee.'

'Okay, wow.' Maisie said, surprised. She pushed past the queue and back into the bar. 'Well, did he tell you that just now?'

'Yes. He said they broke up months ago. But he still seems so attached. I dunno. The way he was watching her at the gig. And they're doing this duet. Oh god, she's so beautiful and talented. I can't compete with that.'

'Amelie,' Maisie said firmly. 'Enjoy tonight. Enjoy his company. He's going back to America and this – whatever it is – is just for tonight. Just enjoy yourself. Quit with the second guessing. He seems straight up to me.'

Amelie squeezed her friend's hand. 'Thanks, Maisie. I don't know what I'd do without you.'

'Also, I have a slight confession to make.'

Suddenly, Amelie was aware someone was calling her name. As the room came back into focus she realised it was someone on the mic.

'Amelie Ayres?' said the voice.

'You didn't!'

'I did. Well, Julian and I did.' She smiled as the microphone squealed with glass-shattering feedback.

'Why does that ALWAYS happen?' Maisie said, covering her ears.

'It's like a fear klaxon,' Amelie said, remembering her audition.

She squirmed, but was totally trapped. She looked across at Clint and Julian and scowled, and then she saw Maxx's face.

He smiled at her and nodded his head towards the stage. 'Do it!' he mouthed, grinning.

'There she is!' shouted Julian, pointing her way.

Amelie looked at Maisie and then back at Maxx.

'Fuck it,' she said, as she took a deep breath and marched forward to the stage. 'I have literally nothing to lose here.'

Amelie took to the stage, picking up the house guitar. She

looked out, the basic lighting shining into her eyes, obscuring most of the room – she knew they were there, but she couldn't see them. She looked across to Maisie, who looked like she might explode with excitement, and then she locked eyes with Maxx, who smiled in gentle encouragement. With the warmth of the wine in her veins and the first flush of love in her heart, she began to play.

This was nothing like the studio, or at home uploading anonymous tracks to invisible listeners. Here in this room, with people watching, there was a warm exhilaration that lifted her up and transported her right into the heart of the lyrics.

As she played the last note, she closed her eyes, and heard gentle clapping fill the room. She opened her eyes and, as they adjusted to the light, she grinned over at her friends.

'Hi, everyone. I'm Amelie. I think I'm allowed to do another song but I'm going to need help from my friend.'

She looked at Maxx who, for the first time, looked more uncomfortable than she did.

'Come on, Maxx. Don't leave me hanging,' she begged.

Maxx sighed, looking down at his hands, before taking a slow and steady sip on his drink. Amelie's heart began to sink. Come on, Maxx, she thought. They'll love you.

He stood up slowly and shook his head at her. He seemed annoyed and she felt her cheeks begin to burn. The silence in the room hung heavy. Just as Amelie thought he might turn to leave, he began to slowly walk towards her. He stepped up on stage and, like a pro, pulled a stool over and took a seat.

'Hi, I'm Maxx,' he said into the mic while he shook his head at Amelie. 'Max with one X. Max Cooke'. He paused to smile to himself. 'And this is a song that she basically wrote most of.'

'You should play it,' he said, nodding at the guitar.

As their voices wound around each other in beautiful harmony – and as they stared into each other's eyes, Amelie knew that she was utterly, completely, hopelessly falling for him. She remembered his words, that first day in the studio. *It's just acting. You just have to pretend.*

It *was* just pretend. But she was happy to get lost in it.

# CHAPTER 26

# Sleepless

Max knew it had been a reckless, but for the first time in years he felt good.

He hadn't meant to do more than accompany Amelie on that one song, but sitting up on that stage, playing in that authentic, pared-back way – this was what he wanted. And there was no stopping him.

He walked the pavement with one foot on the road and one in the gutter, with both arms out for balance. The sky was clear and the stars were twinkling and he was walking around London on a cool summer's night with a beautiful girl next to him, and the career he should always have had starting to take shape. He couldn't wait to quit the band. He never wanted to see a white three-piece suit, a flaming rotunda, or jar of New Wave hair gel ever again.

And the endorsements. He no longer had to pretend to only

drink Pepsi, or wear a specific brand of headphones. He didn't have to flog a range of Keep dress-up dolls or that goddamn toothpaste range to tweenagers, or turn on the Christmas lights at Macy's. He didn't have to appear on Fox! Or worse, Disney Channel.

'That felt too goooood!' he laughed. Holding onto Amelie's shoulder to keep him steady as he balanced on the edge of the kerb. 'And you were great! How do you feel?'

Amelie smiled, her beautiful blue eyes catching the bright streetlights. She shivered slightly, though Max had already given her his shirt to wear around her shoulders.

'A bit more sober. But on a bit more of a high.' She smiled. 'It was pretty awesome. I can't believe you stayed up there and did three songs! There's a two-song limit you know.'

'Ha. I couldn't stop it. I was possessed.'

'Those other songs. I haven't heard them,' Amelie said. 'Are they new?'

'Yeah. I wrote them this week. They just shot out of me.' He laughed. 'All tour I'd been banging away at writing and not a damn thing sounded good. Then, a few days with your dad. Well, with you ... '

'It was awesome. Modern blues. Soul. A little Bluegrass edge. 'You know your genres.'

'I know every genre,' Amelie laughed.

'Cloud rap? Witch House? Chill Wave?' Max laughed.

'Rudimentary,' she countered. 'Try Porno Grind. Nerdcore. Japanoise.'

'Baby Metal. Alpen rock. Nintendocore.'

Amelie raised her eyebrows. 'Nintendocore?'

'Another punk/metal subgenre.'

'Arghh. Well, electronica subs are even worse. Fidgetbass? And what about Happy Hardcore? That sounds like a mood disorder.'

'No electronica in your collection then?'

'No, no. There's plenty,' Amelie said earnestly, rubbing her hands up and down her shoulders and shivering.

Max stopped. 'We really need to get you into a taxi,' he said, looking up and down the deserted street. 'Where *are* all the taxis?'

'Welcome to east London.' Amelie grinned. 'I'll try Uber again.'

As soon as he left the stage Max had been mobbed. He was extremely sensitive to Amelie, who had had a terrible experience of mob mentality after her brush with Charlie a few weeks back, but luckily Clint came immediately to the rescue and hustled them out a back entrance.

'He knows every back door in this place.' Julian had winked, showing them the exit through a supply door. 'Be quick, I think there are photographers here already.'

Max had grabbed Amelie by the hand. 'Which way?'

'This way,' she'd said, the anxiety in her voice clear.

'We'll be fine. Let's get a cab as quickly as we can.'

But though it had proved impossible to find a taxi, under the cloak of the London night they'd managed to get away.

Maisie hadn't followed them. It was clear she'd wanted to give Amelie some time alone with Max, and he was thrilled to have her all to himself. After several beers, and high on the news that Amelie did not fancy Charlie, he wanted nothing more than to be alone with her before she disappeared from his life.

'So, if we can't get a taxi, what can we do at ... ' He looked at his watch. 'One-ten in London on a Saturday morning.'

'Well, I'm not sure what YOU are doing, but I need to get home and finish packing my things. I've got my train in a few hours,' Amelie laughed.

'Let me help you!'

'Help me?' Amelie snorted.

'We can play records and I'll make coffee.'

He was sure he could see the hint of a smile on her face, and grabbed her by the hand. 'Come on, Amelie Ayres. Let's go to your house!'

'It's a good thirty-minute walk from here. But I suppose we can jump on a bus when one comes.' She pulled her hand away, her eyes dancing with that alluring coquettishness he found so magnetic. Her bus timetable app thing was extraordinarily precise. 'Eight minutes actually. Shall we just wait under the shelter?'

'Ooh, the bus.'

'No, my friend. Not just the bus. The *night* bus,' Amelie said wickedly. 'You're going to have to keep your head down, and follow me.'

The number 38 arrived, its harsh fluorescent bulbs highlighting the capricious state of fifty-odd young, drunk revellers heading back to their Hackney lofts after a night out. Max felt a touch nervous about being recognised in this environment, so under Amelie's strict orders he kept his head down as they climbed the stairs and she ushered him into the front seat.

'This is where you sit. With your feet up here,' she said, swinging her legs up onto the front rail.

He obliged, enjoying the view out over the east London streets.

'We're coming up to Dalston, where we were the other night with my dad. Which is really cool, by the way. You wouldn't be allowed back there without some more facial hair.' She grinned.

'What's the area called where you live?'

'Victoria Park. Well, Hackney really, but it's a little bit posher round the park. My mother's flat is tiny by the way, and I'm really not into taking a multi-millionaire there.'

'Well, I still technically live with my parents, if that makes you feel any better.'

'No!' Amelie burst out laughing. 'You DO not!'

'I do,' Max said. 'My residential address is with my ma and pa in a four-bedroom house with a wraparound porch and a double garage. Actually, I still have a single bed with a Spider-Man comforter. And posters on my wall. And I'm twenty-one next month.'

'I seriously need to get off this bus.'

'It's true. It's like I died in 2010. They have not changed my room one bit.'

'Do you miss your parents?'

'Every day. I don't see them enough, but hopefully that's all about to change.'

'How?'

'Well, for one, I'm going to quit The Keep as soon as I'm back in the States.'

'What? Really?'

'For realz. I'm saying farewell to my white satin open-front shirts and tossing out the hair straighteners.'

'Wow. That's big news,' Amelie said. 'But shouldn't you wait? You know, to see if your label likes the music? I mean, how will it work?'

'I don't really care,' he said, though he knew he did. He would be following in the footsteps of a long line of aging boyband members breaking free and nauseatingly desperate to be taken seriously.

'Yes you do,' she said, flatly.

'Well, I care that the EP is well received, but I don't care about waiting for that. My decision is made either way. I don't care about *the band* any more,' he said, doing air quotes to emphasise how un-bandlike the band was. 'I'm just happy to be writing and playing again.'

'Ahh! This is us!' Amelie squealed, reaching around to push the big red button on the post next to Max. 'Quick!'

They both jumped up and darted quickly off the bus and onto a darkened street by the park. It was quiet and creepy compared to the buzz of Angel.

'It's just down there.' Amelie pointed just ahead.

'I hope you never walk home alone.'

'It's literally one minute! And no, Mum makes me get a cab if it's dark.'

She led him down a metal staircase and opened a small door on the basement floor of a terrace house.

'It's seriously tiny,' she said, without her usual sarcastic defensiveness. 'And a bit weird.'

'Oh, shut up.' He pushed past her and flicked on the light switch. It was an Aladdin's cave of china tea pots and Bakelite furnishings; a perfect little curiosity of a house, tightly packed and a bit ramshackle, but wonderfully cosy. The sideboard was purpose-built for storing records and within about ten seconds he was flicking through it, pulling out each treasure one at a time to carefully select the perfect record.

'God, it's late,' Amelie yawned. 'Cuppa?'

'Coffee? Yes please,' he said, switching on the 1970s record player and fixing a Stevie Wonder album down. She switched the kettle on.

'Tea? I'm afraid my culinary skills only extend to tea.'

'Sure, with lots of sugar!' He put the needle carefully down on the groove, and turned the volume up slightly to hear the warm scratch of the start of the record. 'I love that sound. Man, you're so lucky to have this collection.' He continued to flick through each wonderful record, pulling out a couple more to add to a shortlist.

'My dad gave them to me.'

'No *Pet Sounds* though.'

Amelie rolled her eyes. 'You were just being so smug.'

'Is this collection actually yours?'

'Well, most of it. Not the French jazz. My exquisite tastes won't allow it,' she laughed, flicking off the main lights in favour of tiny fairy lights that were enchantingly arranged around the room.

She walked over with two cups of tea and a couple of biscuits. 'A digestive,' she declared, 'with sweet, strong tea. You've reached peak English. Can you give me two mins and I'll just pull my suitcase together? Then it's done.'

While she was gone he lay back on the sumptuous rug and pulled a cushion underneath his head. Staring at the yellowing ceiling with its ornate light fixtures, faint damp stains and quick-fix paint patches, he remembered something Mike had told him. He jumped up and followed Amelie through the tiny hallway.

'Amelie?' he called. 'Let me see your recording studio?'

'My what? No!' she shouted from the bathroom. 'You can't go in. My room is mortifying!'

'Too late,' he laughed, throwing open the adjacent door, hoping it was her bedroom. At first all he could see was an unmade bed with some Spider-Man PJs crushed up half under the pillow.

The studio was incredible. Like some kind of steampunk labyrinth of gear cobbled together with tape and wire and love and time and passion. There was a hum coming from the wall socket and he was sure he could smell a whiff of hot plastic. Instinctively, he moved the mouse and her computer lit up.

'You know, you ought to power down when you go out. This thing is a fire risk,' Max shouted.

'I know.' Amelie was standing at her door. Her eyes were wide, and he was shocked to see her looking almost frightened. 'Please . . . '

'What *is* this?' He turned round to see her SoundCloud account open. 'You're on SoundCloud? But why do you call yourself Lou? Is this your account? You've got so many listeners.' He hit play on her latest track. 'Is this you? Oh. God. It is! Wow!'

'They're called followers,' she smiled meekly. 'Please, Max. That's really private.'

'You're famous!' he said clicking through her messages.

'My songs are. Which is nice,' Amelie said. 'But I'm not.'

'Just let me hear this and then I'll stop. You're a great song-writer. What's this called?'

She sat on the edge of her bed, looking at her hands. 'I was thinking, this week, you know, that maybe I should focus on songwriting and producing. Try to get a publishing deal or something. I've had some interest from an independent label.'

'Oh, wow. That's amazing,' Max said. 'But it's not what you want, is it?'

'No. But tonight, playing in a little pub in Angel ... that's not performing, really. That's just drunk jamming.' She laughed a little, playing with the edge of a nail on her thumb.

'Well, today it's there, and tomorrow it's a bit bigger, and each time you take to the stage you get a little closer. You have to work at it.'

He watched her staring at the computer screen, glancing down the list of tracks, the hours of work, of time, of energy she had put into her music.

'I do,' she said flatly, standing up and flicking the machine off at the wall. 'Come on, that's enough.'

He followed her to the other room in silence as she flopped down on the rug and yawned, pulling a blanket around her shoulders. 'I'm sorry it's cold. I *would* put the radiator on but it takes ages, and I'm leaving in the morning so I shouldn't really be wasting money. I'll light the gas fire though. Do you ever worry about money?'

'Not really,' Max said, feeling a bit ashamed at the vast chasm of difference in the way they lived. But here he felt the warmth of a loving home, just like his own back in Tennessee. She turned the switch on the little gas fire and struck a match, holding it close until the heater lit up blue, then slowly red. Max picked up a record.

'Put that on. It's *good* electronica,' Amelie smiled.

'AlunaGeorge,' Max read on the sleeve as he slipped the record out. 'What time do you need to be at the train?'

'Eight a.m.'

'Okay, well, let me book you a taxi now so you don't need to worry.' He watched her start to protest. 'No, I won't have it.'

'Do you need a number?' He shook his head, and after a couple of minutes typing into his phone, she poked him.

'*You're* not actually booking my cab, are you?'

'No.'

'Who is?'

'Alexia. Our assistant. She's in New York but it's okay, it's still evening there. She wants to know your zip code.' He grinned.

'I can't believe you're messaging New York to book you a cab in London. Ridiculous,' Amelie laughed.

'Well, let's make the most of it. It's all going to be over next month.' He pulled a face. 'I will miss Alexia's amazing way of finding whatever you fancy at that exact moment before you've even realised you need it.'

'Thank you for hanging tonight,' Amelie whispered.

'The pleasure was mine.' He smiled as they lay side by side, staring at the ceiling.

The record came to the end of the first side, and Max turned it over as Amelie stifled a yawn and lay her head down on the rug.

He lay next to her as the second side played.

'Being in such a massive band. What's it like?' she smiled.

'I dunno. It was pretty addictive. The money, the attention.

Obviously I had Dee as well, so … you know, I was kinda happy.'

'There must have been something liberating, I guess, about totally selling out,' she said bluntly.

'Yep. Every gig. Every record.' He grinned.

'NO. I mean, you're a sell out.'

'Yeah, I got it.' He looked at her. 'You know, a bit of advice, if you want some. Not everyone is going to like what you do. No matter how *real* you are.'

'Well, I'd rather be disliked for being me and real and an artist than for all that … stuff.'

'And how's that working for you?'

'What?' She sat up.

'Well, you're talented, no doubt. But there's no point being an artist in your bedroom.'

She looked at the wall, her eyes trailing the windowsill up to the light fitting, her mouth down. 'You told me that I didn't have to give myself away every time I perform. You said just to pretend, but how do you do it when it means so much?' Amelie said timidly.

'I was wrong when I said that,' Max said, turning to her. 'That's what I did in The Keep, and that's why I couldn't write music any more. I didn't know how to be me. The magic comes when the music comes from the heart, and is performed from the heart.'

Amelie looked glum. 'I don't really know how that's supposed to help.'

'Maybe you should try singing to one person in the crowd. Like you did tonight,' he said gently, reaching out for her hands, which she let him take for a moment.

'Well, there won't always be *someone* there,' Amelie said cautiously. 'But I guess I could at least pretend at that.'

For a moment, they looked at each other, and Max saw a vulnerability behind her eyes as she looked longingly at him. He wanted to kiss her. Badly.

Amelie slowly pulled back and lay down on the rug.

'I forget what that was like. To be starting out. It gets easier, you know. And at least, if you're doing something that is *real* ... well, I'm guessing a little piece of you won't die every time you perform,' he laughed.

'Do *you* want some advice?' she asked.

'Sure.'

'You should take some time out and come back and record another time.'

'What?'

'I just think you're not ready.' She burst out laughing. 'That sounds bad. I mean, you know. You need to live a little.'

'Another truth bomb from Amelie Ayres.'

'I'm sorry, that wasn't very subtle. I'm really tired.' She yawned again.

Max looked across at her and realised he only had one thing on his mind. As if she could read his mind, she turned her head to his and he pulled himself up on one arm.

For a moment it looked like she was hesitating, then she

closed her eyes and breathed out gently. Opening them with a small whisper of a smile. 'Well, hurry up then,' she said in the quietest voice, her cheeks turning red.

Pausing for a moment to look into her eyes, he gently pressed his lips against hers. His mouth opened slightly, and he lingered for a moment, before pulling back to look at her face again. Her cheeks were flush and her breathing fast. He kissed her again on the forehead and then lay down next to her.

'I wish we had more time,' he said.

'Me too,' she smiled, her eyes fixed on the ceiling.

'I might come back to London. In a month or so. When everything is done.'

'It would be great to see you, for a visit.'

'Why don't you just close your eyes? I'll set my alarm just in case ... well, the driver will call anyway.'

He watched as she closed her eyes. As her breathing began to slow he felt for her. His instinct was to protect her, to show her the way, to lead her where she wanted to go – but she didn't want his help, and she didn't need it.

For a moment he fantasised about living in London, working with Mike and dating his daughter, and then his mind wandered to the conversation he would be having with Geoff and the rest of the band.

He felt surprisingly sad. And guilty. Guilty because of the likelihood that they'd be made to press on as a foursome for a while, but ultimately knowing that when one member leaves – the jig is up.

He wondered what they would do next. Would Charlie end up on Disney Channel? Would Art do a degree and disappear into obscurity, only to reappear on a reality show? Would Lee move to Hollywood with his girlfriend and buy a huge bungalow in the hills? And what of Kyle? He was sensitive and he genuinely loved being in a boyband. He thought Kyle would probably remain committed to The Keep until the bitter end, playing solo gigs in Vegas with wrinkles and a fully realised paunch, definitely out of the closet, belting out hits to an audience of gay men and housewives. Still with the fire, and still with the white costumes. And loving every minute. He smiled.

# CHAPTER 27

# Jealous Hearted Blues

Amelie stood sulking on the Eurostar platform at Gare du Nord as her mum came rushing through the crowd, pushing aside haughty Parisian business people on their way to do business with equally haughty business people in London.

'Amelie, what's wrong!?' She threw her arms around her daughter, but Amelie pulled away.

'Nothing,' Amelie said, rubbing her eyes. 'Nothing. Oh god, sorry, I just had a big night.'

'New guitar?' Her Mum grabbed her case and coat. 'Looks flash! Your father said you were going out last night. I hope you didn't drink too much, Amelie.' She tried to lift her chin up so she could look into her daughter's eyes. 'I hope you didn't take any crack.'

'Mum! Jesus.'

'Well, you never know. I was doing all sorts of . . . well.

Regardless of that, you're seventeen now and I suppose I worry.'

'I wasn't doing crack,' Amelie said dryly, the tears gone and an all-together more familiar emotion of parental irritation taking over.

'Well, that's great news, darling. Now, I have a car. We're going to brunch at a place called Oliver's and then I'll take you to the apartment I found – I hope you like it – and then to the restaurant in the afternoon.'

'Is there time for sleep?' Amelie said, hearing the teenager in herself.

'Sure, of course.' Her mum threaded her arm through hers. 'This way.'

She led them through the massive station. A filthy welcome to Paris, Amelie thought, as they strode under the grand architecture, past the lost tourists, charity collectors, homeless people and thick plumes of cigarette smoke by the main doors and out onto the street, where the sun was blazing hot.

Amelie tried to focus on the day ahead, though her mind kept wandering back to Max and the events of that morning.

She had hardly slept, drifting in and out of a blissful doze. Both of them had been the same. She would stretch and turn to see his sleepy eyes on her, and he would touch her cheek, or kiss her fingers. He was gentle and a gentleman.

At around 6.30 she was stirred by the vibration of a mobile phone. Max was fast asleep next to her, his arm draped heavily around her middle. Managing to wriggle free, she searched for it, only to find Max's iPhone had slipped from his pocket. Without thinking, she read the message on the screen.

> FROM DEE: Arrived. I can't wait to see you baby – The hotel? Or Studio? Besos. Dx

Amelie felt as though she had been punched. She sat back against the sofa, dropping the phone with a thud. She felt a cold chill rush through her and a wave of nausea about Max, who lay there, completely oblivious, the faintest of snores escaping his slightly open mouth.

She had to wake him if Dee was on her way.

She shook his arm and he woke with a huge start, looking around confused yet still managing to look ridiculously hot, even with the imprint of the rug across his cheek. He lunged forward to pull her close.

'Morning, beautiful,' he croaked.

'You've got a text message.' She tried to sound steady but could hear the fragility in her voice.

He looked surprised, then confused as he fished around for his phone.

'Here.' She pointed to the floor where she had dropped it. 'I'm sorry, I didn't mean to read it, I thought it was mine.'

Max looked at his screen for a moment and then at Amelie. 'Oh, Dee's here. Shit. What time is it?'

'I'm going to take a shower.' Amelie got up to leave the room.

'Okay, sure,' he said without looking up, shaking his head, furiously typing.

'Amelie!' Her mum shook her. 'What is WRONG with you? Here's the car.'

Amelie towered above the old, beaten-up Citroën that looked like someone had tried to make a VW Beetle without the correct plans. It was pale blue with one dark green door that didn't open properly. 'You have to give it a good jiggle, then a bump, like this,' her mum was saying as she heaved Amelie's things into the tiny back seat, and wedged the guitar through the middle of the front seats.

Max apologised profusely for ordering the car to come earlier. Asking over and over if she would be all right at St Pancras on her own.

'I'm not that early,' Amelie retorted.

'I feel like an ass, rushing off like this,' he apologised, as she pointedly dropped her bag to create a barrier between them in the back seat of the most luxurious cab Amelie had ever seen. 'Damn it,' he said several times under his breath, no doubt freaking out that Dee would discover he'd been out all night.

'Can you wait here? I have to get something for you. I think you'll want to take it to Paris.'

She tried to protest but he was already speaking to the driver. 'Five minutes. I'll be right back,' he said.

She watched him run inside his hotel, and immediately saw Dee through the window. Dee rose, bounced even, and gave him a warm hug. She looked incredible. Blonde hair pinned pack in braids around her head, gold shimmering top hanging loosely over her scuffed designer jeans. Who had she been kidding? I'm nothing next to Dee, she thought bitterly.

He had been gone no less than ten minutes before he came back panting with his guitar.

'It's a Gibson J50. Got a righteous vintage sound, as well it should. It's from 1965. I think it will suit your voice. I had it fixed up and it plays perfectly.'

She sat there dumbfounded.

'It's a thank you, for everything you've done. For the music. You have to take it.' He looked unsure of himself for the first time, and as Amelie sat frozen he slid the instrument into the back seat next to her. She knew she had to speak next, but she couldn't, she could feel the tears welling and would certainly crack when she finally uttered something in return.

'I have to go,' she managed. Not even thank you. She couldn't find the words. She wasn't sure what she would be thanking him for. For the kiss? For the guitar?

'My contact details are in there. My private number. My

email. Please send me yours. I have a lot going on over the next month. I need to speak to Geoff and the guys and go home and see my folks as well. But I ... I will try to be back next month. Go back to the open mic night!' he pleaded as the driver started up the engine. 'Shit. Why do I feel like this is goodbye?'

'I suppose because it is. Good luck in the studio. I hope you get a great vocal from her,' Amelie said, the bitterness thick in her tone as she pulled the door shut.

Her mum was fiddling with the radio, which was stuck on an angry talk show punctuated by shouty French adverts every five minutes or so. Ella was gesticulating out the window at almost every car that overtook them or honked at them – even the odd parked car got a fist wave – although it was clear that it was her mother who was a little precarious driving on the other side of the road.

'Honestly, the traffic here,' she sighed, shaking a fist at a lovely old Parisian woman in a very flash red sports car. 'Money, style, no licence ...'

Her mum pulled up at a tiny *épicerie*, as French as they came, with strings of onion and garlic hanging in the window and a basket of baguettes at the door. All that was missing was a guy in a Breton top with a red scarf and a small dog.

'Cute.' Amelie grinned at last.

'You like?' her mum said, proudly pushing a side door open and leading Amelie into a cold concrete hallway with small stone steps leading upstairs to the apartment. 'I still have the key from the agent. Well, I say agent, he's the shop owner from downstairs. Cheap cheese.' She winked.

The flat was almost exactly as Amelie imagined. Small and impossibly cute, with a tiny bathroom and one small bedroom with a gorgeous window seat adjoining an elaborate cast iron balcony, just big enough for one. Utterly Parisian. Romantic even. She smiled at her mum.

'It's lovely.'

'My summer home! And it's just a short walk from work.'

Amelie sat on the edge of the radiator. 'Mum, you don't need to sell me this.'

'Oh, I'm sorry. I just feel bad. Leaving you alone.'

'I'll be with Dad. Don't worry about it.' She looked out the window and onto the busy market street below. She took a deep breath and lied to close the conversation down. 'I'm happy for you.'

'I know you're not. But I really appreciate it, darling.'

She was happy enough.

Later that evening, after Amelie had been dragged the length of the Seine and back, she rolled over on her pull-out sofa bed and checked her phone. Two texts from Maisie wanting to know how her night with Max ended up. Then one asking why she wasn't returning her texts. Then another dramatically declaring Amelie 'the worst friend that ever existed' for not replying. There was one from her dad asking her if she had had fun last night and telling her to enjoy Paris. A missed call from an unknown number. And, finally, two missed calls from her mum from earlier that morning.

She closed her eyes and tried to get comfortable on the soft and sunken mattress.

For a few minutes she allowed herself to forget all the complications and sink into a moment's indulgent bliss. The feeling of that one solitary kiss on her lips. Soft, gentle, and sweet. The feeling of his hand on her face, and the warmth of his body against hers. She felt a shooting sensation down the base of her spine and warmth spread through her body.

But then she shook herself. He lives in America. His talented, beautiful, incredible ex-girlfriend is with him – right now – recording *their* duet, *their* love song, together in a big love fest full of fucking love. Amelie would be erased from the final track, and Max would be heading back to the States imminently to get on with his life without her.

She called Maisie.

'Amelie.'

'Hi, I am safely in Paris. What are you *doing*?' She could hear her friend breathing erratically.

'Sirsasana. A headstand. Just a sec! Let me come down.' She heard the thud of Maisie's feet hitting the floor, her friend unwinding from some crazy yoga posture. 'What happened, Amelie? I'm dying here!'

'Hmm ...' She could feel her eyes welling up. 'I feel ridiculous.'

'What do you mean? Did you kiss?'

'Yes.'

'Oh my god, what was it like.'

Amelie closed her eyes. 'Magic.'

'I knew it! He couldn't take his eyes off you! He was totally smitten all night. And, oh my god, when you guys sang together it was literally the cutest thing I've ever seen. You, my dear, are even more talented than even I thought.'

'But, you know, Dee is with him now. I don't know. I don't think it's totally over between them.'

There was silence on the other end of the line. And then the sound of a blender. 'But you asked if they were together! He said no, right? What's the problem? Where did you kiss?'

'On the mouth!' Amelie shrieked.

'No, I mean *where* did you kiss?'

'Oh. At my house.'

'OH MY GOD. Hang on.' The blender whizzed again. 'Nutribullet. I just made a Green Goddess to help cleanse. I'm still suffering. I've been a wreck all day – so hungover. YOUR HOUSE? You had that hot thing in your house? And you only kissed? Once?'

'None of which is the point,' Amelie said dryly.

'Oh, Amelie, it was always going to be a long shot. What did you expect? A relationship? He lives in AMERICA.'

'I know. I need to let go.'

'You do,' Maisie agreed, and then her tone shifted to serious and concerned BFF. 'I wouldn't worry about Dee. They're old friends and they have music business to do.'

'I saw her text. It was very . . . familiar.'

'You went through his phone?'

'No, it flashed up. She called him baby. She was heading to meet him. We had to leave really quickly.'

'Hmm.'

'When I told him I'd seen it he seemed very rattled.'

Maisie let out a long sigh.

'That's not the worst. When I dropped him at the hotel, she was there, waiting, in the lobby. They were so warm with each other. What if they haven't actually broken up? I mean, we've only got his word to go on, right? All that media attention yet the press don't know yet? I'm just not so sure.'

'Duh.'

'Uh huh.'

'I dunno, Amelie. I think you might just have the wrong end of the stick.'

'Well,' Amelie mumbled, 'I suppose it was a bit ridiculous to think anything . . .'

'Well, I'm not sure whether to tell you this next part or not.'

'Tell me what?'

'Well, someone took a video of Max on stage. There's a few minutes at the beginning of you and him, but it's mostly his song after. It's all over Twitter and YouTube. Haven't you been online?'

'Oh, good god. No.' Amelie shook her head. 'Not again.'

'Well, at least this time the speculation is more about why he was there and why he was singing original songs. Basically, the press are speculating about him leaving the band and going solo. No one is speaking about you being a love interest or anything.'

'No?'

'No.' Maisie paused. 'Is that a bad thing?'

'No, no,' Amelie sighed. 'Of course not.'

'So what's the plan then, with Paris?'

'I told Mum I'll come for a full week later in the summer, but otherwise I'll be in London working with Dad when he's around, I guess. Well, you have to come with me, at least for a long weekend or something.'

'I will! Whenever you like.'

'Okay, I'd better go. I need to do some cleansing of my own, and by that I mean sleep. Bye!'

The next morning Amelie and her mum went for breakfast at a tiny café on the corner of their street-to-be. It was tiny in every sense of the word. Tiny tables, tiny chairs, tiny coffee cups, tiny waiter and tiny menu but, luckily, enormous croissants and pain au chocolats – Amelie ordered one of each.

'I'm starved,' she told her mum.

'Thank goodness, since you didn't eat a *thing* yesterday! And all that free food on offer.'

'I wondered, though, Mum – why *this* job?'

'It's just so prestigious, darling. Imagine me, an English woman from Devon working as a *chef pâtissier* in a fancy French restaurant under Monsieur Lamont.'

Under. Amelie cringed.

'It's just that I thought you were going to do the market stall?'

'Come on, Roman Road is hardly Paris, darling. I mean, I can't spend the rest of my days making croque monsieur for people who call it a cheese toastie. Honestly.'

'But it *is* a cheese toastie.'

Her mum laughed, a giddy high-pitched shrill, which Amelie recognised immediately as the sound of nervous uncertainty.

'Okay, but you're always saying I should make it on my own,' Amelie said gently. 'I just, well, it would be good to see you—'

'But think how amazing it would be if I make a good impression over the summer. I mean, if I spent even a year or two working here with Monsieur Lamont my cooking could be incredible. Imagine that! It's such an amazing opportunity! Then they would really take me seriously. They'd have to!'

'Who?'

'You know, the customers.'

'You need the good patrons of Roman Road market to take you seriously? The cheese toastie people?' Amelie raised her eyebrows. 'You would have gotten a stall place this summer – you said so yourself.'

'Oh, Amelie, I really wish you wouldn't put a dampener on this. I will be such an amazing cook at the end of a summer here.'

'You already are!' Amelie lectured her mum. She had spent

her whole life looking at this optimistic, confident, happy woman, and wondering how she could be her daughter. But for the first time she could see it clearly. Her mum was crippled with fear of failure, just as Amelie was. She hadn't done the market in London because she didn't feel she could pull it off. She was here in Paris because working for someone else was easier than trying to go it alone. Amelie got it. The parallels were unmistakable.

Amelie had tried and failed at that audition. Max and the week she spent in her father's studio had been her own perfect 'French Restaurant and Monsieur Lamont'. She didn't need to be the star of the show under her own steam, she could draw on Max and her dad for the strength to shine. Sure, she'd been able to perform live for the first time – but was that only because she'd been forced into it? Because Max and the others had been there?

'Amelie, don't you see that I'm getting there?' her mum laughed.

'Yeah, Mum.'

'Oooh! Isn't that the musician you were working with?' Ella said suddenly, flicking through the lifestyle supplement of the paper to the celebrity gossip section. There he was – a photo of Max, his face slightly obscured by his hair, leaving his hotel. The caption below was in French.

'*Chut. Maxx du groupe The Keep a été repéré dans l'est de Londres alors que les rumeurs concernant son départ du groupe pour se lancer en solo continuent de circuler. Mais bien qu'il soit possible qu'il quitte le groupe, il ne semble pas prêt de quitter son amoureuse de longue date, Dee, puisqu'on les a vus sortir de la même chambre d'hôtel vendredi matin.'*

'In English?' Amelie said dryly.

'Amelie, your French needs soooo much work!' She patted her knee. 'It just says that there are rumours he's leaving the band, and that his girlfriend joined him in London on Friday.'

Amelie bit into the crisp, flaky croissant and sipped on her strong, tiny coffee and tried to shake the sadness that enveloped her.

# CHAPTER 28

# Goodbye England

When Max rushed back inside the hotel wondering how he'd managed to screw up the timing of Dee's arrival so badly, he saw her curled up in the bright-purple lounge suite, hair immaculate, hands folded in her lap and looking as ethereal and feline as ever. At a table just feet away sat her driver and an assistant having a coffee, next to an enormous collection of matching, black shiny luggage. A small entourage, but an entourage nonetheless. Gah.

He was mortified that he had kissed Amelie and then run off, but he would need to deal with all that later on. For now, he had to focus on the job at hand.

'Hi, Dee.' Max walked over, slipping easily back into the habit of scouring his surroundings for paparazzi whenever they were together.

'Max!' She jumped out of her couch and flung her arms

around him. 'Darling! It's so good to see you! I've actually missed you this last week!'

'Actually?' He laughed. 'Good to see you too.'

'Well, shall we get to it? I'm so absolutely sorry but I only have four hours then I have to get to Heathrow.'

'Right,' Max nodded. 'Okay, well, it's just a vocal I guess. Can you give me five minutes? We can take your car to the studio, right?'

He ran up to his room and back to the car as fast as he could and tried to give Amelie the guitar he'd bought her. But after their evening together, the gesture seemed strange, and strangely unwelcome. It wasn't the grand 'thank you' he'd had in mind. Why didn't he just get her number? As Max watched the car pull off with Amelie inside he felt completely stupid, and angry with himself for how he had handled it.

At the studio, Dee sat quietly opposite Max, typing away on her phone as she had been doing all morning. She looked tired, maybe a little jaded, by being there. Everything felt different to Max without Amelie there. The enthusiasm had left the room like a balloon being slowly deflated, until he found himself wishing Dee's flight was even earlier.

Mike had recorded her vocals in two takes. Not because it was perfect, but because Dee felt that she'd nailed it.

'I don't like to do too many takes, ruins the authenticity,' Dee had said, strolling back out from the studio where she'd barely broken a sweat. 'Really good song though.

Better than the first version you sent. Will you release it as a single?'

'Yeah, that was the plan.'

Mike hadn't said much that morning, and Max could feel his displeasure at the new vocal, a feeling he shared. It had lost its raw edge, its beauty. Its Amelie. He thought of her gloriously sulky face and grimaced.

'So, how has the week been?' Dee asked casually.

'Oh, it's been great actually. I've loved it,' Max said.

Dee was fidgeting, nervous and extremely distracted, and Max began to wish he'd never invited her to take part in the record. When they'd first discussed it, she'd been a catalyst for his taking this leap on his own, but now he didn't need her. And he wasn't even sure he wanted her any more, despite the commercial advantages it would yield.

'Yeah?' Dee said flatly, then looked at him with a sudden fixed determination. 'Shall we get a coffee?'

Max studied her for a moment, and realised it wasn't a question. She wanted to talk.

'What is it?' he asked, sitting next to her in the reception area.

'I have to talk to you.'

'Yeah? What's up? What's going on?'

'There are two things, really. Firstly, if you want to use my vocal on the single as we discussed, we will need to speak to Geoff ASAP. He knows something's up because none of us are back in the States.'

He thought about that phrase – *none of us.*

'Okay. Well, my plan is to speak to them next week. I'm going to the New York office on Monday.'

'Well, good. I know I thought the song was a good idea, but I'm worried about the wider implications. You know, of *us* having a single.'

'Okay, I get it. If you're unsure ... '

'No. Just run it past Geoff. There's something else you need to know.'

'Yeah?' He felt his chest tighten. 'What is it?'

'Well, I'm just going to come out and say it, Max, because you're not going to like it. So just saying it straight is always the best way.'

They were someone else's words. Dee had never been great at talking straight – she was ultimately too concerned that people would dislike her.

'What is it?'

She took a deep breath and looked at the floor, losing her nerve as she spoke, her voice wavering. 'I'm dating someone.' She swallowed. 'And you know him.'

Max took a minute to register what she'd said. He repeated the words to himself, and as he watched her switching her irritatingly busy phone to silent he realised he had somehow heard the words already; somewhere in the back of his mind he already knew Dee was seeing someone, and he already knew who it was.

For reasons unknown to him he had never quite put it

together, but it was suddenly glaringly obvious. His mind went back to London and the first night of the European tour. The night Max had decided he wanted to leave The Keep and had reached out to Dee for advice in that late night car ride to their hotel. He pictured Charlie's annoyed face when Max had slipped into the car with Dee – that was who she'd been ferociously texting during their journey to the hotel.

Charlie.

Dee shifted in her seat, waiting for Max to say something, but the pieces just kept clicking into place. Amelie had been a pawn for Charlie – a distraction – a tactic Max himself had used when he had first started dating Dee to stop the press getting wind of the relationship, and it had been Dee's idea. 'Just flirt with some fans online,' she'd said. 'Play it up. No one will suspect us if they think you're playing the field.'

But how long had Charlie felt this way about Dee?

'Max?' Dee took his hand and he looked down at the immaculately manicured nails, kept short for playing, but perfectly kept. Both of her pinkie fingers were daintily painted blue, red and white, like French flags.

He thought back to the early days of their dating. It had happened really quickly, not long after their first tour together. Charlie had been spiteful about Max dating Dee – using management's rules as his reason – but there was ferocity in his disapproval that Max had always found perplexing. Jealousy, he now realised.

'Um.' Max couldn't find the words. 'How long? I mean . . . '

He knew already, it must have happened before they had split. The red wine incident, that night out, when he had tried to kiss her and she jumped back like a frightened cat and spilled her drink all over him. She hadn't wanted to be kissed because of Charlie, not the press. The Buzz's coverage had been just the reason she needed to end the relationship – 'an unwanted spotlight on a mess,' she'd said. Indeed.

'Well—'

'Dee,' he stopped her. 'It's okay.'

He pulled his hand back from hers and saw the dark under her eyes for the first time. He felt a surge of compassion for a moment, and then an altogether emptier emotion – indifference.

'But it's . . . well, I'm seeing . . . ' Dee looked down, fidgeting with her gold iPhone.

'Charlie,' Max said.

He remembered Charlie on the stage in Copenhagen, the argument they'd had over Amelie. Max realised that his fondness for Amelie, even after that first meeting, must have been obvious, and Charlie must have been out for some kind of revenge.

'Why did you do that to Amelie?'

'Who?'

'Amelie. Mike's daughter.'

'Oh, her. I dunno. You know how it is, you grab a distraction when you can. She fancied him. The photo of her arriving backstage at the London gig was a bit of a bonus really; the press can be so desperate,' she laughed, rolling her eyes. 'She's okay though, isn't she?'

'But he's still contacting her.'

'Not really. A few messages. He showed me them. He wanted to make sure she didn't hate him. He felt bad.' Dee sighed. 'I know what he's like – he's got a terrible reputation. But it's just this stupid image thing. He really does care. It took a long time for me to agree to see him. But he loves me. I know he does. Max, he's kind and a good person.'

And just like that, the room cleared and the haze lifted. Max could no longer see the beautiful, captivating woman he had fallen for way back when he was wet behind the ears. He could see a woman who had spent too long having people tell her how wonderful and amazing she was. She was hollow, and fully in thrall to her own ego. He could see how Charlie and her could work.

'Well, I'm happy for you both.'

'Really?' The weight had lifted and she smiled meekly.

'I think I am,' Max nodded. 'No, I am.'

'Oh, thank you, Max. Charlie will be pleased. He's been really worried about telling you. He looks up to you, you know. He's terrified you'll leave the band.'

'What?' Max scoffed. 'Charlie HATES me. He always has.'

'He doesn't,' Dee said gently. 'He just hates the way you look at the band. He's quite sensitive, you know.'

'The way I look at the band?'

'You've always looked down on the band,' she said. 'I guess

you should know that didn't always make him feel great. He can't sing like you, Max. Or write. This is it for him. When The Keep are over – so is he. With music at least.'

'Well, hell,' Max said, 'now *I* feel bad.'

'Don't feel bad,' Dee said, and then with her best pleading eyes, 'Just don't hate him. Or me.'

'I could never hate you,' Max said. 'I can't say it isn't a bit weird though. Probably a good time to leave the—'

Just at that moment they heard a huge crash as a glass smashed into a hundred pieces behind the reception desk.

'Shit. Balls. Shit.' Julian appeared with a cut hand and a look of faux surprise.

'Don't mind me!' He tried to do a cool dance out from behind reception and into the kitchen.

Max jumped up, laughing. 'Are you okay, Jules?'

'Fine as fuuuuuuck. Owwww!' Julian called back, running the cold water tap as Max followed him into the kitchen to help. Dee started forward as well.

'It's fine, Dee. I got it,' Max said, turning to her.

'I'm just ... what did he hear?' Dee looked nervous.

'It's fine. He's not going to say anything.'

'But, it's just, you know ... well ...' Dee stammered as she shied away from the blood gushing from Julian's right hand.

'It's fine,' Max said, his voice rising. 'Don't worry about it.' He held up Julian's hand.

'Just a scratch.' Julian winked at him.

'Hi, is it Jules?' Dee started. 'I wondered if you heard anything, it's just that it's very confidential—'

'DEE!' Max shouted. 'Enough!'

Silence followed, interrupted only by the running tap and the constant vibrating of Dee's phone.

'Sorry.' Dee looked hurt. 'I just want to keep it for myself.'

'Dee.' Max walked over and put his hands on her shoulders. 'Julian is totally trustworthy. Don't worry.'

'It's tiring.' She looked at the ground. 'I'm tired.'

'I know the feeling.' He smiled and then pulled her in for a hug. 'I want you to be happy.'

'I want you to be as well,' she sniffed, tears welling up in her eyes. 'Good luck, Max. I hope this all works out for you.' She waved around at the studio as she picked her bag up and left, with her security in tow.

'Sorry,' Julian whispered when the door shut. 'It's just I was dusting and there wasn't an appropriate moment to leave.'

By the end of the afternoon there was a feeling of intense gloominess in the studio. Mike had set up the final mixes, ready to be mastered, while Max sat hunched over the desk listening through all the final tracks.

'Happy?' he asked Mike, who had been quiet for the last couple of hours.

'It's not me that needs to be happy,' Mike smiled. 'Are you sure you've got all the takes you want? I have to finalise now, as they've got you booked in for the master over the weekend.'

'I think so, yeah,' Max said, unsure, trying to ignore the

elephant in the room. It was still commercially beneficial to do the duet with Dee, no matter how much he preferred the version with Amelie.

'If you're sure,' Mike said once more, the slightest hint of disappointment in his tone.

'Mike, I really love Amelie's version. I actually prefer it. But I need Dee on the EP to help with the transition. She's got the profile.'

'You don't,' Mike said. 'Do you want some advice?'

'Sure.'

Mike looked at Max and opened his mouth to speak, before letting out a huge sigh and turning back to the desk. 'It doesn't matter. Let me get this ready.'

'Mike,' Max spoke like he did to his own father. 'Please, tell me.'

'Well,' Mike started. 'I'm too long in the tooth for mincing words, Max. So I'll lay it straight. The version with Dee is not a patch on the one with Amelie – and not just because she's my daughter. You know it too.'

'I know. But—'

'But she's a nobody in the industry. Hell, I didn't even really *know* her until recently, but you're right – having Dee on the record will help it sell. Probably get you in the charts! But the other version is the authentic one. If you really want to break free of the factory, you need to trust yourself. Stop thinking like someone who's already in the industry.

'You kids,' he continued, 'you think you need to play *their* game to make it. You don't. You just need to be extraordinary. And you are.'

At that moment Max's phone rang. It was still set on full volume from earlier in the day when it was to be his and Amelie's alarm. The ridiculous default iPhone ringtone filled the room. He glanced down to see if it was Amelie, but it was just Alexia.

'And those bloody phones,' Mike muttered just loud enough so Max could hear.

It rang off, and Max stood for a moment wondering what to say. He hadn't been told off like this since he was a kid, by his father.

'Mike, um . . . I . . . ' he started, before his phone went again. 'You'd better get that.'

# CHAPTER 29

# And Your Bird Can Sing

Maisie was wearing a blue and white halter-top bikini, hand-stitched by a Japanese art student from some cool market stall in Spitalfields. She looked like a supermodel, with her incredibly tall and statuesque frame oozing chia seed and almond butter health from every pore. Amelie looked at her in amazement, vowing to try another green smoothie – although the mere thought of it made her reach for another sip of her coke.

It had been all work and no play at her dad's studio, so Amelie finally gave into Maisie's relentless requests for that promised long weekend visiting Ella in Paris.

In celebration, Amelie's mum had bought her a new swimsuit – new in the sense that it was new to Amelie of course, in reality it could be fourth- or fifth-hand. Ella had found the pink and green striped gem in a flea market for just €2 – a fact that thrilled her far more than it thrilled Amelie. She tried not to think of all the bums that had been in it before hers as she tugged at the awkward frill adorning the single shoulder strap.

They were perched on loungers on one of those fake beaches that Paris puts up every summer along the banks of the Seine. There was a cycle path between them and the water, but you couldn't swim anyway, what you could do is sunbathe and eat gelato and stand under one of the vast portable water features when the sun got too hot. And, of course, for the authentic European touch, there was bad house music playing on the speakers.

'I've decided I'm going to go to Music in the Park,' Amelie announced, peering over her red-rimmed sunglasses at a couple of handsome, shirtless young French boys who had clapped eyes on them, in particular Maisie. 'Those guys totally fancy you.'

'Really?' Maisie looked flattered and terrified all at once.

'Really,' Amelie said, lying back and irritated by the attention. 'I'm quite ready to face my failure.'

'I promise we'll make sure it's a great day,' Maisie said quietly. 'You should stay with me the day before and we can get ready!'

'A whole day to get ready?' Amelie said coolly. 'That's a lot even by your standards.'

'Well – hair, nails, skin, fake tan – if that's your thing, a twenty-four-hour hydration program ... Mum can make us some pretox smoothies.'

Amelie imagined early mornings Chataranga-ing before a breakfast without bacon, and shivered.

'What time do we have to meet your mum at the restaurant?'

'In half an hour.'

'That chef is awful.'

'I know, he's the pits. Mum fancies him though – it's so obvious. It's bloody catering college all over again. I hope he's not married,' Amelie winced.

'He's not married. No ring.'

'I don't think the French *men* do rings.'

'*Excusez moi?*' said a French man, as if appearing to suddenly explain. Amelie put her hand up to shield the sun. It was the two shirtless handsomes that had been staring at Maisie.

'WE ARE ENGLISH!' said Maisie pointing at herself and Amelie, as if she had a hearing impairment.

'Oh, I'm sorry,' he said in perfect English. 'My name is Michel. We were wondering if we could buy you a drink?'

'No! And, wow, look at the time!' Amelie said, looking at her empty wrist. 'What do you know? We have to go.'

The two boys looked a little stunned as Amelie threw on a sundress and pulled her bag up over her shoulder. Maisie pulled on her shorts and apologised to the boys as best she could, 'I'm so sorry. We're tired. Long day.'

'Can I have your number?' Michel was not going to give up easily.

'Um . . .' Maisie nervously slipped her shoes on, looking up to Amelie for help.

'No. Sorry, she has a boyfriend,' Amelie said, and grabbed her friend by the arm. 'He's a boxer. Or something.'

As they walked back along the river, Maisie was silent and Amelie felt dirty and angry at herself. They made their way back up onto the boulevard and to her mum's apartment to get changed for dinner.

'What was that about, Amelie?' Maisie finally asked.

'What?'

'You were quite mean to those guys.'

'I don't know what you're on about.'

'Um, yes you do. It's not like you to be so nasty. Sarcastic, yes. Mean, no.'

Amelie brushed her hair and pulled it back into a tight ponytail. 'Sorry.' She sat on the edge of her sofa bed while Maisie pulled on an effortlessly chic and equally expensive dress before pulling out her make-up purse.

'What's going on? Has something happened with your mum? The studio?' she asked. 'It's not still Max?'

Amelie threw herself back on the bed and felt the tears welling in her eyes. 'No.'

'Why don't you get in touch with him?' Maisie asked. 'What are you afraid of?'

'I don't care about Max.'

'Okay, okay, okay,' continued Maisie, now on an uncharacteristic roll. 'Well what is it? Are you sure it isn't the festival?'

'I'm happy for Tara, she was really good. She deserves the place. It wasn't my year.'

'Okay, so why don't *you* aim to get the place next year? You said yourself playing that night live gave you confidence. Max—'

'Urgh! I don't care what he said. He's gutless, and a liar. He didn't even leave the band. Dad says he hasn't been in touch since the recording, and he's heard nothing about a release.'

Maisie turned around, her face perfectly and almost miraculously made in under two minutes. 'Well, you need to get over him.'

'Wow!' Amelie said. 'You should REALLY do this for a living.'

'Amelie, don't change the subject.'

'I know, I know, I know.'

'I know. I know. I know,' Maisie mimicked, starting to lose her temper. She picked up her handbag. 'I'm getting a bit tired of the woe-is-me stuff, Amelie. Life is not that hard, you know. You're a seventeen-year-old with your own place in London for the summer! There's got to be a way to see that as a good thing! And if you don't want to be alone, surely you can stay with your dad, or you can come to Paris . . . oh, and you had a kiss with a really, really, really famous person and you fell for him but he lives overseas. And I know it's a bit *Pretty Woman* but at least you got a shit-hot guitar out of it, right? And so what if you didn't get a place at Music in the Bloody Park? Try again. It's hard to be around you at the moment. You're wallowing in your own self-pity. It's like you're enjoying it.'

Amelie was floored. She had never heard Maisie speak like

that – she was angry but it only served to make Amelie more defiant. She was up for a fight.

She stood up slowly. 'Well,' she met Maisie's eyes. Her friend was shaking, and Amelie knew that she could unnerve her further. Maisie was deeply sensitive and it wasn't hard to upset her. 'Thank you for that. You don't have to be here, you know.'

Maisie put her hand on the counter next to her and Amelie watched with satisfaction as the perfectly applied foundation could not hide the rising red flush in her cheeks. 'I want to be here. I'm sorry to snap, I just . . . I want my friend back.'

'I'm sorry I disappoint you.' Amelie knew how to out-manoeuvre her.

'You don't . . . don't . . .' Maisie stammered, and Amelie could hear the faint breaking of her voice. 'Amelie, please.'

Amelie leaned over, picked up her handbag and said as coolly as she could, 'Do you want to come to dinner? I'm going to go.'

And with that, a single tear fell down Maisie's cheek. 'Amelie, I'm sorry.'

'It's fine,' Amelie said stubbornly, trying to ignore her friend's pain.

'Amelie,' Maisie pleaded with her.

'Let's just go,' Amelie said. 'Come on.'

They walked in silence along the boulevard and down the cobbled side street to her mother's restaurant. The market shops were still open, with big baskets of vegetables, flowers and other assorted produce outside. The evening sun was almost gone and huge fairy lights hung across the street. A small band was playing on the corner to a crowd of locals sitting on the steps of an old church.

It was romantic, and beautiful, and Amelie felt herself softening ever so slightly.

They arrived late, just as the dinner service was in full swing. Unusually for a French restaurant there was a large open kitchen at the back, and Amelie could see her mother working hard under the heat lamps, wiping her brow as she piped something delicious onto something equally delicious.

The maître d' marched over in a bit of a tizz. She mumbled under her breath in French and sat them at the worst and most pokey table at the back of the restaurant, but Amelie didn't mind.

'We have food coming,' she said in a thick accent. 'Because you were late, um, cannot order. We just bring?'

'No problem,' Amelie replied, knowing that they would get whatever was easy, fast, and available at that moment, as the restaurant was rammed.

Before they had a chance to take their bags off, two glasses of mineral water and a small carafe of red wine arrived at the table. As they sat down, two French onion soups appeared straight from the grill, with bubbling cheese croutons drowning in the thick, beefy onion bowl.

Amelie poured the wine. They had yet to speak a word to each other since the flat, although Amelie was starting to feel desperately bad for her friend, who was looking utterly dejected and miserable opposite her. It took almost every ounce of her will to find the words, 'Sorry, Maisie.'

Her friend breathed out. 'No, I am.'

'No, I am.'

'No, really, Amelie. I'm so sorry.'

'No. You really don't have to be.' It was deadlock, and both the girls laughed. 'It's not your fault,' Amelie continued. 'Everything you said was right. I am wallowing in my own self-pity.'

Maisie cringed. 'I'm awful.'

'Look, I'll come to the festival with you and I'll be happy about it,' Amelie promised her friend. 'And I'll try to let go of Max. You're right – I'm not over it.'

'Okay, I understand,' Maisie said with half a smile.

'We just really connected and now he's gone and it's like nothing ever happened, but nothing is the same and it seems really unfair,' Amelie said. 'And I want my mum to come home. It's usually me and her versus the world. I miss her.'

'I just want you to be happy again. At least Amelie-happy, which is mostly grumpy,' Maisie joked.

'This summer didn't go the way I had hoped. At all,' Amelie said. 'I've lived in eighteen houses since I was two. That's more than one a year. I've owned thirteen different school uniforms. I've had to stand up at the back of class and introduce myself a dozen times to a room full of strangers who were already friends with each other. I've been the posh kid, the poor kid, the foreigner, the Londoner and almost always alone. Victoria Park is the longest I've been in one place! Three years. I've had one consistent thing in my life, and that's Mum. I go home after the studio and I'm lonely.'

'Well, as much as I ADORE Ella, she's all over the place. There's always something new. Job. Man. She's always changing her mind,' Maisie said. 'I've never met anyone who could benefit from a mindfulness course more than your mum.'

They both laughed as Amelie continued, 'And Dad. My whole life I've wanted him to be proud of me. When I get on stage it's sometimes all I think about. What he will think.'

'Oh my god, that's so much pressure on yourself.' Maisie grabbed her friend's hand. 'No wonder you ...'

'... Get stage fright?' Amelie said grimly. 'Yeah, I guess. But I think he's starting to see what I can do. Oh, Maisie, if you could see me in the studio ... it's amazing. I'm totally at home. And the open mic night ... when I sang and played. I dunno. I feel like I was just starting to get there. Things were starting to happen. I wish I had that spot at the park. I just know how good I could be now.'

Before they had fully finished their soup, it was whisked off the table as abruptly as it had arrived, to be replaced without a word by a plate of steak frites for Amelie and coq au vin for Maisie.

'Wow. However did they guess?' Amelie managed a grin and looked up to try to catch her mother's eye, who was stressed and sweaty – buckling under the weight of dozens of dessert orders. Amelie felt a huge surge of empathy for her.

As they finished their meal and enjoyed their rather mean allowance of wine, Amelie watched her mother working behind the stove and felt the smallest twinge of excitement in her belly. She looked at Maisie and then back to her mother, who managed a small wave and smile towards the girls before Monsieur Lamont lambasted her for not paying attention. Her mum pulled a slightly embarrassed, silly face, which Monsieur Lamont of course caught her doing, causing him to throw his hands in the air shouting and slam the stainless steel bench next to her. He stopped short of heaving a twelve-inch knife across the kitchen.

Amelie winced and looked at her friend, and back at her mother again. And then she put her fork down.

'Maisie, how long until they choose the wildcard place?' she said with excitement.

'The what?'

'The wildcard spot. For Music in the Park.'

'They announced Tara weeks ago.'

'No, the YouTube/Google unsigned one. The one where you enter by video?'

'But that's not for schools. That's open to everyone. EVERYONE, Amelie.'

'Well, I'll just have to be extra good then, won't I?'

Maisie's eyes brightened as she pulled out her phone and did a quick search. 'They choose it in two days.' She paused. 'But, Amelie, that spot is for the main stage.'

'I know. And I'm going to get it.'

Maisie's eyes brightened and she clasped her hands together with joy. 'Oh, at last! Let's bloody do this!'

'Does that fancy camera of yours do video?'

'It sure does, and it's at the apartment.'

'Well, we'd better get back then.'

Amelie had twenty-four hours to send Maisie home with a video. The rules were pretty simple. It had to be one song, live and a single take, and you had to accompany it with a short bio, a headshot, and an example of your other work.

She took a deep breath and opened the guitar case, where she saw the card from Max still tucked under the strings. She fingered the edges and ran her thumb under the flap as Maisie walked out of the bathroom with a hairbrush and her make-up bag. Amelie flicked the luscious white envelope open, inside was a note on perfect, thick white card. He had his own stationery.

*Thanks for everything. You're a star. Stay in touch. xM*

He'd underlined where his email address and phone number were printed along the bottom of the card.

'All right, headshot first? May as well – the overhead lighting in here is nice and bright.' Amelie stuffed the envelope into her jacket and picked the guitar out of its beautiful, velvet-lined case.

It was exquisite. She ran her fingers down the strings and let out a small gasp.

'Wow.'

'Is it good? Looks pricey . . . ' Maisie said, flicking the lights on and clearing space against the roughly painted wall for Amelie to stand.

'Oh, it's pricey all right.'

'Well, he can afford it, don't think about it.'

Maisie held up the hairbrush and tugged Amelie's hair out of the severe ponytail.

'Nothing too OTT, Maisie.'

'Don't you worry about a thing.'

As Maisie worked, Amelie tuned the guitar as best she could by ear. She warmed her fingers and the strings up by playing though the song, then retuning, then resting her fingers, then playing again.

Maisie ran her finger across a red lipstick then across Amelie's lips.

'It's subtle,' Maisie assured her, handing her a pale grey loose T-shirt, which she then tied around the waist with the black curtain tie-back to create a loose cinch. Maisie used some kitchen foil to create two identical silver cuffs – which looked exactly like two cuffs fashioned from kitchen foil. 'Trust me,' Maisie smiled, forcing them around Amelie's wrists.

Maisie pinned the neck of the T-shirt high up under Amelie's hairline using a couple of hair grips, and, with Amelie's hair falling straight and centre-parted, it gave a smart, extremely high-fashion look that Amelie was simply bewildered by.

'I was waiting for you to use the toilet brush for a head piece,' Amelie laughed. 'You know, you should REALLY—'

'Do this for a living. I know.' Maisie grinned. 'Now stand up there on the wall with your guitar. Just hold the neck. That's it.'

Amelie smiled as Maisie took several photos of her from all different angles, but soon her smile started to fade.

'Oh god, hurry up,' Amelie moaned, pushing one side of her hair back from her face.

'You're beautiful,' Maisie said from behind the camera.

Amelie shot her friend a grateful half smile, feeling exposed and vulnerable.

'Got it,' Maisie snapped. 'Perfect.'

'Let me see.'

'No. We've got a song to record now. Shall we do it here as well? I can probably make the lounge area look cool?' she said doubtfully. 'There isn't enough space to do it against the wall.'

'I was thinking we could do it on that street. The one where Mum works. It was so pretty.'

'It might be too loud.'

'I don't think so, the band stops playing at ten, and the shops will be closing. There might be a little foot traffic from the restaurant but the song takes three minutes.'

'Let's do it.'

The girls sped off to the foot of the church steps, and Amelie positioned herself under Maisie's orders – Maisie planned to blur out the fairy lights in the background and use the light of a street lamp to keep Amelie in the foreground.

She took a test shot and showed Amelie.

'It works,' Amelie smiled broadly. 'Let's do this, Maisie.'

'Hang on, your mum.'

Amelie turned her head, and without a thought waved her mother over. Her mum ambled across, looking wrung out and apologetic. Amelie leaned over and gave her a kiss on the cheek. 'I love you.'

Her mum was taken aback for a moment. 'I love you too, darling.'

'You need to move over there, Mum,' Amelie said, pointing to the step behind Maisie.

'Was it so bad at the restaurant?' She plonked down and yawned, exhausted. 'Erghh, it's really tougher than I imagined. I thought I'd be making cakes and chatting to old French regulars about art. What's happening? I thought you two went home?'

'We're filming Amelie. She's going to try to get the place at Music in the Park.'

'I thought it went to your school friend?' Ella's eyes widened.

Amelie shook her head. 'Sshh. Let's do this quick, before I lose my nerve.' She looked at Maisie and ran her fingers down the strings.

# CHAPTER 30

# Please Mr Postman

Amelie waited idly by the computer for news on her video audition – they were due to announce the winner before midday. It had been some time since she'd been online, swearing off social media and any kind of news since Max had left. For days afterwards, she'd found she couldn't go anywhere online without a reminder of him – even a seemingly safe article on travel in a discarded *Metro* included a ridiculous special on Memphis, featuring shots of Max and Justin Timberlake with the caption 'The Home of Rock and Roll'. No Sun Studios. No Graceland. Just boyband singers.

But now she allowed herself a little look. She opened the The Buzz, but unusually there was nothing there about Max or anyone from The Keep. She turned to the *Sun*, then TMZ, and apart from some reference to Lee not attending his girlfriend Jessica's red-carpet event, the news on The Keep was scarce.

Becoming more brave, she logged onto Twitter. There was nothing new from Charlie in her private messages, and Max's feed gave nothing away – was he keeping up appearances? Were they all? Or had he bottled it?

@maxxedout95: Hello Memphis. Hello Summer!

@maxxedout95: Chillin' on the porch with Dad & some ice cold lemonade. Listening to toons.

@maxxedout95: I'm melting.

She clicked onto her own profile and read her very last tweet – *that escalated quickly* – and thought about all that had happened since the night of her seventeenth birthday. She had some sense that she had been chewed up and quickly spat out by The Keep machine; one of a string of teenage girls who got a text from Charlie, or kissed one of them during a tour after party. It felt like the aftermath of a huge tornado that had blown through her tiny flat in east London and left her heart scattered all over the city.

11.42 a.m.

She turned to The Keep's Facebook page, where there was just one post since the end of their tour:

*Taking a Summer Break here to visit our folks and rest our bones. See you in the Fall. Love Charlie, Art, Lee, Kyle & Maxx. X*

Well, that kind of explained it, thought Amelie. Maybe the

break had changed Max's mind. She was annoyed at herself for thinking of him and closed the social network windows abruptly, then she saw a notification in her inbox.

'Maisie!' she called. 'There's an email!'

Maisie came rushing through, tossing a tea towel onto the growing washing pile in the corner of the lounge. 'I did your dishes. And the kitchen.'

'I can't read it!' Amelie said, covering her eyes. 'You have to!'

Maisie leaned over the computer and fiddled with the screen. 'How do you ...? Um ... that's it. Do I just click on the one at the top?'

'YES!' Amelie yelled through her fingers. 'Oh god, what does it say?'

'It's just loading.'

They both waited a moment as the computer took its time, slowly opening the window and then loading the image-heavy message.

'Jesus. The suspense,' Amelie whined.

'Okay, okay, it's up.' Maisie started to read out loud, 'Thank you for your entry to the Music in the Park wildcard placement competition. The panel have watched over 1000 entries ...'

'Oh god.' Amelie's heart sank.

'ARGHHHHHIIHHH!!!!' Maisie shrieked.

'I know. It's okay, really.'

'Listen! Listen! ... and have decided that we would like you to represent us on the main stage. Congratulations, Amelie

Ayres! Please fill in and sign the attached form to formally accept the place, and return it to us by the end of the day today. The public announcement will happen on YouTube at one p.m.'

Amelie felt a smile creep across her face. 'I did it.'

'YOU DID IT!' Maisie threw her arms around her friend and they hugged and screamed, jumping up and down until they collapsed onto the sofa in a heap.

'I can't believe it.'

'I can, Amelie. You've worked so, so hard. You've worked hard and dedicated yourself and you've achieved what you set out to do. That is *amazing*. No one can ever take that away from you. Oh, your mum and dad will be so happy for you!'

'I'm so happy. I can't believe how good this feels,' Amelie said, knowing the *chat* with her mum had to be next.

Maisie jumped up. 'Let's get prosecco!' She clasped her hands together, buzzing with excited energy. 'I know a place that will serve us on Broadway Market.'

'No, I just want to lie here for a sec,' Amelie said, basking in the warm, delicious feeling that was radiating through her. 'Then I need to call Mum.'

'Oh, how can you just lie there!? We have to celebrate somehow!'

Amelie smiled at her friend. Her energetic, excitable, beautiful friend, and felt a surge of compassion and love. Maisie handed her the phone and got up.

'Okay, I'll take a shower, you call your mum and afterwards, we have to celebrate. Okay?'

'You got it.'

Amelie waited until she heard the bathroom door shut and the shower run and then she snuck into her room and turned on her computer. She logged onto SoundCloud while she dialled her mother's number, who answered immediately.

'Amelie, I've been waiting by the phone. Tell me!'

'Hi, Mum.'

'Yes, darling. You didn't get it? Or you got it? Amelie, tell me!'

'I got it.'

Amelie heard a loud crackle and the muffled scream of her mother, and couldn't stifle a laugh.

'Wow! Amelie, I'm so proud of you. I wish I could kiss you!'

'I wish you could do. Maisie wants to go for prosecco. You'd love it.'

'Oh, my darling, I'm so happy for you.'

'Come back to London,' Amelie said bluntly.

Her mother sighed. 'Amelie, we've talked about this. I just need this summer here, and then we can do what we want!'

'We both know it's not just the summer. Mum, it's my last year of high school and really, probably, my last year at home. My music is here. Dad and the studio are here. My best friend is here. And I want you to be here too. In our little flat by the park. For one more year.'

There was a silence on the line and Amelie knew her mother had heard her. Really heard her. She felt her stomach tighten and desperately wanted to reach out to her, but she held strong.

'Oh, darling Amelie, I wish I had your determination and drive. When I watch you with your music, you're so dedicated. You get that from Mike, lord knows, you don't get it from me.'

'Come home,' Amelie said again.

'I'll think very hard about it, darling. I really will.'

'Look, I have to go, Mum. There's something I need to do.'

'I love you.'

'Me too.'

Amelie clicked on her SoundCloud profile and then 'Update Image'. She searched on her desktop for a photo and found one of the headshots Maisie had taken in Paris. She clicked upload. She clicked 'Edit' and changed her display name to Amelie Ayres, her location to London. She then did the same on her YouTube channel.

When they were both updated she looked at the screen. This was it. She hit 'Share' – and posted a message to Facebook and Twitter.

*You guys. I wanted to share some music I've been writing. If you like it, it would be great to connect. AAx*

# CHAPTER 31

# Sun It Rises

Max sat back in the swing on his parents' porch, his father next to him plucking their family brand of country blues, just as he had for so many years when Max was growing up. It was hot and humid, and the smell of damp foliage and rotting magnolias filled the air with the heady scent of his childhood. It had been almost a month since he'd arrived at the meeting in New York to announce he was going solo and leaving The Keep, and he was nearly out. The rest had done him good; he was relaxed and ready to continue his next chapter.

At the meeting, Geoff leaned back in his leather chair with his chest hair exploding out of the neck of his Hawaiian shirt.

'Okay, I guess I win,' he said, with raised eyebrows.

'What do you mean?'

'With every pop group we create, me and the marketing team pick a horse. I mean, a member. You know, who will leave and go solo first.' He smiled mischievously. 'I picked you. Jacob out there went with Kyle, but I told him Kyle would come out before he got out.'

'Oh.' Max would have been angry if he'd had anything invested in Geoff or this record label, or anything to do with The Keep any more.

'Anyway, the writing was on the wall after that stunt you pulled in London. Playing an open mic night? Fuck me. Rookie mistake, kid.'

'Sorry about that. I got overexcited, I think. Yeah, it was dumb.'

'Here's how it will work,' Geoff said, leaning forward and picking up a piece of paper from his desk. 'You need to take a cooling-off period of one month, as per your contract. During that time, we will prepare the rest of the band as a four piece – I'm assuming you haven't told them yet?'

'I'm meeting the boys for lunch. Everyone's here for the Christmas single video, so it seemed like a good time.'

'Okay, cool. Well, you won't need to do the shoot. We'll pull your vocal. You can tell them that. Whinging little pricks. This is going to be a pain in my goddamn ass. Charlie will be thrilled, mind. Might get some lead vocals back,' Geoff said, before adding with a smirk, 'Or not.'

Max shook his head.

'You need to tell them this is TOP secret. They can't tell

anyone, Max, and neither can you. Got it? I'll arrange for them all to come in tomorrow.'

'After the month is up, we will get you all back together here in New York to put a statement together about the split. You need to follow our narrative for that, I'm afraid.'

He smirked at Max, who was staring at the gold records on the wall behind Geoff; a catalogue of boybands and girlbands who had been through these doors over the last twenty years. He was just another one – another one who leaves to go solo. Even in leaving the band he was a cliché. It was inescapable.

'Okay, so we do a press release or something?'

'Yep. You are then contractually forbidden to record or release any new material for a set amount of time. Maybe another month or so, I'll need to check.' Geoff put his hands on the desk. 'I know you've been recording with Dee. We might be able to find a way to work with that, but the record will have to be released under us, and maybe on Dee's album, due to *her* contractual obligations. I'm not sure off the top of my head how that will work. I'll need to speak to Legal.'

Max was floored.

'So, do you want to head back to Memphis? What are you going to do for the month? You can't give anything away or you'll be in breach of contract. To be clear,' Geoff said, handing Max the piece of paper he'd been holding. 'You will actually be in breach of contract if you take one step out of line in the next month. No one can suspect you've left.'

'Why do we need a cooling-off period?' Max asked, feeling aggravated. 'I'm not going to change my mind.'

'We need some time to decide how we want to present your story.'

'My story?'

'Why you're leaving.' Geoff picked up the phone. 'Can you send Alexia in please? … Yes, your story. As to why you're leaving.'

'Aren't you going to just ask me?'

'I already know. You think the band is shit, embarrassing, and you're old enough now to know that we're the ones making the real money off your talent and you feel trapped? About right?' Alexia walked in.

'Hi, Max!' she said cheerfully.

'Hi, Alexia,' he managed to squeeze out.

'Can you tell John in Legal that Max will need to speak to him? Tell him to pull out the exit contracts?'

It was moving so fast Max's head was spinning.

'Max, we're sorry you've decided to go. But I've seen so many bands come and go in my twenty years here, I'm not going to beg you to stay. I've seen the tension building and in my experience it's better to have someone go quietly than force them to stay and dance like a monkey to my tune. Literally.'

'I guess that's good.' Max stood up. 'So, one month then, and I can do whatever I want?'

'Pretty much. Just not the Dee record, remember. I'll

contact the studio and get a copy of it, unless you could send one? We'll take it from there.'

'I'm not using the recording,' Max said.

'What?'

'There was a better version, with a local singer.'

For the first time, Geoff looked surprised. 'Oh. Does Dee know?'

'Not yet.'

'I guess there's no issue then. One month,' he reminded him. 'We'll be in touch. Go back and spend some time with your folks, Max. I know you want to just get on with the next chapter of releasing some angsty fucking rock pop or a cover of "Freedom" or whatever, but trust me, taking time out is the best thing for your career right now.'

'Okay.' Max stood up and, to his surprise, Geoff walked around the desk and put his hands on his shoulders.

'Kid, you're a good musician. It's a shame your career has been completely fucked by your decision to join The Keep, but maybe you can claw back a small ounce of integrity, somehow. I hope you can. There are not many youngsters I feel genuinely bad about putting through the factory – but you're one of them.'

Then he hugged him. A sweaty, stinky but sincere hug.

'Good luck, Max.'

And that was it. He was out of The Keep. Like so many things in the music business it was unceremonious, and a little bit dirty, and over quickly.

\*

Max's mum came out onto the porch and sat down next to him.

'Well, I'm sorry we're losing you,' she said, resting her hand on his. 'It's been great to have you back.'

'I missed you too, Momma.'

'Are you ready for this?' she asked quietly.

'Yeah, I'm ready,' he nodded.

His dad stopped playing and put his guitar down.

'I'm proud of you, son,' he said. 'I mean, we've always been proud of you – but this feels right. You should never have been in that goddamn—'

'Honey ...' Max's mum warned his father, as she always did, when his temper was rising.

'Well, Dad, it made me a lot of money,' Max said, pointing to the beautiful but totally beaten up 1967 Chevy he'd bought his father – he knew he would like nothing more than to spend a good five years banging away in the shed fixing it up. 'Even if you won't let me fix the drive.'

'Gah,' his dad said, nodding at the car. 'It's going to take a lot of work, that car.' His way of saying it was perfect.

'So what's the plan?' Max's mum asked, rubbing his arm.

'No plan really, Momma,' Max sighed. 'I'm going to go to London for a while. Then, I'm not sure.'

'A long way from home,' his mum sighed.

'Well, I can come back more often now. I won't be tied up in big world tours any more.'

'That's good news for us, honey,' she called after him as he headed back inside.

He hadn't heard from Amelie, but on a number of occasions had tried to work out what she might be doing. She was on Twitter, although she hadn't tweeted in weeks. He could see she was on Facebook – she had a photo of her old guitar as her profile picture – but since they weren't friends he couldn't see if she was active there. Nothing on her Instagram either.

But that morning something changed. He'd flicked through the usual places to get a hint of what she was up to, and there was a tweet.

@callmeamelie98: I'm alive. And I'm delighted to be playing at Music in the Park on the main stage this Saturday. Come say hi!

She'd attached a link to the festival website where he skimmed through the main stage listings and saw that she had won the Google place for unsigned talent. 'Amelie Ayres', it read, 'Google Unsigned Artist Winner'. She was on at four p.m. There was also a link to her winning entry, he clicked it.

There she was, sitting on the stairs playing the guitar he had given her, singing a beautiful song of her own. A quirky and complex arrangement, beautifully written and perfectly executed.

He wanted to speak to her so badly, his heart lurched.

He picked up the phone and rang her father without hesitation.

'Hey, Mike.'

'Max? How are you doing? You never collected the masters.' He was straight down to business.

'Oh yeah, it was legal things, with the label. A long story, but I want to come back and pick them up in person.'

'Okay, that seems a bit unnecessary.'

'I heard Amelie got a place at Music in the Park?'

'Yeah,' Mike said, slightly hesitantly. 'She did. I'm so damn proud of her.'

'It's brilliant news.' He paused awkwardly. 'I want to thank her myself. Is it possible, I mean, could I get her number?'

Mike said nothing for a moment, and then his voice stiffened. 'Sorry, mate, I can't do that.'

Max could tell by his tone that that part of the conversation was over. 'Okay, no worries. Well, tell her I asked after her.'

'Will do,' Mike said. 'When are you coming then?'

'Maybe Friday?'

'Oh, that soon. Okay, well I'll have Julian pick up the masters then.'

'Great. I've been writing. A lot,' Max said nervously. 'You were right. I wasn't ready before but I think I am now.'

'Well, you just call me and I'll find the time.'

'Thanks, Mike.'

They hung up and Max wondered what his next step should be.

He went back online and looked through Amelie's followers on Twitter. Since the incident with Charlie there were many of them to go through, but he was determined to find Maisie.

After about thirty minutes, he came across @aMAISIEng1 and recognised her face immediately. He clicked on her time-line and was thrilled to find she was active. He kicked himself for not checking sooner – there were a bunch of pictures of the two of them in Paris days before, including a gorgeous shot of Amelie that wouldn't have looked out of place as a cool arthouse album cover.

He had a quick look at Maisie's profile and realised with delight that she was following him. He opened the direct message box:

> TO MAISIE: Hi. Sorry to bother you, but I want to contact Amelie. Could you ask her if I can have her number? Thank you so much. Max.

Then he opened his phone and texted Alexia.

> TO ALEXIA: Can you help me with one last thing before I lose you?

> TO MAX: Absolutely. Still so sad you're going. What can I do?

> TO ALEXIA: I need a ticket to London. For Thursday if poss. And can you find me a hotel in east London?

> FROM ALEXIA: You got it.

He ran upstairs to pack. It didn't take long to throw his stuff back into his suitcase and organise his passport and the rest of his belongings.

Almost immediately he got a notification from twitter.

> FROM MAISIE: Hi Max. Nice to hear from you. I'm sorry but I don't think you should contact Amelie. Sorry. Take care. x

It was all so strange. He didn't understand what was going on, the only thing he could think of was getting to London.

# CHAPTER 32

# The Ballad of Beginnings

Amelie and Maisie climbed out of the car, Amelie's guitar in her hand and Maisie carrying a backpack filled with bits and pieces for backstage. Amelie pulled on her wellies and strode up to the side entrance of the festival. She felt a surge of pride as they approached the two girls sitting at the desk under a sign that said 'Artists' Entrance'.

The sun was beating down, it was stinking hot, and the queues to get in were starting to form at the gates.

'I'm Amelie Ayres,' she said with a big smile.

'Hi, Amelie.' The girl stood up and grabbed two badges, one with 'Amelie Ayres ARTIST' printed on it and the other with 'Maisie Stone AAA'.

'And you must be her plus one?' the other girl said to Maisie.

'I am! Ooh, it says "AAA". What does that mean, then?'

'Access All Areas.' The girl looked a little surprised.

'Sorry, we're completely new at this.' Maisie grinned and put the pass around her neck.

'That's okay,' said the first girl, and turned to Amelie. 'Here is the map of the site. Here is the food tent, and here are the artists' toilets and the lounge area.' She put a couple of big red crosses on the map and handed it to Amelie. 'Do you need help with your stuff? It says here it's just you and the guitar?'

'That's right,' said Amelie.

The other girl handed them a couple of canvas bags with 'MUSIC IN THE PARK' printed on them. Inside there were all sorts of goodies.

'Oooooh!' Maisie pulled out gift after gift – sunscreen, make-up, bottled water, a pair of fold up Ray-Bans and a necklace from a local artist. 'And perfume!' she said, squirting some of Ellie Goulding's latest scent around them. 'Oh god, that stinks.'

They both giggled as they made their way to the artists' area.

'What time are your parents coming?' Maisie asked.

'Soon, I think. I'm going to meet them for a beer before the crowds get too big. I wish they could come backstage.'

Amelie took a deep breath as she waved her badge at the security guard outside the artists' area.

'Hi, ladies,' he smiled at them.

'This is the best.' Maisie clung to her friend as they found a seat on a picnic bench and watched the other less-famous artists milling around. The really big ones were in trailers to the back of the artists' area, and the rumour was that the headliners were arriving by helicopter just before they went on.

'LADIES!' They both turned to see Julian come squealing towards them, his arms in the air and Clint following close behind. 'Oh my god! So awesome.'

They all hugged and kissed, giddy with excitement.

'What are you doing here?' Amelie said with delight.

'Darling, how are YOU?' Clint asked.

Amelie smiled. 'I'm good. Surviving the summer and recovering from ... you know.'

'Well, no, I don't. Julian insists you haven't said a word. What happened? I take it you didn't fancy him in the end or we'd have wedding bells by now?'

'No. I mean, I guess. Well, he's gone back to America. And, I'm just not sure ...'

'They kissed, but we're not sure what his deal is with Dee. I mean, if they're not together why does literally EVERYONE say that they are? Unless he played my Amelie,' Maisie said, waving her hand. 'We don't like.'

'WHAT?' Julian looked confused and looked at Clint. 'What do you mean?'

'Dee,' Amelie said flatly. 'I even read in the paper a few weeks back that they were still together. Well, my mum read it because my French is totes provincial.'

Julian and Clint both looked at each other uneasily.

'He's not with Dee,' said Julian. 'I know that 100 per cent for sure.'

'And he's left The Keep,' Clint added. 'I know *that* 100 per cent for sure. That's why we're here. Well, Julian's my plus one. I was supposed to be finishing the tour film but I'm here filming the main stage for the organisers, because The Keep are taking a "break", a. k. a. preparing to announce Max has left, a. k. a. probably breaking up because the best singer has gone, a. k. a. I'm looking for a new job.' He rolled his eyes.

'He did it,' Amelie said in shock.

'He did,' Julian nodded.

Amelie looked at them both, a little stunned. 'That's great. I'm happy for him. What do you mean you know 100 per cent he's not with Dee?'

Julian looked a little uneasy. 'Well, um, they had an argument in the studio, or rather, she told him some very spicy news.'

'What!?' Amelie and Maisie's eyes widened and they leaned in close.

'Well, she's been seeing Charlie. Apparently for months. There was even ... cross-over.' He pulled a face.

'So, she ended it that day, or what?' Amelie pushed.

'No, no, she just wanted to tell him because it was Charlie and, I guess, you know, they didn't want to sneak around any more. It was hilarious because she TOTALLY thought he still loved her. And he was all like, girl, I don't care.'

'Oh my god.' Maisie looked across to Amelie. 'Amelie!'

'I can't believe *you* didn't know,' Julian pressed.

Amelie suddenly felt her heart swell. The feelings she had suppressed for the last few weeks began to sizzle and she longed to speak to Max. 'Well, it doesn't really matter, I mean, it's not like he's exactly been in touch.'

There was another unnerving silence. 'What now?'

'Amelie, I have something to tell you.' Maisie looked at her friend. 'He got in contact a few days ago.'

'WHAT THE WHAT!?' Amelie screamed. 'WHAT?'

She stood up and paced back and forth, rubbing her head and trying to take it all in.

'What we have here is your classic, tragic misunderstanding,' Julian said dramatically.

'Yeah, he messaged me . . . ' Maisie looked distressed as she recounted their brief interaction. 'I just didn't want him to screw you around because you were doing so well. You know, things are really starting to happen for you.'

Amelie shook her head and tried to laugh about it. 'Jesus. It's almost funny, really. Me and Charlie, him and Dee, Dee and Charlie. The *Sun* couldn't make this shit up,' she sighed heavily. 'Oh man, I should have messaged him. I nearly did so many times.'

'Well, thank god he's here.'

'He's here!?'

'Well, he's coming. To London at least. I had to arrange for him to pick up the masters. This is all very strange, Amelie, we *so* thought you knew all this. I feel really bad. But you guys were getting on so well I just assumed you were in touch all summer and you just didn't want to talk about it.'

Amelie felt her stomach turn, and a huge rush of emotion overcame her. She put her head in her hands and shook her head quietly. Maisie was in full fix-it mode.

'Shall I message him back, Amelie? That's what I'll do. Shall I?' she asked frantically.

Amelie stood up. 'I need a beer,' she said. 'I can't think about this right now.'

She wandered over to the rider, reminding her of the day at the Apollo when she first spoke to Max. She thought about all that had happened in the weeks since, and wondered what she should do next. She felt dizzy suddenly and leaned forward to steady herself.

'Amelie!' Maisie was beside her at once. 'Amelie, you need to put this out of your head and you need to go on stage and perform. Then we can get in touch with Max. We can sort this out.'

'I didn't know. I'm such an idiot.'

'Let's go meet your parents, and have that beer.'

Amelie felt in a sun-soaked daze as they wandered through the grounds. They were filling up steadily and groups of people were parking up on the vast lawns with picnic blankets and Pimm's in plastic glasses. Amelie spotted her parents immediately, about twenty feet from the beer tent, perched on a tartan blanket drinking bubbles.

'Celebrating, are we?' Amelie squeaked. Though it happened

rarely, she was always delighted at the sight of her parents hanging out.

'Amelie!' They both jumped up and threw their arms around her. 'We're so proud of you!' Her mother kissed her for the hundredth time.

'How was the train back? Did Monsieur Lamont get mad at you asking for a Saturday off?' Amelie asked.

'Actually,' her mum took a deep breath. 'I quit.'

'What!? You quit?' Amelie felt bad that she couldn't hide the delight in her voice.

'Yes, I quit. I had to, Amelie. I should never had contemplated moving to Paris at such a time in your life.' She kissed her daughter's cheek. 'You're a young woman now and I need to listen to you. And anyway, the Roman Road market would only hold my new stall slot until next weekend.'

'What? Really?' Amelie threw her arms back around her mother. 'You got the place! That's brilliant. Oh my god, what did Monsieur Lamont say to *that*?'

'I don't know. I left a note,' Ella said, biting her lower lip. 'Never again. I'm never working for anyone else ever again.'

'Champagne?' Amelie's dad held out a glass each for the girls.

'This is better than beer,' Amelie nodded, taking a huge sip, unable to remove the smile from her face.


Amelie stood at the side of the stage waiting for the act before her to finish. She looked down at the guitar around her neck and felt its beautiful edges and thought of Max. The excitement overwhelmed her, at performing and at seeing him again.

The crowd had thickened toward the front of the stage and the applause was growing. She took a deep breath and closed her eyes. She didn't feel frightened, the butterflies she felt in her stomach were of nervous excitement, not fear. She was amped. She couldn't wait to play her opening chord.

'You're on, Amelie!' whispered the roadie who had helped her get set up.

She was introduced over the loudspeaker.

*'And now, the Google Unsigned Talent Winner – who will certainly not be unsigned for long – let's give a warm east London welcome for our local girl, AMELIE AYRES.'*

The applause was perfect, the modest afternoon crowd getting behind one of their own and thoroughly revelling in their sun-soaked afternoon.

Amelie was bursting with pride as she looked out across the field.

As she stretched her fingers she searched for Maisie and her parents, who were standing just to the right of the stage, exactly where they said they would be. Her mother waved and her father smiled, while Maisie clapped her hands in delight.

'Hi, I'm Amelie,' she said into the microphone. 'And this song is called "Two Tuesday Blues".

She began, her nerves steady and her fingers strong. The music was so loud, the sound lifting her so she could float away, be carried through.

The crowd cheered. She allowed herself to look around and drink in the feeling of performing. It was everything she hoped. Her eyes moved across the front row where drunken teenagers swayed along, back to the picnicking crowds holding up beers and cheering, to Brooke and Ashleigh who were stood carrying hotdogs and cider cocktails – their mouths agape. Tara stood next to them with a smile spreading across her face; she raised her hands and gave a mighty cheer. Amelie allowed herself a little triumphant grin in her direction.

Then Amelie looked down at her set list and across to the side of the stage, where she saw him. Standing there.

He was standing in the wings watching her. His face lit up when they locked eyes and she felt that familiar warmth flowing through her. He looked the same. Maybe more relaxed. Happy. He waved. In his other hand he was holding an old copy of *Pet Sounds*, with a big red ribbon around it.

She managed a smile before pushing on to her second track, allowing the feeling of excitement to rush through her. He was really here, in the flesh. Here and not in a relationship with Dee and – almost the best news of all – not in a terrible boyband any more.

She looked down at her mum, who was weeping uncontrollably, and her father, who was shaking his head at her mother and giving Amelie the thumbs up. Maisie looked drunk on champagne, dancing and singing along to all the words. It was the best day of Amelie's life.

'Um, I've got time for one more,' said Amelie, glancing back to Max. 'This is a song I wrote with a friend. Well, hopefully more than a friend.'

The crowd whistled and cheered and Amelie closed her eyes. She wondered if anything would ever feel this good again.

'It's called "The Ballad of Beginnings."

# Acknowledgements

I want to firstly thank Julian Friedmann for answering my hastily written DM on Twitter. I will be forever grateful to you, Julian, for taking a chance on me and for pairing me up with my smart and kind agent and now dear friend Hattie Grunewald. How did I get this lucky? You are both incredible.

And to Sarah Castleton (you are a wonder) who bought the first messy draft and helped bring out the best of *me* in my book. Thanks also to the team at Atom Books – Stephanie, Olivia, Nico and Sam. You amaze with your creativity and cleverness.

A very big hug for the support and answering of groveling emails begging for help, in particular Tim Dellow, Kevin Molloy, Nick Abbott, Ardon Taylor and Matt Ingram. And a special mention to my dearest Toby L (and darling Deb) and all the Rockfeedback crew past and present who inspired this series and were part of one of the most fun, carefree and hazy times of my life.

It would be seriously remiss not to mention the crew of Dunedin gals (special nod to Lisa & Marissa) with whom I lived and breathed music. Here's to sneaking into gigs, $4 jugs and perfectly stable table for dancings. Oh god how I loved being 17 with you.

A virtual pint (until I can buy a proper round) for lending their valuable time and expertise to: Flash, Alex Thompson, Chris Sweeney, Rachael Bollard, Thomas Hannan and Dennis Weinrich. Also to my designer Donya Davis. THANK YOU for making me look far cooler than I am, and please keep painting!

A dancing gif to Frankie Hulme, Mya Punter-Bradshaw and Lily Cole for their invaluable critiques.

A humble thank you for lovingly helping with the kiddies so I could write: Mum, Anna, Edith, Jula and Juliet. And ALL THE GIN to the mums (and dads) who held my hand during those first months – The Maybies, Vicky Shields, Torie Chilcott, and my Hackney NCT crew, Foxy and my big, wonderful online village.

A trio of pink loveheart emoji's (because there are no words) to my lady writer inspirations: Dolly, Laura, Emma, Katz, Aleks, Kate and Allison.

My girls: Nicki, Chloe, Cathy, Aimee, Carolyn, Sara, Kylee and Marta. Thank you for the emails, support and encouragement in this journey.

Always thanks to my awesome family, Mum, Dad, Michael, Tom & Sonya. Oh how I wish we were all in the same place.

Eternal love and gratitude to the person who started me on this journey: Rachael. I'll never forget our lunch in Swan Valley, you are an inspiration as a cousin, a mother, a writer and a friend.

And biggest thanks of course, to Bernie and my baby girls, Billie and Georgia.

# JOIN US ONLINE

FOR THE LATEST NEWS, REVIEWS AND SHINY
NEW BOOKS FROM THE WORLD OF

# ATOM

Sign up to

*the Journal*

at

http://bit.ly/AtomTheJournal

🐦 @AtomBooks

📘 /AtomBooks

📷 @atombooks

🎵 atombooks

WWW.ATOMBOOKS.CO.UK